Mother

Mother

A Novel

LINDA ANN RENTSCHLER

MADISON
PARK
PRESS™

NEW YORK

Published by Madison Park Press, 15 East 26th Street, New York, NY 10010. Madison Park Press is a trademark of Bookspan.

Book design by Christos Peterson

ISBN: 978-1-58288-256-7

Printed in the United States of America

For Emily, Elizabeth, and Sam

Remembering JRT

ACKNOWLEDGMENTS

With deepest gratitude to Stephen, who never lost faith. Thank you, Andy Fau, for your creativity and tech support with the Web site. Thank you, Leigh, for a great dog, and two careers. Thank you, Beth Goehring, Carole Baron, and all of the wonderful people at Madison Park Press.

We are never ready to let go of our mother's hand, but her death shapes our hearts one last time. Without her, our love spills out in all directions, falling here and there, in the most unlikely places. Perhaps it is her greatest gift, to leave us aching for each other.

Mother

*I*t began as Mary Sullivan, bored with the late August after-noon, wandered into a store so old it was still called a luncheonette. Her eyes scanned the rows of candy bars as she recalled the taste of peanut butter cups, chocolate-covered co-conut bars, and cool mint patties, none of which seemed ap-pealing enough to buy. Remembering how many unopened candy bags she had already in her kitchen drawers, she reached for a roll of peppermint Life Savers, too embarrassed to leave the store empty-handed.

Time shifted. Her hand felt for the single dollar bill that had dived to the bottom of her purse like a runaway fish in a pond of boulders. She felt it happening, a current come alive, dominating, controlling everything, even the rhythm of her breath.

The unsuspecting salesgirl smiled opposite her. Mary's sweaty fingers dug deeper and deeper, until she found a dollar and held it out with the blue and silver roll, toward the young woman.

And then the voice, or remainder of voice, like an unacknowledged phrase left dangling amid bits of childhood verse or prayers, rose up unleashed, triggered by the sight of that deep blue roll of mints, the voice, the vibrant likeness of voice rang out with timeless impact and clarity.

"Think of me whenever you have one," Mary's mother, dead five years now, whispered to her daughter in the luncheonette.

Her mother's voice brought on an outpouring of tears so generous that not even Mary could have sopped them up with her handy packet of pocket tissues. She sniffled and she shook. She had been taught to prepare for such circumstances. To carry a comb or brush, aspirin, spare change. Her mother was, it seemed, item by item, contained and portable in her purse, warning by warning, truth by holy, heavenly truth, inescapable, uncapturable, absent, lingering.

There, in the luncheonette, with the sun streaming through the beveled glass windows on a seemingly ordinary afternoon in Schenectady, New York, Mary Sullivan bobbed against the drift of her tears, Life Savers in hand, unable to jump the emotional wave. In her warm and plentiful tears were vegetable soup bubbles as she watched her mother cook at the stove. There were champagne bubbles as she and her mother toasted the New Year. Mary did her best to hang on to those images, but predictably they dissolved into the others, the life-supporting bubbles that were pushed through the plastic hoses delivering medicine and oxygen.

The young clerk put the change in Mary's hand and, as if she had handled this sort of behavior regularly, sat her upon a wooden step stool behind the glass counter where customers didn't belong, tearing off sheet after sheet of paper towel from the roll she was using to shine up the globe on the bubblegum machine.

Grief felt like the final string of a loose tooth, so concentrated, so precise, but to pluck it was to deal with the bleeding, jagged cavern it left, so it was encouraged to cling there holding a space, wrapped up tightly, safely preserved, a blown-glass miniature, a kiss good night, a melody, a scent, a harsh word, a joke, a sentence sleeping in the mind's shadow, an indistinguishable hair trigger linked to the peppermints.

Mary had wept in many places over the past five years, but this seemed the oddest to date. This was not a lonely place by any means, or a dark place like the attic or basement that contained some of her mother's possessions, which she occasionally took out of the boxes and held to her heart, or sniffed for the remains of her perfume, or searched for notes in her mother's handwriting. Sometimes, Mary imagined her mother giving an opinion, for it was the conversation that she missed most, not the visits or the holidays or her presence with the extended family. It was the idle passing of time as they laughed about silly things by phone, while her husband watched television and the children played in the background, and the dinner pots soaked in two separate households. They remained attached, mother and daughter wired together, words and laughter passing through the airwaves, accounts of this or that minor event flowing uninhibitedly as it only could from flesh and blood–fed connections.

Mary managed to utter a few soggy syllables to the clerk with the ponytail, her eyes focusing on the girl's many ear-rings. She wondered how her life would have been enhanced if in addition to her two teenage sons, she had been given a daughter to raise, a person who wore jewelry, whose face stayed soft and hairless, who smelled like perfume or coconut shampoo, who could eventually share cosmetics and maga-zines and stories.

An elderly customer was playing the lottery as Mary promptly and self-consciously began to rationalize the blessed fullness of her life, her loving husband, her two sons, her home, her extended family, church, and friends. But in the af-ternoons, particularly this summer, she noticed she was mak-ing dinner earlier and earlier, keeping a spare half gallon of sun tea in the already overstocked refrigerator, and writing birthdays in next year's calendar. On days like this one, she forced herself out to walk, or ride, or shop the local stores, fearing the onset of loneliness, or laziness, or perhaps even agoraphobia. It was easy to stay home as the television blared out the bad news repeatedly, loved ones lost by fire or storm, drowned in an underestimated current, tangible connections severed. Mary detested such reminders.

Throughout the dull routine of her life, she consciously

avoided thinking of her mother while she hurried needlessly in and out of the post office, shopped the same supermarkets, bought the same brand of tuna fish, and confronted on foot or by car the funeral parlor where her mother had been laid out. The loss, invisible to others, was still completely evident, all-consuming to Mary, there in the black-beaded jewelry resting upon another woman's bosom, in the galoshes and plastic hair caps of older women, in the discolored eyes and gray hair of the sickly, in the bright red lipstick of the younger women, in the scuffing of men's shoes leaving church service, in the ubiquitous smell of fresh coffee.

"I miss my mother," she confessed to the young woman, sounding like a lost child who accidentally wandered down the wrong aisle on a shopping trip, or took the wrong hand in a crowd. "She's dead," Mary added firmly, just in case there was any doubt in the salesclerk's mind, to clarify that her mom had not been one of the fortunate relocators, off to Florida for perpetual sun and all-you-can-eat senior citizen buffets.

"I'm sorry," she said, her clear, blue eyes widening, her long, blond hair looking almost silver in the afternoon light. "How about a Coke?" she offered, the way the police chief might give a grape lollipop to ease the fears of a child inadvertently left behind.

"Oh, no," Mary choked out, appalled enough by her present imposition. "I'm sorry for troubling you. I should go."

"It's okay," the clerk continued, waving a hand for Mary to follow. The young woman's rings glistened on her lengthy fingers, and Mary decided they were Austrian crystal. She had seen a lot of those on the Home Shopping channel, but always resisted the temptation to buy one.

"The store's slow this afternoon. I'll get two Cokes and we can sit at the counter," she continued, making her way toward the glasses. She seemed so sincere, Mary couldn't help but relax.

Mary tagged after her, for the moment a non-grown-up, pulling tissues out of her handy packet, feeling some relief as she blew her nose, feeling even more juvenile as she climbed upon the slow-spinning counter stool. She watched the girl scoop pre-crushed ice into old-fashioned Coke glasses. The refreshing rattle of the chips deepened her thirst, reminding her how much she had preferred carbonated beverages to her own home-brewed, sugar-free, lemon tea.

"Thank you," Mary said with sincerity, grateful now for such hospitality, for the move from the rickety wooden step stool to the swivel seats at the counter where plate-size chocolate chip cookies were kept under glass, and potato chip bags hung in simple symmetry from an old metal display. "You're very kind," Mary added, having been around teen boys and a husband who would have eagerly accepted her declination at face value and gone off to play ball or rent a movie, relieved that they didn't have to cope with her.

"Chocolate or cherry?" she asked.

herry," Mary decided quickly, unwilling to brave the familiar taste of chocolate Coke, another memory that may have resulted in another round of tears.

A sense of well-being drifted through Mary as her eyes followed the young woman. She thought perhaps the store's old-fashioned decor in combination with the peppermints had set her off, been too much of a reminder of how many years it had been since she had visited such a place with her mother, felt so close to any other woman. There was plenty of floor space, and the tin ceilings were at least eleven feet high with attached wooden paddle fans circulating the air. She remembered looking forward to such places for ice cream the day before grade school resumed, her mom letting her order the large sundae with extra whipped cream as a special treat.

Mary blew her nose a final time, feeling her breathing calm, sighing peacefully. That the loss of her mother could have dragged her down so immediately through, ironically enough, a candy Life Saver, seemed a peculiar wrinkle in her otherwise uneventful day, but her mother, even grave-ridden, managed to find joyously creative ways of reaching her. Mary could have given the mints up forever, like she did the Marilyn Monroe movies they watched together, the fabric softener used in the household, the scent of which she once trailed a block in a crowd before realizing that she was tracking the invisible ghost of her mother in fluff cycle. One after the other, Mary had let them go, the big-band records her mother sung obnoxiously loudly with, the vivid images of her dancing on the hardwood floors around the pedestal table as she taught Mary to conga, the offensive color of her Canarsie-orange lipstick as she dressed for a night out, the brick-size bars of Ivory Soap that turned the tub water white, the well-onioned chili dog so unfeminine and so sloppily eaten, the Winston cigarettes, the smothering Aqua Net hair spray, the abundant statues of the saints. Mary had pieces of her mother's jewelry in a hatbox at the bottom of her closet, most of it costume, which she would have sooner passed to a daughter than put on herself, such was the thread of grief still attached to it. And then there were the knitting needles, a full set rolled into a pocketed cloth and tied with a red ribbon. Although she didn't knit, she couldn't bear to pass those on to the seniors she visited, because she couldn't remember her mother without a ball of wool, knitting or crocheting something for someone.

Mary sipped her Coke, a real cola, not the diet stuff she had been forcing upon herself for the past twenty years, but a delightfully, sugary, teeth-rotting Coke with just the right squirt of cherry. Her pretty hostess moaned with delight at her own chocolate Coke and sat beside Mary, introducing herself with an outstretched hand as Cathy with a C. Mary told Cathy her name and shook her hand, noticing first the infinite blue of her eyes, young with promise and vitality, and next, the exquisite, yellow rosebud tattoo just above her thumb knuckle. Mary couldn't help lifting Cathy's hand to get a closer look.

"Yeah, my mom didn't like the idea," she confessed. "So I got it painted on instead. It fades after a while, and you don't have to worry about needles or infections."

"That's a much better idea," Mary said, admiring both the flower and the commonsense mother. Slowly, she released Cathy's hand, adding an affectionate squeeze.

"It's an Indian custom, actually," Cathy volunteered.

"Cathy, I can't thank you enough for your kindness," Mary forced in, apologetically. "You're really very sweet."

"Well, I wouldn't be working here if I didn't like people."

So Mary, who couldn't remember having a conversation in the past three days, confessed that the Life Saver eruption had hit her out of nowhere, and explained she really didn't cry all that much anymore. But Cathy shrugged and tossed it off, saying she too was an emotional person, and thought it best to cry rather than bury your feelings.

"I'm always surprised by my tears," Mary admitted. "You think you've gotten through the grief, and then something hits you," she rambled, knowing how difficult it was to understand unless you had been the unenviable target of such a life-altering thunderbolt.

"I don't know what I'd do without my mom," Cathy volunteered. "We used to fight a lot when I was in high school, but now we get along great."

"You're not in high school?" Mary blurted out, sincerely stunned by the girl's adolescent features.

"I'm twenty, in my second year of college. This is my summer job. So in two weeks, I'll be going back."

"Where do you go?"

"State University at Potsdam," Cathy groaned.

"That's definitely out of commuting range."

"About three hours from here. I can come home on weekends if I want, or I can say the weather's bad and stay if I have a hot date."

"My son Matthew may go to Rensselaer for engineering. He's seventeen, just starting his senior year. And Brian," Mary couldn't help but smile. "Brian is one of a kind. He's fifteen and always ready for a good time."

"You don't look like you have kids that old," Cathy said, returning the compliment.

"It's the extra layer of fat," Mary giggled, now quite comfortable and composed, and made extra jovial by the supremely delectable mix of cherry sugar and caffeine. "I really think an extra ten pounds helps you look younger. So if you manage to bounce back to your pre-pregnancy weight, which I didn't, you get all those lines in your face and neck. It's not so bad to fill out the wrinkles with a cheesecake or two."

"My mom should hear this," Cathy offered. "I don't think she's had a full meal in the past five years. She eats the outside of everything."

"She what?"

"You know, potato skins, apple skins, the crunchy part of a roll, the tops of fat-free coffee cake."

"She must be a hundred pounds," Mary exclaimed.

"I'm not sure," Cathy continued. "But a size six. And I take an eight."

"Eight is a fine size," Mary encouraged. "Not that I would know that from experience, except in a shoe."

"My mom models occasionally."

"Really? That's wonderful. I haven't done anything in a while, like that, like work I mean, unless you count volunteer stuff. How about you? What are you studying?"

"Liberal arts. I just can't make up my mind. I'm not good with big decisions. I always know what kind of ice cream I want, but I don't have a clue what to do with the rest of my life."

"What do you enjoy?"

"This."

"This?" Mary asked, confused as to whether she meant talking or the retail business.

"Working with people," Cathy answered emphatically. "I like being here, seeing the daylight through these big glass windows. In the afternoons, kids come in to buy Bazooka with pennies in plastic bags, and they count with me. I see the same faces all the time. The retired men have their favorite stools at the counter, and read the paper while they eat their eggs and have their coffee. Some of them are pretty crabby when they come in, but they leave here smiling."

"It does seem like a warm place to be," Mary agreed, and then felt her maternal persona argue that she shouldn't encourage such a bright girl to spend her life dishing out ice-cream sundaes. "But I'm sure you'll find something at school that interests you more than anything. If I were you, I wouldn't rule out psychology. You've had a soothing effect upon me already," Mary added, understating just how calm she felt.

"Mary, do you mind if I ask you what it felt like?"

"What?"

"When your mother died."

Mary took a breath, remembering, tugging the thread. "Well, first it was like relief. She had been very sick, and every waking moment we spent caring for her, worrying about her, wondering if she would make it through each crisis. My dad died when I was eight, so it was really just always my mother and me. For weeks after, I felt like someone had shot me right through the stomach, like there was a huge hole the size of a bowling ball. I remember thinking it was visible, that everyone could see that I was like a ghost. That was the weird part, the grief was a physical experience. I walked around, but the water, it was always right there, behind my eyes, swelling in my throat, like a veil or a shadow. But very gradually, it spilled out, a little every day at first, buckets every now and then, until I could finally open my eyes all the way. They were always swollen. Throughout the first year, I felt it at certain times of the day, then at certain times of the week, especially when the seasons changed. You catch the smell of a spring flower and know Mother's Day is coming. It surprised me. I wasn't prepared for the intensity or the sheer volume of it."

"How did you ever get through it?"

"I'm still getting through it. I cried a lot at first, because if I didn't, I'd cry in my sleep and wake myself up sobbing. My husband, even in the middle of the night, would wrap me up in his arms and try his best to console me, even though he knew he couldn't. Ted, my husband, seemed to know when it was affecting me. I can still feel my face in his chest because he would fall asleep holding me. And my boys were great about it, they kept at me for things they could have done themselves, as if to remind me they were not going to let go of me. And then, of course, there were the dreams of my mother leaving. She always wore this long black coat. She'd wait for a bus, and I would try to go along, and she would tell me I couldn't, that she had to go alone."

"Wow," Cathy said, impressed by the details. "I really can't imagine having to cope with all that."

"Well, I think that's normal. I notice now I'm much more understanding with people who have lost parents or spouses. I can sit and listen to them talk about everything. I know what they're going through. Before, I thought people wallowed in their grief intentionally. Now, I'm pretty sure, if you don't get it out, it can drown you."

"Do you still dream about her?" Cathy asked. "I've taken a course on dreams, and I keep a dream journal, so I'm always interested."

"I can't find her anymore. It's like I'll be on my way to her house, the house I grew up in, and I'll get to the porch, ring the doorbell, and then realize she's dead and I can't see her. I bang on the windows, and then I wake up."

"That's sad. It sounds like your conscious mind should stop interfering."

"It's disappointing, that's all. Because I can't tell you how many times I've thought, if I could just talk to her again for five minutes, even in a dream, it would mean everything to me."

ary had enough energy to start an indoor herb garden when she returned home, during the time most people were cooking the dinner she already made at eleven in the morning. She'd been meaning to plant the seeds for several days, but it always seemed like too much of an effort.

She spread old newspaper on her tiled kitchen island and enthusiastically scooped the soil into five containers, carefully sprinkling in the seeds. Instead of watching the news, she flipped on the radio, singing "Help Me, Rhonda" along with the Beach Boys, remembering all the lyrics. Usually, as the afternoon progressed, her thoughts seemed to evaporate in the heat. Time had been endless some summer days. Tonight, her mind seemed to conjure up ways to make concrete changes, and she looked at her home thinking some redecorating was in order, maybe exchanging the heavier drapes for sheer curtains to bring in more natural light, or going with a more neutral palette on the walls and rugs.

She made herself an iced coffee, and wished her family would take a drive to Lake Placid to breathe some cool air, smell the evergreens, and see more stars than they could from the backyard. Her clay pots rested in line on the windowsill, and Mary watered the basil, oregano, parsley, and lemongrass, certain they would get more than enough sun, worrying not whether she would remember to water them but if she would accidentally water them twice. At least six plants had gone yellow in the past two months. She attempted to water them on Wednesdays and Saturdays to spare them her failing memory, but Wednesdays were hard to distinguish from Tuesdays or Thursdays, and soon she was dousing them irregularly again.

Summer was never her favorite time of the year, and she was happy it was almost over. Ted and the boys could never get enough of the backyard pool, and swam enough laps each night to train for the Olympics. The family's vacation was arranged for mid-July, always at a beach, which Mary never objected to but never really enjoyed.

Late August was always better, a pledge in the atmosphere for more frequent breezes, clocks rolling back, an approaching season free of pastels. Mary was liveliest when she noticed those few, half-red leaves announcing the fall, when she could return to the security of her long-sleeved shirts and pants, and go back to drinking hot coffee in the afternoon. She supposed she was happiest with both her ovens on most of the day, timing her muffins and meat loaves, surprising the senior citizens with dessert trays, providing the Sunday school with enough gingerbread and icing to build quaint little villages, having occasional afternoon teas.

She noticed she could bake for the holidays as early as October, and freeze dough, cakes, or cookies. She would spend one day mixing and the next baking, just as she alternated shopping and wrapping days. The warmth of her home enveloped everyone who came to her door, the neighbors, the deliverymen, even the teenagers who stopped by with her sons. She loved the winter best. She made it her business to arrive home before the boys. She kept a wood fire burning, and even if most of her baking was done by noon, she held back at least one tray for dinnertime, to refresh the smells of cinnamon, of vanilla, of warm sugar.

Closer to Christmas, she focused her attention on the forgotten senior women who loved to be invited anywhere. They arrived in crisp cotton dresses, in scarves, gloves, and hats, with polished, holiday brooches pinned upon their coats. Even though Mary took a lot of her baked goods to the senior citizen center, she tried to have each of the women over individually for lunch or tea, just to spend an afternoon with them, to listen to their reminiscing about past holidays. She wondered if they would enjoy visiting the luncheonette as much as she had, where simplicity seemed preserved and Cathy and her kindness were on duty.

Every season, no matter how much baking or cooking or brewing or packaging she accomplished, Mary ended up with time left over. She could assess each and every domestic task and approach housework in an order that would make the most of her energy and effort. She made the beds a side at a time, worked clockwise with furniture and glass polish, cooked dinner as the laundry spun, made tea while she watered her plants, and vacuumed almost daily. If she were ever to calculate the time she saved assigning an order to such mundane jobs, she was certain the sum would be quite impressive. But saving time without a purpose was as ungratifying as saving money without a goal. There was really no reward for it other than boredom.

This year, the boys' back-to-school clothing had been bought in June, even before they began their summer jobs. Only shoe sizes were unpredictable, and the boys handled that locally and quickly with Ted when they went for their back-to-school haircuts. Mary always spent a solo afternoon with each of her sons in the mall, shopping first, and then over hamburgers, trying to coax out any details about their lives. Matthew was nearly impossible to converse with, "Mom, I'm the same person I was last year at this time. Really, there's nothing to tell. I'm consistent. If you want to worry about someone, worry about Brian."

"Matthew, the world is in constant motion. There must be something different, some growth, some new like or dislike. Did you make any new friends this year?" she asked, trying to suggest without suggesting, the possibility of a girlfriend.

"No, Mom. Hey, is Dad serious about going away for an extra week this summer? Because if he is, I'd better work the extra hours while I can. In fact, I could pick up four today. What do you think?"

Mary couldn't recall with any clarity what Matthew had shared with her a year ago, if in fact their lunch had ended in the same abrupt manner, or whether he was any more communicative. To Matthew shopping always meant buying a new set of whatever he already owned, the same pants, the same sweats, the same sneakers in all the same colors. It made lunch seem a disruption in his schedule. Matthew, if possible, appeared to have grown even more serious and private, but was charitable enough to give the illusion he was enjoying his mother's simple, innocuous traditions—even if he routinely cut them short.

Mary found herself trying to make him smile, and then remembered how hard he always tried not to laugh—which was so opposite of Brian. On their day out, Brian kept her store-hopping until dinner, making jokes about Ted and Matthew and their inability to enjoy any part of their lives without the two of them.

It was six-thirty when Mary summoned her family from the backyard, knowing the boys always did a few extra laps before climbing out of the pool. She allowed herself twenty minutes to set the table and toss the salad, and knew it would be at least that long before the boys were dry and dressed. They arrived looking tall and bright-cheeked, hair neatly parted, with sun streaks of often-denied red highlights, skin softened from the water, reeking of chlorine. Mary looked each of them over, their big hands, their thick, straight hair, their mild brown eyes and generous eyelashes any girl would kill for, their bumpy, ever-hardening arm muscles. Brian looked the spitting image of Ted, thick boned, round-faced, dimpled, with an ever-present smile escaping, while Matthew's face was angular, his cheekbones pronounced, his eyebrows so dark and linear, his intensity was immediately evident.

"So what did you do today?" Ted asked politely of his wife.

"Let's see, I was so busy, I barely had time to iron the place mats," Mary answered good-naturedly, not willing to share any of the emotional details of the afternoon.

"So that wasn't you I saw in the clown suit handing out balloons in front of the florist?" Brian teased.

"No, unfortunately, they gave that job to a more mature candidate," Mary answered, playing along.

"So then it had to be Matty. He's the only person I know who's more mature than you," Brian continued.

"As if you knew what the word meant," Matthew offered.

"How about you?" Mary asked Ted, returning the courtesy.

"Nothing special," he answered automatically. "Matt?"

"Nope."

"So this clown is handing out balloons in front of the florist . . ." Brian continued until everyone including Matthew was caught up in his ridiculous story of who yelled what to whom, and another dinner passed, another hour of quality family life.

It was good to hear the laughter around the table, to take in, as Mary so often did, the sights and sounds of her precious family, to believe that nothing was more important than this, and to wonder if her mother, before the illness, had felt as she did. Mary hadn't forgotten about her resurfacing grief, her meeting with Cathy, but saw no reason to burden Ted. He had already heard and endured it all, the reflections, the recollections, the middle-of-the-night sobbing, as much as she could verbally communicate. If he had not been such an extraordinary man, he would never have amassed enough compassion to brace her up, again and again. When they discussed his parents, who were alive and well and capable of sustaining their same level of marital combat for more than twenty years, he actually made her feel relieved that her "parent" issues were already over. Ted would have all the worries about nursing homes or cancer treatments, if his mom really had Alzheimer's as his dad so often accused her, or whether to move them before they became incapacitated by age or disease.

It was these topics of discussion that first led Mary to her volunteer work, strangely feeling as though she had gotten off too young or too easily with the generation preceding hers. Or perhaps she had some inexplicable desire to continue ushering souls on to the afterlife, now that she had done so with her mother. Or maybe working with the elderly made her relax a little, feel slightly more immortal than she had when her mother passed on and she realized she would be the next generation to be shipped, boxed, and consigned to the deep dirt.

Last week, when Mary visited the ladies at the center, she drove Alice to the hairdresser, took Gertie for eyeglasses, and sat looking through Margaret's wedding album. Margaret explained every photo, down to the yellow ribbons on the garden bouquets her bridal party carried down the aisle. Mary loved the women for their sharp memories and strong opinions, and couldn't believe they were all over eighty and just as bold as ever, checking their watches if Mary didn't arrive ten minutes early, and commenting that she shouldn't worry because they could still "make it" if they hurried along. She volunteered to take them anywhere but to the hospital, where she still couldn't help feeling queasy, where the more unpleasant images of her mother's death were a little too accessible.

~ 4 ~

A storm blew in well after the eleven o'clock news. Mary couldn't see the clock on Ted's nightstand, but twice she had gotten out of bed to check a door or a window. The second time she went all the way into the attic and ran her hands along the windowsills, feeling for wet spots, knowing water occasionally forced its way in up there. The lightning and thunder seemed to take turns, so Mary assumed the eye of the storm wasn't over her house as long as she could still count the seconds between them.

Ted stirred as she felt her way back between the sheets. The wind smashed the baby tree branches into the side of the house, and she shivered at the sound. Tornadoes were uncommon in New York State, but there was always a possibility. She considered going down to the den and watching television for a weather report, but undoubtedly Ted would

wake up and follow her, and she would have disturbed his
sleep for nothing.

Mary flipped her pillow. She counted backward from one
hundred. Her own maturity was beginning to haunt her, what
with her night sweats becoming so regular, and these periodic
yet indefinable aches and pains she noticed, headaches, shoulder stiffness, cramps in her legs. She lay there tense and determined to capture at least some sleep, although it took quite
some doing to even get comfortable. Her scalp itched. Lately,
she gritted her teeth, noticed soreness in her breasts when she
lay upon her stomach, and awoke when her hands hurt from
being balled up tightly into fists.

A short while after she dropped off into sleep, it was Ted
who abruptly sat up and asked if she'd heard the doorbell.
Mary said no, having learned to rely upon her logic instead of
her senses, thinking no one would ring the doorbell at three in
the morning in her neighborhood. But then the second time,
she heard it too, this time in undeniable fear-provoking clarity.

Ted pulled on his jeans. Mary felt blindly through her
closet for the soft familiarity of her robe, settling for a long
denim shirt. Ted headed directly down the stairs while Mary
quietly opened both her sons' bedrooms, relieved to find that
neither of them was out and involved in a crisis.

When the door opened, at first Mary didn't recognize her.
Ted had no clue, of course, having never met Cathy. She was
drenched. Her hair looked six shades darker than the bright
blond it had been in the luncheonette sunlight earlier that day.

"Mary," she seemed to sigh with relief. "The police gave

me your address," she added, having been through an obvious ordeal. Mary looked back toward the street for a car, but there was nothing to be seen in the lamplight except a soft, misty rainfall, weightless and quiet.

"Cathy, come in," Mary said, pulling her out of the rain in a snap maternal decision. She stood there dripping on the rug in the front hallway, half folded into herself, arms crossed, shivering. "Ted, get a blanket," Mary continued, dispatching her confused husband who flew into action, pleased that Mary was connecting this event to her life in a manner which perhaps made sense, but didn't necessarily involve him.

"My mother," Cathy said, choking on the words, closing her eyes and nearly collapsing under the weight of the words. "She's gone. Dead," she finished in a crackly whisper.

Mary shouted "No" clearly and loudly enough to not only wake her sons but propel them down the stairs to zero in on the location of the bad news, and there they nearly collided with Ted who was making his way back from the den with a blanket, the striped L.L.Bean one that the family always took on vacation, that he wound around Mary during thunderstorms.

Mary wrapped the blanket tightly around Cathy, and it seemed the weight of it took her last half ounce of strength. Cathy went down into a grieving human puddle, fell almost soundlessly down upon the oriental runner like a rag doll, an empty heart of a girl. Mary took the ride with her, down to the floor where she had so often found herself weeping the week her own mother died.

Matthew asked his dad who the girl was, and Ted now answered confidently, "Cathy, a friend of your mother's," all he knew of this collapsed, pathetic soul in his hallway.

"The teakettle," Mary told no one male in particular, as she stroked Cathy's wet head, listening to her soft moans.

Mary refrained from speaking. Without words, she comprehended the degree of anguish, the inability to generate more than a low-pitched hum, as though the loss of your mother had removed every power you had acquired through her since infancy, your speech, the ability to stand, to hold your head erect, to keep your limbs from flailing out unpredictably, to guard against tumbling from a high place, hurting yourself. What high place had poor Cathy fallen from? A college student with a cheery disposition pushed off an emotional cliff. It would never be the same again, this life, this unprotected, abandoned young life.

When it was her mother, Mary had her husband, her two sons to cushion the blow. She was prepared for years by the doctors, by her mother, by her priest, and still, it was a long, long painful way down, and an ever-painful struggle to rise again.

Mary heard the shrieks of the teakettle and the deep scraping of male voices from the kitchen. They were confused, she knew, but at least wise enough not to come into the hallway.

As Mary held the young crying girl, she waved her family to bed. Ted was lingering, mouthing something about the tea, asking silently if she was sure she didn't need his help. Her work with the seniors had sometimes spilled into their home.

Ted had answered the occasional phone call from a mourner, and he often wondered why Mary continually subjected herself to such pain. She held up her hand to him, he shook his head as if to say wasn't it a shame, and tiptoed cooperatively up the steps.

Mary waited in the dim hallway for Cathy's grief to subside. When she could hear only whimpering, Mary said, "Let's have some tea," and helped Cathy up, steering her into a wooden chair at the kitchen table. Mary gave her a full box of tissues, which she always kept accessible on the second shelf of her island. She extracted the tea bags and put milk and two sugars in both teacups, knowing her guest wouldn't care, feeling that grief changed or pronounced your tastes for things, but tea with milk was always a safe bet. Mary put lemon cookies on a plate. Chocolate chip would not be a taste you would want associated with the worst night of your young life.

"What happened?" Mary asked after Cathy had sipped at her tea. Mary's hand rubbed Cathy's, the one with the yellow rose that maintained its detail throughout the awful downpour.

"An accident. The car and a truck. She was killed instantly," Cathy said defeatedly.

"I'm so, so sorry," Mary said, placing her hand on Cathy's arm for support.

"I just can't believe it," Cathy added.

She bit into a cookie as if doing something normal would convince her to behave that way, and she looked into Mary's eyes and apologized for coming to her home in the middle of the night. "I don't even know why I'm here," she continued, wiping another tear from her cheek. "I just felt . . ." she paused with a shrug of her shoulder, "that you would understand."

"Don't worry," Mary told her, eager to help this young woman who had hours before exhibited such kindness to her, forgetting they had just met that day, feeling as though the amount of tears they shared had glued them permanently together.

"I know I have to take care of things. But they didn't know when she would—" Her blue eyes seemed completely drowned in sorrow, lifeless except for the pain. That pain had a life of its own.

"Oh," Mary sighed, as Cathy's head went down to the table in another wave of sobbing. This time, she continued talking, with one hand massaging Cathy's back. "Tomorrow we can take care of things," Mary told her. "The night my mother died, I didn't want to sleep, so I stretched out on the couch in the den. Ted, my husband, was on the floor next to me. We turned off most of the lights, except for the white Christmas twinkle lights, and we turned on the television to watch reruns of old shows, not movies, but things with commercials. Looking at someone selling aspirin or muffin mix seemed to reassure me that tomorrow would come and I would be able to get up, get dressed, and function. I would try to picture myself a few months down the road, watching that same commercial and saying to myself, 'There, you made it this far, you'll make it the rest of the way.' Somehow, those stupid commercials helped."

"I can't imagine tomorrow, Mary," Cathy said, pulling her head up, her eyes squinting from the pain.

"I know you can't now, Cathy," Mary agreed. "But try to trust me. Everything will ever so gradually improve, and that terrible feeling in your stomach will let go."

"I have an empty feeling," she quickly added. "Not quite pain. And I don't know what to do. It feels like a dream."

Mary nodded. "Let's go into the den. I'll get you a night-shirt and toss your clothes in the dryer."

"Thank you," Cathy said, taking the hand of her friend.

Mary cleared away the cups and the cookies while Cathy changed. Mary led her into the den and tucked her into the sofa. She pulled pillows out of the closet and an afghan for herself. She turned on the red, white, and blue twinkle lights that framed a large bay window in patriotic fashion, and clicked on the television, thinking only of a lamb, a fright-ened, helpless lamb, motherless now, and wandering. Mary positioned herself on the floor next to Cathy.

"*Raymond* or *Ally McBeal*?" Mary asked.

"*Ally McBeal*," Cathy answered firmly. "I hope it's a snowy one."

"I love those," Mary agreed.

"Mary, I'm afraid," Cathy confessed.

"I know. I'm going to stay right next to you," Mary promised.

"Does it sound crazy? I would love to see my mother, but I'm also afraid to see her."

"That's why we keep the lights and the television on. I

don't think I slept without a light for six months. In fact, I got pretty dependent on those twinkle lights, so I decided to put up different colored strands for each holiday. The boys kind of liked the idea. They think it's festive."

"I'm glad you understand. It's so cozy in here. I'm actually feeling tired. I didn't think I'd be able to sleep."

"Try to get some rest," Mary told her. "I'll be right here if you need anything."

"Thank you, Mary. My mother would have liked you."

ary recalled wandering into the luncheonette, her mind full of scattered thoughts. But why? Why not the Hallmark card store where she had so often gone before, where she could stand and read through birthday sentiment, or look through the rolls of new wrapping paper?

Her imagination was now leaping about to concoct an explanation. Of course it was just coincidence, a random meeting. Mary wasn't even going to go out. She was going to clean the basement. Then she spied the boxes of her mother's things and changed her mind. She simply drifted out and wandered off. Yet there was evidence that it might not have been just a whim. Cathy was sleeping on her sofa, vulnerable, motherless.

Cathy stirred from the sofa, moaning slightly. Mary's curiosity deepened. Who was this stranger now so effortlessly tucked into her home as tightly as one of her own? Yesterday

Cathy seemed everything wonderful, a college girl, a young and pretty face, a head full of blond and beautiful hair, blue eyes that tonight seemed nearly green, a young girl blessed with warmth and intelligence, an unmarred personality. A wall had fallen on her, and it would probably be months before she could find her way out of the dark.

Uncomfortably awake in the den, Mary feared for a moment her aching heart, her chronic wish for a daughter of her own, may have prompted Cathy's circumstance. There were other explanations, Mary presumed, but none of them arising from any logical dimension. Transferable mental energy was plausible in spheres Mary had never visited. She had encountered the subject lately in women's magazines, pop drivel about positive thinking, where thoughts were acknowledged as tidbits of energy. She couldn't help noticing that such firmly forwarded thoughts never proved effective when you were behind the wheel and you wanted to inform the driver next to you that her blinker was on. There were all those how-to articles on visualizing oneself thinner or more confident or in the Bahamas, and in sending those positive vibes out to attract more money or romance. For the moment, Mary rationalized that if it didn't work for good, it couldn't possibly work for evil. But she couldn't help considering the possibility that somehow her grief in the luncheonette had bred more grief, that this most horrible event had been psychically induced by her dark emotional state.

If that was so, what on earth was next?

Mary grew up listening to aunts who would never let you say the word *accident* while they were driving. They believed the mere mention of the word would exact the event. Had she become a jinx, a calamity breeder? Mary could not fathom letting that much darkness seep out of her soul into such a beautifully, bright, lighthearted woman. She mentally retraced her steps looking for answers. Details seemed routinely elusive. This day had been an empty day, like most others. There had been nothing memorable, breakfast, a cup of tea, a wash of dark clothing, a bleach-wash of towels, lunch, just boredom, nothing out of the ordinary or significant that she could recall before the Life Savers, and even they were only an impulse away from being a chocolate bar.

If only she could talk to her mother. She would know what this incident meant, or at least offer an entertaining superstition. Oh how Mary missed the unshakable "rightness" that was her own mother, Stella. She was the ultimate authority, an embodiment of common sense and intuition.

Each time Mary was pregnant, she never managed to get the words out before her mother guessed. The first time, Mary didn't even make it all the way into her house before her mother blurted out that she had "pregnancy eyes." The second time, Mary attempted to tell her on the phone, but the minute she paused, her mother filled in the blank with "You're pregnant again!"

Mary couldn't imagine having lost her mother at twenty, before she had even been married. Did Cathy understand the maternal bond was impossible to sever, that her mother could never be withdrawn from her, no matter how many lifetimes apart they drifted?

Mary knew she shouldn't try to replace Cathy's mother, but if Cathy needed her, there was no harm in helping. So why now did she feel so instantly committed to this stranger?

August was the month abundant with shooting stars, and one had simply crash-landed in her den this night as the raindrops fell upon her home. Mary was uncertain what exactly she would be able to do for this brokenhearted soul, other than guide her through the rituals through the burial. But watching the snowflakes falling on Ally McBeal in Boston, and considering the maternal power of her name, Mary couldn't help thinking some spiritual connection, an invisible thread from one heart to another, a voice perhaps from beyond, maybe her mother's so brutally clear in the luncheonette, had encouraged this relationship.

And of all things, Mary was feeling excited. She admittedly grew enthusiastic at the wrong times—like when Matthew got the chicken pox. Before she picked him up at school she stopped at the store and bought Jell-O boxes and new crayons, cherry ice and apple juice, a bottle of calamine lotion, and a cut-up chicken and carrots for soup, as though she were shopping for a vacation. And when she saw him, fever-cheeked, drowsy, with reddened ears, she touched his hot little head, and knew she would give him cherry Tylenol and wrap him up tightly in his bed, and read to him, and surprise him with all kinds of treats, and kiss his warm little forehead as often as she could, for as long as his illness would last.

Perhaps it was just loneliness that enshrouded her, and only in a crisis or during a holiday, when people came to her with a request or sorrow, did she come alive, really alive, the kind of alive that allows you to stay up all night and watch re-runs and commercials because you can always catch up on sleep, the kind of alive that keeps you wrapping Christmas gifts or baking one batch of cookies after the next, or suspends completely the grip of time.

Time was all there was some days.

Mary's mind raced. How long would Cathy need her? Another day, a week?

The rain kicked up hard again, its drops hitting the windows, which looked as glittery as Cathy's green crystal rings had in the bright afternoon sunlight. Mary loved those tiny twinkle lights. Her body seemed to let go of its tension, her pillow smelled of peach sachet, and the wind and weather reminded her just how protected she was from the elements — at least for the moment. She would have liked to have shared this room with her young friend in a better circumstance, the green plaid curtains, the warm wood framing the wide windows, the bookcase with the pictures of her boys at different phases of their lives, the wreath she had made the year she quit smoking. Her antique clock was a treasure, and in the small room, its Westminster chimes seemed just the right tone and volume. There were large hanging plants, a philodendron and a spider, both of which came from her mother's room at the hospital, which she brought back instinctively, the way she kissed the flower she threw upon the casket when the funeral service concluded.

In the morning, Ted would have questions, not that he had ever stopped her from doing anything, but he would be concerned about this unexpected presence in his home. Mary could do nothing for the moment, except rely upon the pattern of her ordinary life to spin its way back.

The rain on the roof grew lighter. The darkness slowly faded. In a dim, groggy moment, even as she could feel the day approaching, Mary thought she heard the whisper of a familiar voice, like the lazy flutter of a warm breeze passing over her face. Mary touched her own face, her ears, as though she would find some evidence of what she had felt. But there was probably very little that couldn't be attributed to her racing thoughts or the summer heat.

~ 6 ~

At dawn, Mary set an extra place at the table and went about buttering sets of wheat toast, preparing coffee, pouring orange juice into actual juice glasses, using cups and plates that coordinated with her blue and white patchwork place mats, the way she always did when company came. She made a full pot of coffee and kept to her normal schedule, breakfast ready at six-thirty for Ted, pancakes, eggs, and bacon for the boys who had to leave at seven-thirty to work for a local landscaper. Mary had just filled the creamer when they all appeared, the father and sons descending from the stairs, the houseguest arriving from the den.

"This is Cathy," Mary offered. "My husband, Ted, my sons, Matthew and Brian."

Cathy said a quiet hello, nodding in the direction of each name. Ted gave a sympathetic half smile, his warm brown eyes managing to communicate his acknowledgment of her ordeal,

37

while the boys just seemed momentarily paralyzed. Matthew, looking overtly confused by this additional female presence, seemed to note the decorative style and casual elegance of the table settings, but reserved his commentary for a more private family moment.

"Would you mind if I showered?" Cathy asked, crossing her arms over the part of Mary's pale pink nightshirt that read: I HATE MORNING PEOPLE.

"Not at all," Mary answered. "There are fresh towels upstairs. Third door on your right."

"Thank you," she whispered. And then, as an afterthought, craning her head over the side of the staircase, so that her long, daffodil-yellow hair draped down past the banister, she added, "Nice to meet you, guys."

The table full of short-haired, brown-eyed brunettes couldn't help but be transfixed by the effortless sweeping of Cathy's hair, like a weightless scarf trailing after her, like fringe of the highest quality silk. Mary noticed that Cathy's hair was blond again, and as the hallway sunlight reached it, pink highlights seemed to streak it as it moved. Cathy, oblivious to the family's fascination, continued upstairs, her bare feet silent on the steps.

The men could manage little more than mumbling at first.

Everyone waited, passing pancakes and bacon, until they were relatively sure Cathy was out of earshot. They made an attempt to whisper.

"Mom, who is she?" Matthew began.

"She works at the luncheonette in town," Mary answered

politely. "She's Cathy," Mary finished, having little more to say.

"What is she doing here?" Matthew continued.

"Her mother was killed in a car accident last night," Mary said, her own voice cracking. "Needless to say, she was upset when she arrived."

"Doesn't she have a family?" Ted asked.

"I'm not sure," Mary admitted, drizzling a scant trickle of syrup over her pancake, pausing, then adding a generous stream.

"How well do you know this person?" Ted began now, taking the interrogation up a notch.

"Well enough for her to come here," Mary answered firmly, adding another scoop of butter, predictably disappointed in her family's attention to practicalities. It was really very simple. Someone had bounced into her life unexpectedly. Someone who needed her help. Someone who had just lost her mother.

"Well enough to be sure she won't go nuts or anything?" Matthew inquired, startling even himself.

"Nuts?" Mary accused.

"You know what I mean. The shock of her tragedy," he continued, snapping his bacon with his fork and spearing a wedge of pancake. "I mean this is pretty rough stuff. How do you know you're not going to find her dead in our bathtub?"

"What? That's enough, Matthew!" Mary barked. "Now, I know this seems a bit odd, but considering the state she was in last night, I didn't think it was appropriate to ask too many questions. For the time she is here, I'll expect you all to be extra nice. You can put up with a slight inconvenience or two if it comes to that. The poor thing's just lost her mother, for heaven's sake."

"Dad, what do you think?" Matthew demanded, reaching across the table to claim another pancake before his gluttonous brother scooped the remaining three onto his plate.

"I think we have enough drama without trying to look for more, Matthew," Ted cautioned, transferring a pancake from Brian's plate to his own.

"I thought you were cutting down." Brian defended himself. And then feeling generous, "She can have my room, Mom," he offered, his cheeks puffed full of food. "Mom's judgment's good enough for me."

"And I'm sure you'd have volunteered whether or not she was pretty?" Matthew inquired suspiciously, rolling his toast to dip into his remaining syrup.

"Who said she was pretty?" Brian asked. "Keep him away from her, Mom. She's already got a broken heart. The last thing she needs is Matty in her life."

"Shut up."

"You shut up."

"Everybody shut up," Ted ordered.

"When did we start saying shut up in this house?" Mary whispered, offended, as if her guest could hear.

"Pass me the juice, Brian. These little glasses are completely useless, Mary," Ted commented further.

"Now, listen to me," Mary commanded. "Cathy has been through an ordeal none of you know anything about. I expect this family to behave with some compassion," she ordered. "Eat, Ted," she instructed, dumping the final two strips of bacon onto her husband's plate. "You'll be late for work."

"Mary, please, I'm trying to cut down," he protested. Hearing that, Brian's fork pierced the top strip on Ted's plate, but Ted defended with his fork and immediately sliced through both pieces. Brian's fork retreated from his father's plate, managing to secure the last slice of toast.

"Honey, the boys were just—"

"I know, being boys. But perhaps they could every once in a while attempt to evolve into sensitive humans," Mary said, depositing her plate into the sink and slamming out of the kitchen.

The boys looked at each other and rolled their eyes.

"How old do you figure she is, Dad?" Matthew asked. "I mean, she looks like she's at least eighteen."

"Matthew, I wouldn't go down this road. After all, it was your comment that set your mother off—"

"Me? You know, I'm the only one here who speaks the truth. I'm trying to protect our family. You just don't know how people are going to react to sudden death."

"What, now you're an expert?" Brian accused.

"I don't need to be an expert. I remember when Grandma died. And Mom doesn't sound like she knows her very well at all," Matthew defended, taking the orange juice container for the third time with a sigh. "Dad, it starts with these little things. Look, it hasn't even been twenty-four hours, and already Mom broke out the juice glasses."

"Son, as your mother said, suck it up," Ted said with resignation, shaking out his newspaper.

"Okay. So no one sees this coming. Fine. I'm telling you, these glasses are just the beginning," Matthew predicted, utterly frustrated. "Maybe I should stay home and keep an eye on things."

"Matthew, take a little advice here. No matter what the girl looks like, you don't want to start a relationship with someone who is going through a hard time. Women are difficult enough to understand when they're happy."

"So I was right? There is a chance she could be a nut."

"Dad, you should know Matty only dates depressed girls. If he found one sad enough, he might actually fall in love. We should keep her."

"Both of you, finish your food and get to work. Become productive citizens. Find a cure for crabgrass," Ted encouraged.

"I'm telling you, Mom seems a little strung out, or was I the only one who noticed the bacon was a little too crisp?"

"She'll be fine," Ted assured him. "And the bacon was fine."

"So we should ignore that stuff you said about charred bacon and carcinogens?"

"Matthew, the orange juice counteracts that. We've been over this a hundred times," Ted said, annoyed.

"Not in these little glasses," Matthew objected.

"Matthew—"

"Dad, I'm just concerned about Mom's involvement here."

"Mom's used to nuts," Brian added.

"That is no way to talk about the senior citizens," Ted corrected.

"I was talking about us," Brian admitted with a shrug.

"I'm serious. I've got a bad feeling about this, Dad," Matthew insisted.

"I can't imagine that you'd want to be part of whatever your mom will be dealing with today. Go to work. Consider yourself lucky."

"He is lucky. A girl with a broken heart under our roof," Brian continued. "Matty's having a windfall."

Mary showered in the master bathroom, skipped the hair conditioner she usually left on for the recommended minutes, did without her facial moisturizer, threw on a navy skirt, white blouse, and tennis shoes, and returned to the kitchen in time to hear the family car depart. Thank goodness. She found Cathy sipping a cup of coffee, and she entered the kitchen with an apology, explaining that the boys had left for work early, probably just to get a ride from their father.

"Are they usually so quiet?" Cathy asked.

"They're a little confused," Mary explained.

"I don't blame them. So am I. I should get back home

and do whatever I'm supposed to do. Maybe I can have a ride, if you don't have plans? My mom was in the only car."

"Sure, I can help you if you want. Is there anyone else who you're close to, who may need to be involved in the arrangements?"

"No. There was only my mother. Now I'm completely alone."

Mary watched the tears fall from Cathy's eyes, knowing what Cathy wanted most could not be given, her mother back, the removal of all last night's events, a way out of the pain, even temporarily.

"You're not alone, Cathy, I promise you," Mary said through her constricted throat. "You'll get through this."

"It hurts so much," Cathy cried, sobbing. "I don't know what I'm ever going to do."

"I know," Mary answered. "Shh."

*A*t the front door of her condo, Cathy's hands shook as she tried to put the key into the lock, something she had done hundreds of times in the dark, after dates, after vacations, after getting a ride home from college, carrying groceries, carting books, with shopping bags full of Christmas gifts from the mall. Mary took the keys from her and opened the door, walking Cathy gently through it.

"Isn't it stupid?" Cathy asked, tears rolling down her cheeks. "I feel like checking the rooms to see if she's here."

"I did that every time I walked into my mother's house," Mary admitted. "Let's go," she offered, walking up the three wide, gray, carpeted steps to the bedrooms, Cathy holding on for dear life.

Mary noticed the bedrooms had distinctly different styles. Cathy's had lavender-colored walls, white lace curtains, a romantic rose-patterned area rug above the ivory wall-to-wall carpeting. It was overloaded with stuffed animals, prints, painted picture frames, dried flowers, a boom box, VCR, and television.

"So, this is what a girl's bedroom looks like?" Mary commented, inhaling cinnamon potpourri and rolling her hands along the lilac comforter. "Did you paint these pictures?" Mary asked, leaning in to get a better view.

"I like to fill up the walls with color," Cathy responded. "Opposite of my mother."

Her mother, Deborah, had accepted the white walls, accenting with a few deliberately chosen, neutral-colored geometrics, and nowhere, except at her vanity, was any clutter visible. At her doorway, Cathy mentioned that she really didn't mind going into her mother's bedroom since she couldn't remember her mom actually spending much time there. She loved the living room, the television, and slept most often right on the sofa.

"I can smell her in here," Cathy said, half comforted.

After they had inspected every room, they returned to the kitchen. Mary offered to make coffee and muffins while they made a list of what needed to be done.

Throughout her five years of mourning, Mary discovered occasional consolations or tributes in the kitchen. With both hands on her scrubbed Farberware, she did her best to reproduce her mother in a soup pot, casserole, dinner roast, or cake. Recipes were the legacy of many women she knew from previous generations, and each handwritten recipe page that survived, despite the oil or coffee stain, was considered a trea-

sure. Combining the ingredients was an optimistic act to combat some of the world's sorrow. The softened butter into the
sugar. The bread crumbs into the beef. The cocoa into the
milk. The food-knitted togetherness of the family. The enticing smells of her nearly done pot roast. The conversations that
were best exchanged at the kitchen table. Anything to feign
control over those unimaginable horrors that could swallow
up a family member. A virus. A stroke. An accident.

"You mean I have to pick out the casket?"

The visit to the funeral home would be difficult, Mary explained, but once all the decisions had been made, wakes sort
of flowed along quickly. It would all be over in a matter of
days.

"I just can't think that far ahead," Cathy admitted. Her
head sank into her hands and she sobbed once more.

Time seemed irrelevant when Mary's mother died, sur-
real. Time was irrelevant yet comforting, for it told her specif-
ically in how many days she would be beyond the rituals of
death, beyond the viewings, the funeral, and the receiving of
friends, fruit baskets, and flowers—that first dreaded look in
the casket that nearly sent her sprawling down on the red carpeting, the overwhelming smell of flowers beginning to decay,
the beginning of her fog. She reduced everything down to
hours. Two hours per viewing, three hours between viewings,
during which Ted seemed to guide her from her home to a
nearby restaurant to join the family, always filling her glass
with chilled chardonnay, to "take off the edge." She ate and
drank and said hello and good-bye to people. She tried to

comfort them when they admitted they hadn't the words, all the time feeling, as this gruesome party played out, something was at peace within her. She wasn't sure what it was, if it had been something as selfish as enjoying the full-time presence of her husband and sons, so handsome in their suits, so manly in their behavior. Perhaps it was the larger hand of power, beyond schools and meetings and petty disturbances.

Cathy explained that her mother had all of their important papers at her writing desk, insurance policies and bank statements, but that she bored easily and had transferred those responsibilities to Cathy back in high school. Mary shivered.

"I know," Cathy nodded. "At the time, I thought it was because she was trying to teach me how to be independent for college. Now I'm thinking maybe subconsciously, she knew. Anyway, I know exactly where the birth certificates, insurance, and mortgage papers are."

"That will make things a little easier for you," Mary added, marveling at how well Cathy seemed to be doing.

They made lists and they talked, Cathy telling story after story about her mother, Mary encouraging her to share as much as was comfortable. Still, Mary couldn't help but be amazed by the girl's composure, remembering how she was unable to touch her mother's possessions without collapsing facedown into the sorrow. Yet Cathy, even after suffering such a shock, seemed to become more animated each time she touched something she knew her mother loved, telling stories, laughing out loud as she remembered the time when their dirty clothes had piled up so high, they dumped five thirteen-gallon trash bags into the trunk and spent all night at the Laundromat.

Cathy went to change out of Matthew's bulky white T-shirt, which Mary had offered when Cathy couldn't seem to touch her own clothing—what she had worn when she learned the news. Mary had passed a lot of her own clothing to charity, as many of her own sweaters and slacks as her mother's, to avoid resurrecting those final days. But Cathy carried only Matthew's shirt, which she promised to wash when they returned to Mary's house, no outfit from yesterday to be donated. Cathy then asked Mary if they could go to the funeral home and make the arrangements, now that she had gathered her papers and put on a skirt and blouse. Mary nodded.

Cathy had her own ideas about grieving. Where Mary struggled to comprehend death as a regretful, permanent separation from a loved one, Cathy preferred to believe that dead was not at any point to be confused with gone. When they arrived at the funeral home, Cathy consulted out loud, uninhibitedly, with her dearly departed mom, during each of the preparatory steps for the burial, choosing the type of wooden casket, wording the obituary, deciding which picture best depicted the personality of her mother. Mary, not wanting to intrude, hung in the background making small talk with the receptionist, writing things into her notepad, running her eyes and hands across the mahogany coffin she remembered choosing for her own mother, admiring her young companion's bravery. Mary added her opinion when solicited, only when it seemed daughter and dead mother had already made their decision and finished their one-sided exchange.

Mary believed it was good for Cathy to be a little strange, to talk to as many dead people as she needed to, out loud, in front of each of the vendors she hired to help transport her mother to her final resting place. Interment would be at Peace Hill Cemetery, where Mary's parents had long ago been consigned.

When they returned to the apartment Cathy fell silent, sat on the ivory sofa, and wept facedown into the teal pillow she had given her mother a few birthdays ago. Mary had no problem comprehending this. This was healthy, Mary thought, to get it all out, as much as she could, to acknowledge the shattering pain. Everybody said so, not just Mary. You cried at the good times, at the memories of struggles, and eventually you began to cry for all the days you'd never have.

In broken sentences, Cathy told Mary that she had picked the two softest pillows she could find, to make her mother more comfortable on the sofa.

"We can drop the pillows at the funeral home on the way back to my house," Mary suggested. And Cathy, wide-eyed and excited, as though she were plotting to give her mom the perfect gift, hugged Mary, hugged her again, and thanked her for her wonderful suggestion. Cathy thought it would make all the difference, knowing her mother's head would lay upon those pillows for all time.

Mary suggested they drive into town for iced tea and sandwiches, just to offer a change of scene, but Cathy, fresh

from a second emotional wind, announced she was determined to continue cleaning up. Together they emptied the
perishable food from the condo, made a dozen or two phone
calls, and, at Cathy's insistence, packed away Deborah's clothing. Seeing the growing emptiness, Mary again offered Cathy
a place in her den. Cathy brightened momentarily, accepted,
then, as if preoccupied, announced that she would like to go
out to get a pizza. At first Mary didn't comment, not realizing that Cathy's conversation, or, more accurately, her mono-
logue, had refocused on her.

"Don't you like pizza, Mary?" Cathy asked, now staring
with the same disbelief Mary had moments before.

"Yes, love it," Mary now replied, somewhat relieved.

Surely Mary was always on the brink of falling down under a sea of tears, at least throughout that first year, if not
longer. But Cathy, to her credit, seemed to lose neither her
appetite nor her enthusiasm for life. She ordered a pie with
everything, and as she sipped her Coke and smoked her
Salems, she relayed anecdotes to Mary as she made a list of
possible attendees at the service.

"She didn't have very strong connections, work acquain-
tances mostly," Cathy admitted. "But I'm sure they'd want to
be there."

Mary approached the next subject cautiously.

"And your father?"

"I don't have one. I never had one," Cathy said, matter of
factly. "You know how family life changed in the seventies. A
lot of people had multiple partners. My mom said she lived in

a type of commune for a while out in California, you know, one big happy family. She was proposed to enough times, but claims she never liked the idea of marriage."

"I knew people like that. I often wondered how they got around the issue of children, you know, who raised them, how they adapted to life outside the commune."

"Well, my mom took me and left when I was an infant. And there was this modeling thing that didn't fit in with the group lifestyle. So she came back east, found a small apartment, and flew to photo shoots when she had to. She never really wanted a lot of money. Just enough for the two of us. She only bought the condo because the accountant kept nagging her."

"And she never saw the commune people again?"

"No. I asked her about it enough. To let me look for these men, see what I think, if I could get a feel for who my father might be. But she didn't think it was the right thing to do. She was a very private person."

"I'm sorry."

"I'm sure she knew who he was, my father. Maybe he never wanted to marry her or be a father. I always encouraged her to date, but she just wasn't interested. I think she was in love with him still. Unless I just romanticize her life. I really don't know. I think I might have liked being part of a family. It sure would have helped me through this."

"That's really what kept me going," Mary admitted.

"I can see that. Your house, your family, it's all so cozy."

"So maybe you'll enjoy staying with us then?" Mary asked.

"I feel bad about imposing. It's probably not fair to your husband, your sons."

"Well, they still have their mothers, don't they? So they don't know what you're going through. But I do. And you're welcome to stay as long as you can stand us," Mary finished.

They returned to Mary's home at eight-thirty that evening, having talked for hours in the pizza place, then gone for dessert at a new coffee shop Mary had been wanting to try, but couldn't bear to go to alone.

The boys and Ted had gone off to a movie, so Mary and Cathy, already exhausted, had some tea before retreating to the den. As Cathy slept on the sofa, Mary sat in the leather chair under her favorite afghan, watching television show after television show, there where her mother's spider plant still thrived, where the twinkle lights and whispered voices of celebrities made it safe enough for two motherless women to close their eyes and sleep, if they so chose.

Mary, who usually found it hard to stay awake until the boys came back from their various sports meets, had difficulty falling off. She felt the impact of change when she realized she had not even bothered to tell her family what to defrost for the evening meal. She knew, of course, they were capable of opening the refrigerator and making sandwiches for once, but Matthew in particular had a rough time when his routine was interrupted. Brian was undoubtedly the one who suggested the movie, and probably a pizza or burgers for dinner. Like Mary, he transformed the worst situation into an excuse to eat somewhere, stay out, do something refreshingly different, create a memorable moment in an otherwise ordinary day.

Mary heard her family come home, and at first she couldn't decide whether she wanted to talk. Ted poked his head in the den to see if she was waiting up. She was, of all things, talked out. Mary pulled on her robe and went into the kitchen, conscious that her boys were eyeing her for signs of regression, for evidence that Cathy's misfortune had now become hers, which would inadvertently become theirs, and they would have to live through yet another bad spell of tears and sadness.

"How is she doing?" Ted asked diplomatically, stooping to deliver a hello kiss, smelling of popcorn and peanut chews, innocuous good times.

"Very well under the circumstances," Mary answered, smiling at them all. "We accomplished a lot today. The service will be Saturday."

"Do you need me to go?" Ted asked, not really knowing what to do with this situation. Others whom Mary had helped had not spent successive nights on a couch in his home.

"No. I think we've got it covered," Mary answered, knowing how he prized his Saturdays, how he just needed to keep mowing that lawn, washing that car, having those quarter-pounder burgers with his beer by the pool on the weekend. After all, there was so little left of summer, and she rather liked the thought of having something to do without him.

"Well, if you change your mind," he trailed off, relieved.

"Doesn't she have any family, Mom?" Matthew, not liking any of this, insisted upon knowing.

"Afraid not, Hon."

"Wow," Brian said, shaking his head. "We really are keeping her."

"No!" Matthew decided. "I'm really not sure you should be doing this. Are you?" Matthew probed his mother.

"There's no one else, Matthew. The owners of the luncheonette are elderly and are taking Cathy's shifts, so they can't get away. Luckily, Cathy's replacement starts Monday, so the owners of the place can have a break. Anyway, it's not going to be more than a morning service and lunch."

"It's too depressing," he grumbled. "There are still two weeks until Labor Day. Don't let her get too attached, Dad," he cautioned his father, going up to his room, two steps at a time, not even casting an interested eye toward the den.

Mary shrugged, not understanding her older son's attitude.

"Don't let him kid you, Mom. He thinks she's a fox," Brian said.

"Boys are the last thing on her mind, Brian," Mary told him.

"That's perfect. Matty loves rejection," he said, jumping

to hit the top of the doorway and continuing on his way up the stairs.

Ted turned off the kitchen light, leaving only the one above the stove.

"Mary, maybe you shouldn't be so completely involved," Ted cautioned. "I mean, I can't help thinking it will bring back all of what you went through."

"I'm okay. Really, Ted. I think it might be helping me."

"Helping you what?"

"You know, move on."

Mary and Cathy both wore black to the funeral service, walked arm in arm to and from the grave site, looking more like a mother and daughter than women who had known each other less than a week. Even with Cathy's head resting upon Mary's shoulder, strands of her long, light hair were shimmering and rising on the breeze like the head of a match in a drafty room, and Mary would brush them from her face, wipe tears from her eyes, kiss her head affectionately, as she would have done with either of her sons. Mary felt instinctively protective of Cathy who only days before had been so abundantly full of life and promise. She felt empathy too for her new friend, and a strange combination of sorrow and gratitude toward the woman she had never met, for having involuntarily bequeathed her this girl.

Mary knew Cathy would remember that August morning forever, the dim sky, the scent of cut grass, the freshly dug, clay-like earth, the single carnations. The only living colors seemed to be the resilient blue of Cathy's eyes and the sparkling gold of her hair.

Without Ted, Mary's strength was more pronounced. She held Cathy up the entire time, through the prayers, through the blessings, through the long and lonely walk back to the car.

Mary had helped Cathy arrange for a small lunch reception at Jolson's, a local restaurant with an outdoor patio. She couldn't help remembering how difficult it was to move from the place they had her mother's reception, back into the light of the day, how the sun seemed to blast out at her, unfairly blinding and bright, against her washed-out eyes. Now she worried about an unanticipated storm. She tried to spare Cathy each and every discomfort she could remember from her own mother's funeral, and she was actually amazed that she hadn't broken down at the cemetery, for she had done so each and every time she visited over the past five years.

At Jolson's, Cathy was friendly and full of social grace. She introduced Mary to everyone she knew, and introduced herself to those people she either couldn't remember or had never met. She was remarkable, crying outright one minute on whomever was nearest, telling each of them over and over again how much she was going to miss her mother.

"She was forty-one, and still so beautiful," Cathy told an elderly gentleman who was a regular at the luncheonette.

"Give yourself time, honey," he advised, patting her hand.

"It's like a dream. I still can't believe it," Mary heard

Cathy say as she bid good-bye to a trio of young women in business clothing.

"It was a beautiful service. I loved that photo of your mom," one of them said to Cathy.

"I didn't think I could take an open casket," Cathy admitted.

The truth of her pain touched everyone.

As the final group said good-bye to Cathy, Mary waited near the car, feeling as though things had gone as well as could be expected. But Cathy lingered on the patio, the grief settling in a little deeper. You could almost hear it spreading out like a virus.

Mary thought better of taking Cathy back home to Ted and the boys, and suggested dropping by the senior citizen center for tea with the ladies. Cathy readily agreed.

Together they picked out an assortment of butter cookies from the grocery bake shop, added a pound of ripe peaches, some vanilla ice cream, and two half-gallons of lemonade. Ordinarily, Mary brought only her own cookies to the center, but she understood the women appreciated the attention far more than the sweets.

As Mary parked the car, Cathy remarked how impressed she was by the charming look of the place. Mary agreed it was every bit as inviting as a bed-and-breakfast, with its blue wrap-around porch and creamy gingerbread accents. The ladies did all their gardening in raised beds, and were even growing some peppers and tomatoes.

"You have no idea how hard they fought to keep it looking this way," Mary told Cathy. "When they were offered funds to modernize, there was practically a revolt against even replacement windows. They did eventually agree to a few chairlifts and some recliners, but they had to be Queen Anne legs to match the tables. And the ladies insisted upon using the rest of the money to buy a van, but the stipulation was that none of them could drive it."

"I'm sure they're happier with the quaint look. I hate those depressing places with the tinted glass. They look too much like office buildings. This is so much better," Cathy remarked enthusiastically.

Mary was relieved to hear Cathy talking again. If this trip didn't help wash away the images from the funeral, she didn't know what would.

Mary pulled the grocery bags out of the car as a few of the ladies began making their way from the house. Cathy couldn't believe the women were wearing woolen sweaters in the summer, and walking so fast.

"Well, they're always cold. And I think they're very competitive," Mary acknowledged with a smile, "although they would never admit it."

Indeed, Penelope Miller insisted her aide, Dolores, roll her wheelchair over to Mary's car so she could greet the visitors properly, and first. Penelope liked to focus on the benefits of her infirmity—such as her ability to leave the ladies traveling on foot in the dust. "Step on it," she'd whisper to Dolores when she felt Gertie or Agnes closing in on her. There really wasn't much competition from the others who were content to arrive anywhere dead last. Beatrice Hammer-schmidt, who still had a spring in her step, usually preferred to stay in the sunroom guarding her favorite chintz lounge chair.

"So you brought the orphan," Penelope announced, offering Cathy her hand. "I'm Penelope Miller, Miss Penelope Miller."

Mary winced and wished she had thought to warn Cathy about the way these ladies approached a matter so directly. But Cathy didn't flinch at being referred to as an orphan. Mary suspected she probably felt more sympathy for Penelope's lack of mobility than her own parentless status.

Cathy immediately squatted down beside Penelope and grasped her extended hand, noting the coolness of her brown-spotted skin, her very deliberate grip, and a gold and ruby ring, twirling loosely about her finger.

"Nice to meet you, Miss Miller. I'm Cathy with a C."

"We're all very sorry for your loss, dear," Penelope began. "It isn't right to lose your mother so young, while the likes of us are hanging on by our dentures."

"Thank you," Cathy said, instinctively hugging her.

Penelope looked surprised by the sweetness of the gesture, and gently patted Cathy's back in return.

Someone tapped Cathy's shoulder as though cutting in.

"Do you bake too?" asked Gertie, a round woman with Coke-bottle lenses who could never wait to ask a question or eat a cookie. She wore polyester black pants, a mint green sweater, and double-knotted, tan Hush Puppies, which allowed her to easily take second place against Penelope's wheelchair, which was not bad at all for an overweight woman in her eighties.

"I've done a little cooking at the luncheonette," Cathy answered modestly.

"Mary's sugar cookies are delicious," Gertie proclaimed, sneezing and sliding out tissues from her left sleeve.

"That's because I always use your recipe, Gertie," Mary reminded her. "The extra confectioners' sugar makes all the difference."

"That's right," Gertie laughed. "In my day I used to make enough cookies to feed all the Cub Scouts in town. You know, they didn't have a cookie program. I would have started one, but they never asked me. Maybe they thought cookies were for girls. It was probably for the best because I would have eaten myself right out of business," she said laughing. "So, what do you do, Cathy?"

"I go to college," Cathy responded, and when that didn't elicit any further conversation, she added, "I work at the luncheonette. And I like to make wall decorations."

"Cathy's very artistic," Mary volunteered. Nothing moved a conversation into high gear quicker than a craft discussion.

"Is that so?" Agnes Morrison asked, stepping forward to assume control. She wore a silvery blue poncho that nearly matched the shade of her tightly curled hair, a navy linen skirt, and two-inch black stack pumps, which may have slowed her down but gave her both height and authority. She extended her left arm and the woolen material spread as if it was a feathery wing, and Cathy obediently moved into it. Agnes clasped Cathy firmly around the shoulder and began walking her toward the entrance. "You come on inside now and tell us all about your art projects. You know, young girls don't seem to know what to do with their time these days unless they're plugged into something. They're not taught to be resourceful. I'm happy to hear you're not like that. I do a nice cross-stitch myself. I passed many a summer afternoon like this one with just a needle and some colored thread."

"Don't you have a sweater?" Gertie asked Cathy, hitting the blue handicapped button to open the door for Penelope and Dolores, and sneezing once more for good measure. "It's so cold inside with all that silly air-conditioning."

"I'm okay," Cathy answered

"Of course you are," Agnes answered. "You seem to be of pretty strong stock. And if you get cold, we have enough afghans to heat you to boiling."

"Oh look, Agnes, Mary brought lemonade," Shirley added, tagging along merrily. Shirley was always easily pleased, with no apparent agenda other than to eat, drink, and socialize. Mary suspected she had suffered at least one stroke.

"I like lemonade," Shirley said to no one in particular.

The pedestal dining table had been set with two porcelain tea services for four, one sporting hydrangeas and the other lavender lilacs. Mary knew from experience that, although the ladies had converted from loose to bagged tea, it was still going to be Earl Grey.

At the center of the table was a floral arrangement in an

opaque urn that included crisp tiger lilies, daisies, and peace roses. The pale pink tablecloth was topped by a white cutwork runner and matching napkins. The ham, cheese, and turkey slices were fanned out on a large yellow platter near a basket of soft rolls. Mary loved how much these ladies enjoyed dressing up the table.

"How pretty!" Cathy exclaimed. "It looks just like a party with those beautiful flowers," she continued.

"Evelyn's our in-house florist," Penelope volunteered. "She's smart enough to never include a horrid gladiola around any of us. Only one thing that flower's known for, and we don't like to be reminded of it."

Penelope began pouring tea while the other ladies helped Mary stash the ice cream and dessert for later. Cathy volunteered to serve tea and sandwiches to the women who were reading or watching television in the living room, and Mary was surprised no one objected. Whenever Mary suggested she take tea to the others, the ladies explained that high tea was always served in the dining room, not in the living room, and if they didn't come for the conversation, they could certainly do without the food. But she guessed they were making allowances and trying their best to help.

Cathy had an instant rapport with Margaret, the painter of the group, who showed a distinct preference for folk art and especially loved doing winter scenes. By the time Mary served up the ice cream and cookies, Cathy had been given a tour of the center, and a watercolor of Central Park which Margaret had painted in her twenties.

"I first began painting on stones because we had no paper," Margaret offered loudly since she couldn't always remember to turn on her hearing aid. She passed Cathy a smooth rock the size of a baking potato, depicting a city snowfall with skaters and evergreens, gentlemen with tall hats, and women in full-length coats accessorized with bright red muffs. "One year, my children came to show me this packaged stone—what was that they called them?"

"Pet Rocks," Mary volunteered at equal volume.

"Yes, that was it! Pet Rocks. Now, here some huckster had decided to sell plain rocks for pets. But they had no faces or ears, no tails or fur on them at all. Some of them weren't even entirely smooth, so you couldn't even use them to paint a picture!"

"People will buy anything," Penelope commented with disdain before biting into a chocolate leaf-shaped cookie.

"Maybe dumb people," Agnes mumbled, taking another raspberry sandwich cookie, and passing the plate to Cathy.

"My kids knew better," Margaret added. "They knew the value of a good canvas, whether it was a seashell or a rock."

"Do they put pictures on the stones?" Cathy asked.

"No, dear. They just sold them plain, the way they came out of the ground." Margaret tried to explain.

"No," Cathy said quietly. "I meant for the cemetery. I just thought it might be nice to have a scene on the stone for my mother. I hadn't really thought about it before."

Margaret looked confused and finally began to fiddle with the buttons on her hearing aid. It was so quiet you could hear

Shirley's stomach gurgle, and Evelyn passed her one of the cookies she had stuffed into her pocket for later.

"I'll tell you this. They charge you by the letter," Agnes told her, smacking the table as though she couldn't quite get over it. Margaret, who had apparently turned up her volume too high, jerked in response.

"It's the nature of business," Penelope added. "Everybody wants a piece of that insurance money."

"I'm sure you can pick out a scene," Mary added gently. "They do a lot by laser now."

"Sure, sure," Shirley added, just to be part of the conversation.

"They laser everything these days, from your eyeballs to your bunions," Agnes said with a wave of her hand. "I'm sure you can have whatever kind of picture you want."

"I just used my husband's middle initial," Gertie added. "He never liked the name Rupert anyway."

"I want my entire name. I earned every single letter," Penelope stated emphatically. "I put it right in my will. I'm counting on you, Mary, to check and make sure the lawyer doesn't stick me with Penny to save a buck. After all, I'm not a cheap coin."

9

here was no further discussion about where Cathy would stay until her semester began; Mary had already convinced her that her home was big enough and that her family didn't mind her staying in the den. Mary now enjoyed how Cathy meant to keep an eye on her, in much the same way Mary was looking out for her. So they sorted through the paperwork, the excess linens, and together they managed to collect and transport the few boxes Cathy elected to keep, which they marked for storage in Mary's basement. Mary was even inspired to send some of her mother's old glassware to charity, to make more room in the basement for Cathy's things.

Matthew offered to move her boxes in for her. This was the young man's first act of kindness toward Cathy, if you didn't count his distancing himself. She had followed him into the basement carrying one of the larger boxes. When he turned and saw her struggling, having already decided he would take his time going back and forth, grabbing a considerable amount of exercise from the staircase, relishing the pleasure of carrying each of those pleasantly scented, square containers from the blinding bright heat of the summer sun into the cool, moist, darkness of his basement, he quickly blew his cool, yelling, "I'll get them." Matthew then vowed to return to his policy of limited interaction, realizing he could not yet endure his proximity to Cathy with any amount of grace.

"Okay," she responded. But Matthew did not just hear okay, but a long, drawn-out, what's-your-problem okay, hinting, accusing, concluding in fact that he was anything but okay, and as the sweat dripped down his handsome, suntanned face, she stood there defensively, her golden ponytail dancing in the shadows of the light from the doorway, before shrugging off her confusion.

Matthew was instantly conscious that he had admitted too much, everything in fact, with his possessive claim to transport Cathy's boxes. Undoubtedly, she thought he was an idiot. On the other hand, he now understood why his father at times fought to pay the dinner check, and opened the hood of a car to stare at an engine he would never understand.

"I just didn't want you to get hurt or anything. You don't know how much junk is piled up here," he said, trying his best to apologize without apologizing.

"I could help you clean it out," she volunteered, smiling,

looking around. "You could have a great spare room here. I'm real good at making things look nice."

Never a truer word was spoken, for Matthew need only look upon that beautiful, pure, tragic face to know just how nice she could make a thing look.

"That's okay. We're used to it," he shrugged, quite comfortable with the cavelike, masculine, unfinished look of his family's disorganized stuff, eager to protect the territory, as it was one of the few indoor places he was sure not to accidentally cross her path. He had even moved his weight bench there, seeing how his mother and this girl were always coming or going from the garage, taking shopping trips, packing clothing away for this or that charity, wrapping glassware, mailing papers, doing things he knew nothing of, but which required a lot of local travel, a lot of strained hellos and goodbyes.

Mary and Cathy took a ride to a Syracuse monument company where they could look at samples for Deborah's headstone. They had an appointment with Harold Lempke, an unassuming man who wore wire-rimmed glasses, a short-sleeved button-down shirt, and desert boots. He offered coffee, but Mary's nose could tell it had been sitting on the burner for a while, so she politely declined. Cathy had brought in her can of Coke, which she had been sipping since the last stop for gas.

As Cathy flipped through a binder of samples, Mary couldn't help repeating she had no idea there was so much available, everything from mountains to flags to skyscrapers.

"Do you have anything that would be appropriate for a seventies-type woman?" Cathy asked, closing the book of "best sellers."

"We have a peace symbol," Harold offered, "and a sun-moon symbol."

"That doesn't seem right for her," Cathy responded.

"We also have electric guitars, astrological symbols, and flowers," Harold suggested, sliding another book toward Cathy.

"What do you think, Mom? Flowers?" Cathy asked, opening the book marked *Floral Motifs*.

"Pardon?" Harold asked, when Mary didn't answer.

"Oh, I was just talking to her," Cathy explained. "My mother," she continued naturally. "These are pretty, and roses were your favorite."

Harold slowly moved his gaze toward Mary, who shook her head and calmly pointed one finger toward the heavens. Harold nodded that he understood, but he looked a little unnerved.

Suddenly, Cathy was laughing out loud. Mary put down the house-pet book she was looking through and ran to see what was so funny. Cathy was pointing to a huge gladiola. "I never realized that flower was so common to funeral baskets. But Penelope was right. They're all over the place."

After flipping through symbols, hobbies, musical instruments, and planets, it was Mary who actually stumbled onto a book of lighthouses that Cathy immediately knew her mother would love. They narrowed it down to three, weighing the pros and cons of clouds versus sun, and decided on a few clouds drifting by.

Cathy loved the idea of putting such a pleasant scene at the Peace Hill Cemetery. It also made her feel like her mother was still on duty from afar.

Ted was grilling hamburgers when they returned home. The boys had set out a stack of paper plates along with buns, mustard, and ketchup. Mary grabbed potato salad and quickly sliced tomatoes and onions, while Cathy put out napkins, silverware, and iced tea.

Both Ted and Matthew went immediately silent as they sat down to dinner, but Brian had no problem making conversation. Eventually, he moved off the subject of what awful choices were on school summer reading lists, to asking for details about the stone.

"So, how'd it go? Did you pick something out?" Brian asked, adding two pickle spears to his plate.

A slight thump could be heard, as though Matthew had attempted a subtle kick, but ended up striking the leg of the table when Brian's reflexes outmaneuvered his. Mary touched Matthew's shoulder, letting him know it was okay to discuss the headstone. Matthew bit off a large piece of his hamburger, as if to hurry this dinner along.

"I bought a beautiful lighthouse scene," Cathy told him. "It's amazing. You can see the water, some clouds, and a really detailed reef."

"Cool," Brian said. "I'm glad it's not just holy stuff you can have. That's kind of boring," he added, squirting out some extra ketchup for dunking his hamburger.

Ted asked Matthew to pass the mustard. Matthew and Ted exchanged looks of incredulity, as though they could not believe Brian.

"You wouldn't believe what nice alternatives they have," Mary volunteered. "You can get absolutely anything. I saw farm scenes with pigs and tractors—" Mary caught Ted's eye and stopped mid-sentence, but Cathy, who had been scooping potato salad onto her plate, picked up where she left off.

"Entire pages of gorgeous horses," Cathy interrupted excitedly. "They have covered bridges, peace symbols, yin and yang, drum sets, and the sweetest-looking cows."

Mary noticed Ted's jawline was tighter than normal, and assumed he was more than a little uncomfortable with the idea of animals or instruments on a headstone. "Of course you can have more traditional pictures too," Mary added.

"I think a lighthouse is a great idea. So when you have to go to the cemetery, you're looking at something happy," Brian said with enthusiasm. "I think I'd want to have a Maserati. Or maybe an F-18 with a good-looking girl standing next to it."

"No one wants to see that at a cemetery," Matthew told him in no uncertain terms.

"I'll bet you're wrong. I bet some poor guy who's just buried his grandfather would love standing next to my stone. I bet it would take his mind off his grief to see a Hornet and hot babe."

"That's completely disrespectful," Matthew growled, expecting one of his parents to chime in and object. But the only voice he heard belonged to his brother, the idiot.

"Says you. Did they have any plain crosses for Matty or other people with no imagination?"

"Would you mind not discussing my death before I'm even out of high school?" Matthew barked.

"Maybe we should change the subject, Brian," Mary suggested.

"Thank you," Matthew sighed, reaching across his brother for another burger and bun.

"Okay. But it might be smarter to at least find out what Mom and Dad want, now that the subject's officially on the table."

"I'm with Matt. Now I'd like the subject off the table," Ted announced, popping open a beer and pouring it carefully into his tilted glass, minimizing the head.

"Fine. Don't say I didn't ask," Brian huffed. "I don't know why you're getting all creeped out about this. These are important decisions. And it would be nice to have your opinion."

"Anything you choose will be just fine," Mary said to comfort him.

"You're going to let him pick!" Matthew exploded, standing in anger. "Fine. Don't blame me if you end up with a circus elephant!" Matthew said, wrapping his burger in his napkin and storming away from the table.

"I'll save the bearded lady for you!" Brian antagonized further.

Mary quickly yelled after him. "I meant you collectively, Matthew."

"Don't mind him. He's the sensitive type," Brian whispered to Cathy, adding a shrug of his shoulders, as if he had no clue at all how he got to his brother.

Ted frowned at Mary and Mary averted her eyes, smiled at Cathy, and watched as Brian claimed the potato salad from his brother's abandoned plate.

As Labor Day weekend approached, the women complained to each other, Cathy for her subjection to the immaturity of student life, and Mary for having nothing else to focus on but her family, home, church, and seniors. Mary decided to take Cathy shopping, a last, long mall fling, the way she had taken Matthew and Brian for back-to-school clothes, savoring the last few days of her young friend's presence.

It was crowded, but sales were everywhere, in the shoe stores, in the specialty boutiques, in the large department stores where dozens of mothers with daughters Cathy's age argued over one style or another, rolling their eyes at each other, angrily clacking hangers back onto the racks.

They ate at the luncheonette. The afternoon sunlight poured through the windows, and not even the paddle fans seemed to do more than blow the humid air about them as they sat on their twirling stools drinking chocolate and cherry Cokes, chatting with Neva, Cathy's replacement. They ate cheeseburgers, fries, ice-cream sundaes decorated with whipped cream and sprinkles, talking about anything and nothing, boys, dorms, courses, and college life.

As the conversation and lunch wound down, Cathy casually announced her plan to contact her deceased mother. For a moment, Mary didn't think she was suggesting anything new, but listened intently. Cathy was talking about visits with a psychic, tarot cards, approaching someone who could, she insisted, bring messages back and forth from the spirit realm, and, hopefully, help Cathy develop her powers to do the same.

Mary was intrigued. She asked questions, as though they were on any other topic. But then, casually, as if Cathy was asking Mary if she wanted to go to Macy's, she invited her to go along to meet the psychic. Mary had been anticipating some symptoms of grief, even suspecting Cathy might have problems separating from her, a maternal presence. But this suggestion made her laugh.

"What? You're kidding, aren't you?" she asked, automatically replying as though the joke were evident.

"Not at all. I believe I can find a way to communicate with her," Cathy continued, unaffected by Mary's incredulity. "And you always say how much you'd like to talk to your mother," Cathy added.

"Okay," Mary said, quietly to herself, the way she might have reacted if Brian had come home and announced he had just had the nicest lunch with aliens. But this was Cathy she was talking to, not one of her sons. Mary took a breath and asked, "And how do you plan to do this?"

"We." Cathy affirmed. "I mean, I don't see why you wouldn't want to communicate, assuming we could learn how."

"Assuming we could," Mary repeated. "And that's a broad leap of faith," she added, trying still to understand Cathy's statement in perhaps a figurative sense. "Do you think that would help you more than what you're doing now? I mean, I can't help noticing you talk to her outright, often."

"Yeah, but I can't hear her talk back. You know, certain people can. And if they can, maybe we would be able to, with the proper training, of course," Cathy finished.

Mary tried to stay open-minded, but, at the same time, responsibly grounded to her view of reality. Not that the idea of speaking to her mother was at all distasteful. Hadn't she tried so hard, banged on those windowpanes and doors, to bring her mother back again in dreams? Perhaps what Cathy was suggesting was little more than inviting contact through some subconscious doorway. And really, what it came down to was that she could certainly use all the female companionship she could scrape up, dead and alive.

"Mary, I know I might sound crazy, but I've seen it done. I've seen people channel and speak to spirits. They can communicate with the dead because they're sort of tuned in."

"I don't know, Cathy. Psychics? I find them in direct conflict with my overwhelming fear of the Almighty. Are these people in cults or something?"

"Not at all. Some are extremely spiritual. And I've seen you read your horoscope, so I know you're at least aware of parapsychology."

"Well, sure, astrology. I mean, we touched on all that mystical stuff at college. I read Linda Goodman, and every magazine has run something on numerology, dream interpretation, all that stuff. Even my mother had a book that would tell you which lucky numbers to play if you dreamt about certain things. I just never delved in too deep."

"So, maybe it's time to."

"When you say these psychics are spiritual, how do you mean that? Are they out there cavorting with the demons, or are we talking holy people?"

"I can't speak for all of them. The people I met seemed gifted, like prophets, although, as I said, I believe we all have it. We just need to develop it. I really never had a reason to before my mother died. But the thought of her in a reachable dimension—I just have to try."

Mary sipped her Coke and tried to remain objective. She tried not to think of her own mother, only the tragedy that Cathy had experienced. Perhaps this was as positive a way as any to redirect that restless energy that kept her staring at the ceiling recounting the final conversations, the soft coolness of her mother's face, the way she looked so peaceful as she sighed her last breath.

"And what do these people do, look into a crystal ball?" Mary probed.

"I've never seen a crystal ball reader. But I asked a lot of questions when I saw the tarot reading."

"And the people you saw told you they spoke to dead people?"

"In most cases, they just listened. They brought messages. Nothing like you see on television. No swaying or moaning or assuming another person's voice. No ectoplasm spewing from their mouths. Like this one girl felt guilty that she was alive, and her sister had died of cancer very young. The medium helped her resolve that. He brought her messages that helped her heal."

"What was he wearing?" Mary asked, skeptically, though she was beginning to enjoy the conversation so much more than her own chronic mourning.

"The medium? You mean like a turban or a gypsy shirt? Mary, he was in a blue work shirt and Dockers. Think about it. Maybe we'd have to use slightly more than the ten percent of our brains everyone talks about."

"Cathy," Mary laughed, "the way I've been feeling lately, I'd be happy to work my way up to four or five."

Having a conversation with her mother had been more than a mild preoccupation of Mary's. If she wasn't inhaling her mother's perfume in stores, she was trying her best to get her dreams to spring for one five-minute dialogue. If the truth be told, Mary always looked for even the faintest presence of her mother. She pictured her before she was sick, walking along the flowers in the park. She stared at the neighbors' tomato plants, remembering her mother working in her garden. Anything had to be better than staring at that carved, gray stone amid the thousands of other carved, gray stones that did no more than announce her name and the number of years she lived.

~ 10 ~

*C*athy's invitation was intriguing, once Mary allowed herself to consider such unconventional communication. It was all coming back to her, how she had gotten from psychology class and Carl Jung to Linda Goodman's astrology sun signs. She knew about Jung's theory of synchronicity, and recognized her meeting with Cathy as a textbook case. Sure, she thought she had heard a voice, but was she really ready to open this strange and scary door?

She could almost hear her mother encouraging her to remember the stories of the other departed souls who had dropped in on relatives. Remember Dad's whistling. Aunt Henrietta's spilling the sugar bowl. Inexplicable physical movement attributed to visitors beyond. She could certainly try for a conversation or two.

In absolute truth, what else did she have to do with her time? Wheel her old ladies in and out of Sunday service? Make ten thousand more cookies for fund-raisers? Be ever accessible to her husband and sons? Something had connected her with Cathy in some capacity. Something had drawn her into that luncheonette on a seemingly ordinary day and precipitated this relationship.

Ted wouldn't like it; she knew he would think she was more than a little nuts. But then again, he still had his parents and couldn't begin to comprehend her desperation, and therefore was denied a vote. Brian would accept it with a laugh—Mom's been sniffing too much ammonia! And Matthew, well, like most things in her life, just wouldn't allow it to affect him, would raise one eyebrow and grumble the way he did upon seeing his third variation of Hamburger Helper.

At the very least, she could help Cathy, who was probably setting herself up for some horrendous disappointment. It was possible the young woman was in tremendously deep denial. But it was also possible that she knew more about this particular subject than Mary, and together they could at the very least learn something, or help each other over her loss. It was so wonderful to be around someone who knew the kind of pain she had been battling these past five years.

"There are books about this," Cathy told Mary. "Not that I'm trying to twist your arm," she added, offering Mary a stick of Juicy Fruit. Mary couldn't remember how old she was when she stopped chewing that flavor, but smiled as she took a stick.

"I would definitely feel more comfortable reading about it first," Mary admitted, already pretty well in favor of the idea. "It really does sound interesting, especially when you consider how I spend most of my free time."

"How did you spend most of your free time? I mean before me," Cathy asked.

"Looking for things to do, ways to be productive. I mean it was all so overwhelming, my mother's illness. Years had gone by while I cared for her and my family. Then it was all so empty, the house, the days. And you know it's getting worse all the time. I could definitely use a new hobby," Mary admitted, handing Cathy a roll of Life Savers, which she now bought in bulk, six rolls to each shrink-wrapped package, to sustain the connection between the mints and her mother.

"For me, it's simple. I know I don't want to live my life without my mother. I'm going to try to talk with her whatever way I can. If I can't develop the skill, then I'll just work through a medium, and for the price of a dinner out, I can get messages."

"This isn't like a 1-900-Calling-Mama, is it? I mean, it's not going to be four bucks a minute to talk through this person?"

Cathy laughed out loud. Mary joined her. They seemed to be laughing a lot lately.

"No. These people, sensitives as they're called, are kind of like counselors. They help you the way a psychologist would, only they have exceptional resources. The guy I saw could read the past, the future, and what's hanging you up in the present."

"When do I meet him?"

"There's one up at college, a former professor, but he in-

sists upon our enrolling in at least one meditation course before we see him. I phoned him yesterday."

"You mean I'd have to enroll?" Mary asked, profoundly
disappointed. One minute she was consulting a professional
psychic, and the next she wasn't. Of course she couldn't go.
She couldn't even consider it. She had immediate thoughts of
Ted, Matthew, and Brian, followed by an emotional rebellion
that had her yelling through the bathroom door at her husband as she packed her most collegiate nightshirt, her compo-
sition notebook, and her loose-fitting jeans.

College was out of the question. She remembered things
from yoga class about a third eye, very easternish, metaphysi-
cal stuff that always managed, during past attempted climbs to
a higher consciousness, to put her right to sleep. Her classmates would brag about their visits to other planes, flying
through the night, writing in joy circles, encountering miniature talking animals, and astrally projecting themselves into
each other's bedrooms where they had instantaneous or-
gasms. Even then, Mary who was already wearing a pre-
engagement ring from Ted, couldn't seem to venture further
than the familiar landscape of her late-for-school dream,
where she ran, half dressed, her hair dripping wet, spilling
books all over campus.

"If I took a course, I'd have to drive out once a week.
Maybe I could spend the night without too much chaos at
home. Although I can't imagine Ted being happy about all
that mileage on the car," Mary sighed again, her voice already
pinched with lost hope.

Cathy was smiling. "You could drive out and stay over. Or why don't you just come for the whole semester? Maybe there are other courses you could take. You can live with me. I never replaced my roommate when she dropped out last year. She was the smart one."

"What? Why didn't you say anything? We could have spent time finding you a replacement."

"Well, until now, I was considering dropping out too," she admitted, shrugging her shoulders.

"It's too soon to make that kind of a decision," Mary advised.

"I know. I heard you say that in my head. What do you think? Would you come for a little while? Crazy, huh?" Cathy asked, flipping her ponytail.

"The thought of actually leaving this town is so absurd, and yet so exciting. Just pack up and leave for a semester?" Mary now asked tentatively, yet with a hint of enthusiasm. She laughed out loud. The thought of it was so impossible. "I couldn't. There'd be an immediate economic decline if I stopped baking in the fall. Oh, can you imagine my family?" She laughed again.

"Well, I guess they'd be upset, really upset," Cathy acknowledged, not wanting to put any pressure on her friend.

"Well, I don't think they'd be upset really, not in the way of actually missing me, but I'm sure they'd miss something— my being there. And they would be shocked. I mean the thought of me going back to college. I just couldn't manage it. Who would take care of them? And what about the seniors?

They'd all have overdue library books in no time. They have all these appointments, foot doctors, cardiologists, church."

"Let it roll around in your head for a while," Cathy suggested, shrugging as though it really didn't matter, as though it were just a suggestion, not a next step in their inexplicable relationship.

But Mary said an automatic no to Cathy, explaining why it would be totally impractical for her to get away, especially just as school was starting, why she couldn't leave Ted, Matthew, or Brian, any one of them indefinitely, and certainly not all three, why they would never understand, and then in the middle of her own discourse, she heard the slightest whisper of her own voice to visit the bookstore anyway, on her way home.

Mary disguised her parapsychology book by placing it inside another, like a teenager with a *Playboy* magazine. Sex would have been easier to explain than this. Ted would never understand her desire for spiritual knowledge, and would attribute it all to some emotional need or an unwillingness to accept her mother's death—exactly what she had initially suspected of Cathy. Still, it was obvious that, after spending the last five or so years with her nose in magazines and cookbooks, she could create lovely casseroles and wonderful cookies, but hadn't experienced any spiritual growth. That she could manage to read this book straight through without nodding off seemed a minor miracle in her life.

There was life and there was death, this life and the next, and it was difficult not to be mighty curious about the goings-on of your beloved, departed ones. The more she thought about it, the more she knew she wanted to leave, had to leave her home, to just pack a few things and head toward this source of learning, had to rejoin the living through her search for ongoing dialogue with the dead.

It all made perfect sense. No, it made no sense at all. It was a feeling, like the one that had drawn her out of her basement and into the luncheonette. The idea was not just rolling around in her head, it was building momentum.

She could try to explain it to Ted. He was an openminded, loving husband. He had denied her nothing. She would tell him it was not so much a choice as a compelling need to follow this thread of a connection with Cathy to the next level. And if Ted didn't get it, if he couldn't comprehend the difference between her pursuing a higher level of life and running off with a drunken sailor, then that would really be too bad for him, wouldn't it?

She had to accept responsibility for her quality of life. Perhaps it had been her mother's life she had assumed, the stay-at-home, be-there-for-her-family nobility, and it was either putting her to sleep or having her slice onions at eight in the morning. The seniors would miss her. They would miss her a lot. But they had lived fully, and Mary was twenty years too young to have become so invisible in the world.

That wasn't anyone's fault but her own. She didn't expect her family to sit with her and sob while the world marched on. Lately, she was always feigning interest in this or that sport, this or that car, and she had absolutely nothing worthwhile to add to family dinner conversations. Even when she offered a story, it was one Ted heard before, and he endured it politely, even occasionally helping her get the details right, which just made her feel even more pathetic. Imagine the anecdotes she could gather if she were away for more than an afternoon.

She definitely needed to get out of her den, and, God willing, this time, get so much further than the Peace Hill Cemetery.

~ 11 ~

Mary was up so late reading, she overslept. She had meant to get up early, speak to Ted, spend a long time explaining the unusual circumstances that drove this desire of hers to leave home for a very short period of time. Instead, she was up most of the night, thrilled, terrified, confused, talking herself into and out of making such an incredible change in her life. Finally, she had fallen into a sound sleep around dawn. She now raced to be dressed, to make it to the breakfast table before her family left.

Ted had made the coffee and Cathy had gone jogging, she learned as she entered the kitchen. Mary grabbed a mug of coffee, her sugar substitute, her milk. She poured a bowl full of granola and sat at the table. She stared at her boys, at Ted. They had managed breakfast well enough without her. One of them had even made toast. She supposed they could eat toast and cereal for weeks and never get a vitamin deficiency, although they really loved bacon and pancakes. Especially Brian. He might lose weight in her absence. If she thought about it, breakfast alone provided dozens of reasons for her not to go. But this was never about logic.

She didn't allow enough time for her own coffee to take effect. Mary simply blurted out to her family that she would most likely be accompanying Cathy to college for "a little while." She could have said a few days, but she didn't know for sure that she wouldn't want more time. She could have said a semester, but she didn't know that she wouldn't rush back missing them terribly in a day or two. Judging from the enthusiasm she was feeling, and her lack of sleep, she had a selfish and energetic thought that she actually might enroll in a course or two for the semester.

Ted crinkled his brow in that conservative, middle-class, husband-disapproving kind of way, as if not quite understanding, but in reality trying to formulate his theory of dissuasion. He slurped a little coffee, collecting his thoughts. Matthew looked to his father accusingly, as if he now had proof that his dad had dropped this most important ball. Brian offered an automatic "cool" and poured a second bowl of cereal.

"I'm sure you'll all do fine," Mary added, smiling.

"Mary, whatever are you talking about?" Ted asked, personally insulted, not to mention embarrassed in front of his sons by his lack of information. There was a time when Mary discussed everything with him in agonizing detail. And certainly, prior to making any decision that jolted the family harmony, he was not only consulted but heavily relied upon for his input. But this was before his wife had gotten herself a coed as a girlfriend.

"Come on, it's not that outrageous," Mary continued. "It's just college for a semester. You'll have numbers where you can reach me, and I'll leave you a list of things that need to get done. If you all pitch in, you'll hardly notice I'm gone," she finished conclusively, not looking at anyone in particular, sweeping and grinding another layer of scrap foods in the garbage disposal. "I'll be back before Christmas."

"Are you guys getting a divorce?" Matthew demanded for effect, now tapping his spoon intolerantly upon his bowl of Frosted Flakes, his one dark eyebrow raised accusingly.

Ted swung his head in Mary's direction, waiting for her to provide the answer, his eyes widening as if to say, "Could be, for all I know," cracking a phony smile, his head cocked to one side, a schnauzer waiting for a tossed Frisbee. His mind raced randomly, searching for any hint of an explanation; ten minutes ago, he had been enjoying his Cheerios, never complaining that breakfasts had gone from hot to cold with dizzying abruptness.

"I don't think so," Mary now toyed, growing more tense and yet more pleasant, sure to be singing her answers at the three of them before long. Ted nodded his head as if to say this news was entertaining, if nothing else, like a tabloid headline of his life that required no contribution from him, and which he wasn't sure he believed.

"This has nothing to do with Dad," Mary added, now flaunting her newly declared independence before them.

"I beg to differ," Ted retorted.

"Great, and in my senior year. It's not fair," Matthew growled with pessimistic certainty. "This family's falling apart."

"Why? Because Mom is going to hang out at school for a while?" Brian argued. "I say, who needs you, Mom? Have fun. I'm the youngest. I'm the one with the most to lose."

"Again, I beg to differ," Ted repeated. But then, he began to chuckle a relaxed, knowing laugh, nodding his head at Mary, having apparently solved the riddle for himself. He chuckled deep and confidently, now quite content with the whole idea. "Oh, I know what this is about," he winked at Mary, and then redirected his attention to his sons. "Don't worry. It's okay, boys."

"What? What's so funny?" Mary asked, dying to know if the big joke was that he didn't think she would actually go.

"Come on, Mary. If you don't want the boys to know—" Ted responded, shrugging for effect.

"Know what?"

"That you're going to one of those places," he whispered now, raising his brows accordingly.

"One of what places, Ted?" Mary asked, sincerely confused.

"You want me to say it out loud?"

"Please do. I have no idea what you're talking about."

"Boys, your mother's just going to one of those spas to get her figure back," Ted pronounced with uninhibited ignorance.

"Oh, you mean a fat farm?" Brian asked.

"Well at least that makes sense," Matthew added, dismissing the crisis, pouring another bowl of cereal.

"Does it?" Mary exclaimed.

"Of course. Frank's wife got back from one, twenty pounds lighter. She developed some upper-body strength and took some courses on low-fat cooking. They're like newlyweds again." Ted smiled, amazingly content in his ignorance. "Take all the time you need, honey. We'll support you in this."

"I cannot believe this family!" Mary exploded. "It's easier for you to believe that I would leave you because I'm overweight than because I'm going away to study?"

"Chill out, Mom," Matthew interjected. "Your secret's safe with us. I mean, we're not going to announce it at the doughnut shop."

"I hear you have to drink wheat germ oil and eat seaweed at those places," Brian informed her. "I can smuggle you some chocolate," he whispered.

"For your information, you are wrong! You're more than wrong. If I were going to a spa I would tell you. But I'm not. Why is it so difficult for you to believe I want to go back to school? I am going exactly where I said I was going, like it or not, believe it or not, whether or not any of you can grasp it."

"Mary," Ted interrupted, "now, hold on—"

"Ted, don't say anything else! You're the worst one, not believing me. Did you hear your sons, thinking it's not really wrong to go off on some physical fitness kick?" Mary asked rhetorically. "All of you listen. Put your dishes in the sink, turn off the coffeepot, make sure you lock the door when you leave, and get used to it—fast! Me and my megatrillion fat cells are going shopping for back-to-school clothes in size sixteen, no, make that an eighteen, and I don't give a damn who knows it!"

No one said a word until the door slammed.

"Boy you really blew that one, Dad," Brian said, breaking the ice.

"Thanks, son. I hadn't noticed," Ted growled.

"Well, this is just great," Matthew began. "I knew that girl would be trouble."

"Why are you blaming her?" Brian asked.

"Because Mom would never just up and leave this way. I mean who's going to take care of things? Maybe we should hire someone to do whatever Mom does."

"Yeah, like any of us knows what that is," Brian added.

"Calm down. Let's not get ahead of ourselves. She's not really going to go," Ted told them. "She'll come to her senses."

"I don't know, Dad. I think that fat farm thing pushed her over the edge," Brian continued.

"Well, I wasn't the one who called it a fat farm, was I?"

"We really hurt her feelings," Brian said, remorsefully.

"Her feelings? What about us?" Matthew demanded. "Dad, you'd better take control of this household. I'm a senior. This is a big year for me. I've got trips and scholarship applications, and the prom. Tell her she can't go," he insisted.

"I told you, she won't go. She'll think it over. She'll look at the pictures of you guys on the mantel. She won't be able to leave us. I know your mother. If she goes more than two days without baking a cake for us, she feels guilty."

12

ours later, Mary knocked on Ted's office door, contrite, hoping to say more of what she meant to say before the fat farm comment had unleashed her temper. He invited her in and closed the door behind her. There, in full view, were pictures of their family, and one of Mary from her engagement announcement. She couldn't believe he kept that picture after all these years—but that was Ted, sentimental, kind, a devoted family man.

She sat on his red leather sofa while he picked up his phone and asked that his calls be held. He sat beside her. Mary thought he looked exceptionally handsome in his suit.

"I'm sorry," she began. "I didn't mean for everything to come out that way this morning. I wanted to talk to you first, alone. I know it must seem strange," she rambled.

"Mary, you know I didn't mean to insult you this morn-

ing. I guess that was the first logical explanation I could think
of," he said, looking at her with all sincerity.

"Let's forget about that, okay? It's not about anything
logical, Ted. That's why it's so difficult to explain. I have to
go. I'm supposed to go."

"Okay, here's where it gets real fuzzy for me. Why do you
have to leave? What could you possibly be thinking? I mean
it's not just me. It's Brian and Matthew. There are other col-
leges if that's what you want to do."

"I know. Believe me, I know. What am I thinking? All the
right things, all the things that you're thinking. But that's not
what I'm feeling. I just have to do this. I'm not even sure for
how long. I can only tell by my own reactions that I'm doing
the right thing."

"So, you've made a decision, pretty much."

"Ted, I don't expect you to understand something I don't
understand. I just, I would really like your support."

"To leave? I'm sorry. I can't give you that."

"Couldn't you think of it as a little business trip?"

"But it's not. And it's not really about education either,
is it?"

"Well, I don't know. I mean, I'm not sure. I only know
that I have to go."

"Fine. Go. But don't act like you don't have a choice. You
have a choice, Mary."

"Yes. You are right. I have a choice. I could ignore all of
this, everything in me that's screaming to do this against all
the logic and emotion fighting inside me. I could choose to

stay right where you leave me in the morning. I could sit still, get a little older every day, ignore everything I don't understand about the way I feel. I could continue to make dinner at breakfast time, water the plants too much, focus on the senior citizens and their appointments. I could let the world go on as it has. But I can't ignore Cathy and the way we met. There was some kind of spiritual connection—"

"That doesn't prove anything!"

"No, it doesn't. But it's not like she's just a feeling. She's alive, right in front of me. And whatever part of my life is opening because of her, I want. Not just a little bit either. I mean, I really want it. And frankly, I'm entitled to it."

"Are you really! And just what am I entitled to as your husband?"

"I guess you have to figure that out for yourself."

Days later, after a leisurely breakfast of extra bacon and eggs, Mary composed a terse good-bye note to her family whom she was about to—in the deliberate and harshly chosen words of her angry husband "abandon." Presenting a united front in boycotting her farewell, the Sullivan men had fled to play an early tennis game. Mary expected as much. It didn't take a genius to guess that Brian, who over the summer had grown to despise tennis, had been in some way coerced with promises of a visit to the pancake house, music store, or computer mall. Mary wondered if he'd been outright lied to or perhaps threatened. She suspected Ted and Matthew convinced Brian that there was a good chance Mary would reconsider her decision if they gave her no support at all. Ted had managed to keep himself and the boys committed to their hostile interactions, to send the not-so-subtle message that if she still dared leave, her return would be met with as much coldness and offensive behavior as she could imagine.

With her family, her home, her overgrown herbs, her senior citizens, and her uncountable miles of blank days soon to be behind her, Mary realized this power game had been years in the making. Perhaps the pleasantries she had been shown by her husband, occasional dinners out, flowers, trinkets from street vendors, winks, pecks on the cheek, postcards from his business trips, were as insincere as they were infrequent, and always part of Ted's agenda to give Mary the illusion of a shared and happy life. It was all so very clear from the highway, how she had bought into all those fake encouragements to find new work, new friends, new hobbies, so long as they were local, so long as they didn't in any way impact the stale status quo of the household. Yet Ted, reluctant though he seemed, could fly off to all points in the country at a moment's notice and, in the holy name of "business," eat lobster at four-star restaurants, tour active night spots, actively seek new and exciting places to impress his clients, knowing the boys were tucked in and safe at home, Mary on her emotional leash, with her protective motherly instinct, always and forever on duty.

But Mary was usually happy for her husband's adventures,

as happy as she would be when the time came for her sons to leave home for a more exciting place. Couldn't they allow her an adventure of her own, even a foolish one?

Mary always did her best to keep Ted's concern on business, freeing him from the more mundane elements of running the household. But she hadn't been so far removed from the world that she couldn't remember how enjoyable it was to sit through a meal without popping up to fetch grated cheese, to slice ham, to substitute green beans for the broccoli Matthew hated, to scrape the skin off the potatoes for Brian, to rise again and again in reaction, for more milk, for yards of paper towels to sop up the spilled milk or orange juice that never missed her newly washed floor. Mary had never forgotten how wonderful it was to eat out, to lean back against her clean, upholstered chair and have someone, a courteous, crisply aproned stranger, remove her plate and bring her steaming hot coffee, and tempt her with exotic desserts. How wonderful it used to feel to reapply lipstick and perfume instead of stain remover, to meet the bathroom mirror slightly woozy from the wine, fluff up her hair, smile at herself, and walk back to her table, watching her husband watching her.

Something about this trip was necessary to Mary. She couldn't explain it, hadn't bothered to mount a huge defense, but knew it was far more significant than a stay at a fat farm or creative revenge. And it wasn't even about Mary's having suddenly become embarrassed by what or who she had become. Cathy had inspired her to leave the comforts of her den, to explore the parapsychological world or, at the very least, college life. Neither Mary nor Cathy could deny the overwhelming feeling that they belonged together.

"I'm sorry," Cathy apologized.

"You have nothing to be sorry for," Mary told her as she beeped at the old man who had just cut her off. "I've been a mother for seventeen years. I've been a wife for twenty-two. And at least two of the members of my household hate change."

"Do you worry about Brian?" Cathy asked. After all, he was her younger child, and really a lot of fun to be around.

Mary laughed. "Not at all. I suspect he's in it for the cheeseburgers."

Cathy had been out swimming and hadn't witnessed the final conversations, how many times they yelled to Mary to find this or that thing before she left, how they expected her to write down instructions for, of all things, the dishwasher, something she had long ago gotten them all to use—well, she had outright refused.

She had done all she could do to get packed last night, trying to get her little bag of belongings together before going farther than she had gone from her home alone in years, full of all sorts of emotion no one cared to acknowledge. At first she had thought she and Ted would talk; he had sent the boys to the movies with Cathy. But talking wasn't on his agenda.

As she opened and closed drawers in her bedroom, Ted managed to get in her way so often, she finally caught on that he was attempting his subtle form of seduction, trying to intentionally collide hips, since he was too proud or angry to admit that he wanted her. That was too bad for him. If he didn't have the decency to speak to her, she certainly wasn't about to jump at the chance to make love. Eventually, he accepted his failure, only to strategically plop himself down upon her sorted underwear on the bed, like a dog hiding a bone, clicking incessantly, angrily, from one TV channel to the next, displaying his restlessness, his masculine aggression, and when that didn't evoke a response, pulling off his shirt to bear his tanned and muscular chest.

All he had to do was say a single word, Mary decided, lift a kind eyebrow in her direction and utter a syllable, and she would have willingly complied. But he wouldn't soften his position enough to look at her, much less talk to her. Mary drew an equally thick line in the sand, yanking her bras and panties out from under his legs and snapping off the bedroom light to continue her packing elsewhere. A balled-up pair of socks took flight into the hallway after her. Mary let him have the last word.

~ 13 ~

Midway into the drive to college, Mary suddenly felt like smoking again. Considering the cigarettes, Mary had a brief image of Ted's judgmental brow and could almost hear his reprimand. "Mary, why would you smoke now? Have you any idea what your insurance rates will be? What about setting an example for the boys?" As if they would ever touch the stuff. Her sons were mostly like their father, sports minded, self-righteously health conscious, and largely thought immortal. But she was very different from any of them, and being with Cathy served as a welcome reminder. Besides, she couldn't even remember being bad, and now was as good a time as any to explore that side of herself, break some rules. Her family already disapproved of her. How much worse could it get?

Mary couldn't help who she was, now that she was beginning to remember. She loved chocolate, coffee, cake, and, throughout the years preceding her pregnancies, cigarettes. It had only made her feel older to try her best to swear off sweets and caffeine. The Sullivan men seemed to think that if they didn't think about aging or dying, it could never affect them, so they fought each sag, each wrinkle, each fat cell with the weight bench, the swimming pool, the tennis court, anything to keep them in motion, running from their inevitable decline.

"What's wrong?" Cathy asked, sensing Mary was having a dilemma. Mary hadn't realized it, but she had been moving her head from side to side again, the way she did when having these internal arguments. Cathy had been the only one in her life to notice the motion, probably because she was the only one who ever paid that close attention.

"Well, I quit smoking cigarettes a long time ago, but I never really gave them up forever. I told myself while the kids were young and in the house, it was just too much trouble to hide them, and too hypocritical. Then, they all became so healthy, working out with weights, eating a bunch of bananas and a box of granola every two days. Anyway, I just didn't think I had the right to smoke. It wouldn't have been worth the criticism."

"You gave up even that?" Cathy interrupted incredulously, half accusing Mary of some crime against herself. "Oh, Mary!"

"Even what?"

"Smoking. You sacrificed it for your family. The more I learn about motherhood, the less I can see myself driving down that road in the near future," she said matter of factly, without insult, just as a statement of observation.

"Okay, maybe I'll take just one," Mary decided with a giggle. Was it to convince Cathy that motherhood was worth all the sacrifices, at least under the right circumstances, and that not every woman went at it with the devotion Mary did? Other mothers smoked, drank, went to work whether or not they needed to, and Mary accepted that. Hell, the world accepted that more easily than a mother who had kids just to be around them. Did she really need to behave so appropriately all of the time? What had it cost her?

Mary lit up and inhaled the cool, crisp, menthol smoke, feeling something so familiar and tender—the reunion nearly made her cry.

"Let out the smoke, Mary. It's not a joint. You'll get a headache if you're not used to it," Cathy teased, laughing openly.

"Oh, you're right," Mary laughed, blowing out awkwardly with a cough. "But for a moment, it was all there," Mary admitted, slightly aware of a light-headedness.

"What?"

"I don't know. My youth. My vitality. My thoughts. The music. My enthusiasm. My sex life. I mean, just having my lips wrapped around this—"

"Really! That does it. We're getting you a pack. A carton. A case!" Cathy laughed, her blue eyes wide in amazement. She really was a bad influence, but maybe that's exactly what Mary needed.

"Oh my, does this feel good! Damn," Mary said, waving the smoke toward the window. "And they say even second-hand smoke is bad. Ted will get so mad at me if I give myself cancer. I'd hate to go to my grave with anyone mad at me."

"I think people get mad at you anyway. You die and you leave them. They resent it. It's the way of things."

"So, your theory is, I may as well smoke?"

"If you want. I mean look at my mother. I don't remember her having dessert, not ever. She passed up brownies, chocolate bars, even her own birthday cake, and what for? All that sacrifice and she's now in a realm where you can't even buy a Clark bar."

Mary took her eyes off the road momentarily, smiling tenderly at her passenger.

"Yeah, I stopped referring to her as dead. It sounds too depressing. My mother is in another realm, Mary," Cathy smiled, and then giggled. "Look at you. You look so natural with a cigarette. Your husband's definitely going to blame me."

Mary wondered how she ever lived without cigarettes. In those deep drags were all the promises of youth, freedom to defy authority in any form, freedom to claim and keep your body to yourself in any condition, or share it, if you so chose, freedom to take five minutes many times during the day and just breathe in and out, think, do nothing, be belligerent, be stupidly and profoundly careless.

"I'm embarrassed to say just how much I'm enjoying this, being out of the house, talking with you, smoking," Mary continued. "Do you think this is a form of regression?"

Cathy lit her own cigarette and took a second to think. "Actually, I think it's more rebellion. You never did rebel against your mother, did you?"

"How could I? It was only the two of us. I just did everything I wanted in a totally sneaky fashion. Confrontation is not my strong suit. I really hate to fight. Smoking wasn't too hard, because everyone did it back then. It was all that other college stuff. May I have another?" she asked, reaching for her second cigarette in twenty years.

"Sure."

"I mean like the sex. I could never admit to it, but it seemed for a while, it was all I lived for," Mary admitted. "I was obsessed. But I guess that's always the way with your first lover."

"And what about your second?"

"I married him."

"Wow, that's pretty conservative."

"I know. I wasn't exactly a guy magnet. What about you?"

"I had three before I got out of high school. I thought I loved the first one, but then I got so infatuated with the next, I had to break up. After that, I didn't go steady. I wanted my freedom. That was something my mother and I always agreed on, that I shouldn't rush to settle down. But she did tell me if I ever found true love I'd know it, so I guess I'll wait until Mr. Right comes along before I have an exclusive relationship, and in the meantime, practice safe sex."

"Your generation's so much more practical."

"We have to be, Mary. Here, want another cigarette?"

"Why not?"

Even if it were only for the time she stayed in the shadow of her young college girlfriend, looking for her mother in foreign vibrations, in memories, in some psychic's tarot cards, she could smoke. She could hold the cigarette in her hand, draw it to her lips, inhale deeply, and release the white toxic air toward the ceiling, feeling satisfied, and at the same time feeling renewed, feeling reckless, feeling alive again.

"I just don't see what I'm doing that's so wrong," Mary blurted out. "I'm only asking for a little bit of space. Ted went away lots when the boys were young. They're practically raised now. They're smart. They're responsible. They can fry an egg. Did you see Matthew? He was downright mean! He wouldn't even look at me, and barely let me kiss his cheek," Mary told Cathy, appalled by her family.

"Brian at least asked for a logo sweatshirt," Cathy offered, to cheer her up.

"That boy knows how to enjoy his life," Mary said proudly.

"Let's hope he rubs off on the other two," Cathy added.

Mary blew a perfect smoke ring. If she seemed adolescent, she didn't care. She was on her way to school. And this time, she didn't have to choose a major, a husband, or even count credits. She didn't have to worry about alcohol, drugs, or fitting in socially. She was totally free to spend her time talking to dead people if that was what she wanted to do.

Mary was in the process of recharging some batteries, refueling. Her last stay at college kept her alive and interested in the world for at least ten years after. Oh, she'd be so grateful for five more like that, for excitement and energy, to be who she once was until the boys were born, and they became all that mattered, until her mother had become sick and left her.

"Don't get me wrong, I loved being their mother. I loved feeding them, and rocking them, and teaching them the alphabet song," Mary acknowledged, trying her best not to miss them so soon.

"You did an incredible job. Really, they're great," Cathy reassured her. "They're going to be fine."

Motherhood was a noble cause, and Mary had embraced it. Her children were her greatest gifts from Ted. She marveled at all they learned, at their progress from the first rollover, through sitting, walking, and saying her name. And when that first year was through, she was always a little sad, because they were not babies but toddlers on their way to independence. She appreciated her role every spring as she watched mother birds dropping food into their babies' mouths; this was the natural order of things. But then, by the fall, they would fly. All of them would fly. No one was left behind to straighten up the nest or make a lifetime's work out of loving and being accessible. Maybe if she had given birth to more children, had a household full of them running up and down the stairs, it would have held her interest. Ted had thought two was plenty, had wanted to be involved in their lives, and had wondered how to manage that with more. He was practical. Mary yearned for a daughter.

Cathy reached over and flipped up the radio volume,

blasting out a version of "Born to Run," and Mary Margaret Sullivan, deserter of two sons and a husband, relaxed in her long-sleeved polo shirt and her baggy jeans, on her way to a college campus, for once was not afraid of anything at all. Mary was evaluating everything, now that she had the perspective of the road. She cooked way too much. She ate way too much. She drank way too much. And she was always playing beat the clock in reverse, trying to look busy in her collapsing, little life, trying to look content, to smile and thrive in her illusion of contentment, to create a house of love, to make everyone comfortable where she belonged—the good mother and wife.

At times, when Mary was asleep at nine-thirty in the evening, awake at two swimming in sweat, the sweat that could only be comparable to postpartum flop sweat, she dreamt a baby had just come out of her. She was infinitely disappointed when she awoke. She worried whether she was reverting, or if perhaps she could hear the Grim Reaper getting his forms in order, his pen poised over her name. The sluggish rhythm was in her breath, in her heart; she heard it like a rake upon the asphalt.

Mary wished she had been in touch with herself enough to know what had forced her to take this trip—grief over her mother, her new friend, or traveling back to the old days to get a perspective on life gone dull. Had this miraculous, pink-cheeked doll been chalked down to her by the generosity of the universe, a prize for having not gone mad among men, a gift from her namesake, beloved Mother Mary? Whatever the reason, this was the best star she could have wished upon, and although it had smashed down upon Cathy's life, it was somehow meant to include her, for her enthusiasm was overflowing, here in this sun-filled car, with her overnight bag of play clothes.

Boldly, she reached for the cigarettes again and again, always asking politely, "May I?"

"Of course," Cathy giggled. "Make a right, and we'll get more at the town diner."

"Are we going to a town diner? I so love diners," Mary exclaimed, doubly excited.

"There's a really good one about a half mile from school."

"I'll have a cheeseburger," Mary decided. "With French fries and onion rings on the side."

"They make really good onion rings," Cathy offered. "The batter's real crisp. And the cheesecake is the size of a brick."

"God, that sounds so good. And the best thing about all of this is I have credit cards. I was never in a college town before with credit cards."

"The jukebox is great. But it doesn't take Visa or Master-Card."

Mary sat in the red and silver booth, reading the paper place mats filled with advertisements of the local businesses in this town she'd never before visited. She had gone to a school half the distance away from her mother, so she could get home easily on weekends. Away with Cathy, everything felt like fun. She could see the waitress walking around with her pot of fresh coffee, eager to fill a half-empty cup before any customer had to ask. And at the counter, in front of the glass case of doughnuts was a line of truckers having the special— some meat loaf or roasted turkey. Salesmen with satchels were strategizing, women were clustered over salads, hungry from some church meeting or Bible study, and there was loud clink-ing and laughing while a cloud of lethal cigarette smoke wafted up from Mary and Cathy's booth.

"You're awfully quiet," Mary commented. "Are you thinking about your mom?" she asked. As they waited for their food, Cathy had been making Mary a choker, stringing beads on some black satin cord, to give her jewelry a more collegiate look. Mary marveled at her patience with little things, remembering how the walls in her room had been filled with her paintings, pressed flowers, fiber and metal wall sculptures.

"No, I'm still too excited about talking to her to feel much else. But I feel guilty about taking you from your fam-ily. They must hate me," she said, crossing her legs Indian-style. Mary never remembered being that comfortable in public, but there was Cathy, shoes off to expose tiny, rounded, pink-painted toenails, horizontally striped shirt barely meet-ing her jeans, dozens of black and golden cords, colored and painted glass beads in plastic bags around her.

"They don't hate you. And don't feel bad for them, they're very capable. I've lived through years of business trips and sporting events and always been very gracious. They'll just have to come to terms with what I'm doing. Besides, I miss my mother. So don't worry. Anyway, if this psychic is good enough, he'll see trouble before we do."

"I guess you're right," she said, unconvinced, pulling her braid from over her shoulder to examine it.

"I feel badly for you, about losing your mother before school began. A nice girl like you should be going to parties. I hope you don't miss them because of me. Don't feel that you need to do anything different because I'm with you. I'll bet there are lots of dances you'll be invited to."

"You know what? I hate those things. Kids get drunk all the time. I'm not interested in that. I haven't even joined any clubs because I'm not sure what to major in."

"Don't worry. You have plenty of time to pick. I changed my major twice. First I was primary education, then sociology, and then I got ridiculously practical and went into data processing. I actually was pretty good at designing and evaluating systems, decreasing manpower, that sort of thing. But you know what? I kept working myself right out of a job. We didn't need the money, so I did some consultation work from time to time, but after a while I felt like it was more effort to find the job than to do the job, so I sort of stopped. I think that's what happened to me at home too. As a mother, you're supposed to build these independent children, and then when you do, you're happy about it for thirty seconds, until they walk away and never look back."

"You never thought of it as a chance for you to be free?"

"No, why?"

"Even though I miss my mother, I feel stronger. No one else can make decisions about my life. I'm on my own."

"You know, maybe that's what I'm feeling now, freedom from my family. I mean, look at me, I'm going to college, I'm smoking, I'm drinking real Coke, I've got a friend who's half my age, and we're going to see how we can tune in to other worlds. Doesn't this all seem bizarre to you?"

"Not at all. I'm in college. Nothing is normal here."

"Oh yeah," Mary said, reflecting. "I think I remember that."

~ 14 ~

The apartment was on the second floor with a living room–dining room combination, a large and small bedroom, and a small kitchen with a huge window overlooking the street. The living room furniture looked worn but inviting, a round, oak coffee table that could double as a footrest, a plain three legged sofa in a beige weave that sported oversized red pillows, an armless love seat in blue denim, end tables that didn't match heights or styles, and some bean-pot lamps with shades that had seen better days, all sitting upon a braided oval area rug.

Cathy took her luggage to her bedroom which was painted a bold, sunflower yellow, while Mary was relieved to find her walls a cool ice blue. Mary dropped her bag and offered to open all the apartment windows, excited to hear new sounds from the very active street below.

From her bedroom, Cathy was telling Mary how she and

her mother had shopped for the daisy sheet sets just a year ago, bought cheap dishes at Wal-Mart, ate lunch in town, anything to stall their inevitable separation.

"I miss her so much it makes me sick."

"I think that's normal," Mary told her. "It hasn't even been a full month," she added. "How about you show me around campus, and we can unpack later," Mary offered.

"Sooner or later, I'll have to come back," Cathy said with resignation, already wiping tears. "And I feel even further away from her here," she added. "Isn't that stupid?"

Cathy flopped on the sofa, put her head into her hands, and then slid down to the floor. Her baby-fine hair slid out of its ponytail and drooped down alongside her face as she sobbed.

"It hurts. How can anything hurt so much?"

Mary put her water glass down and listened, observing as Cathy's body shook with uneven sobs. She understood all too well you could never predict what was going to set you off, a photo, a song, a familiar smell. Grief was nothing like sadness, loss, sorrow, any of the passive terms applied to death that seemed to describe an event outside yourself. It was something that inhabited you, that battered you unpredictably.

"Oh, I don't know how I can do this," Cathy cried.

The pain was in charge, and the little that was left of Cathy succumbed. Mary wished she could point to an easy way through the process. It was like falling through the cracks of a day, a whole other being seemed to occupy you, even though minutes ago you were brewing coffee, washing a floor, baking cookies, making love.

"I guess what helped me was knowing my mother wouldn't want me to be so sad," Mary told Cathy, stroking her head. No matter what, she always believed her own mother could see it all. You had to honor the woman who had kept you from losing your virginity at sixteen, the one who made you collect the money you loaned a friend, the one who reminded you breaking your own heart would break hers too, dead or alive. She was a mirror, a friend, a guaranteed companion and ally, your flesh, your blood, your skeleton, your fan, your critic, your connection to all living things, and the only reason you did not crawl off in a corner and drown in your grief.

"We could always bake a back-to-school cake," Mary tried as she rubbed Cathy's back and waited for her tears to subside. She remembered she always felt numb afterward, like her body was just along for the ride, incapable of keeping itself dry or quiet or dignified, and when she finally did rise, eyes swelling, nose stuffed, hands raw from tightening them into fists, she was never sure how much time had passed.

Cathy looked up, blue eyes drowning, but coming around.

"Chocolate?"

"Absolutely."

Mary wished there was a smelling salt for crying, something that would snap you back with a whiff, but in lieu of that, there was always chocolate. Mary was relieved that Cathy was now listening to her, not her own voice, and she knew she was already feeling better.

"I don't even own a cake pan," Cathy said sadly.

"I packed one!" Mary said enthusiastically.

"You didn't tell me."

"You were busy moving my old speakers and turntable. We have it all in that blue wash basket. Cookie sheets, a mixer, bowls, a Crock-Pot, chocolate chips, and my favorite cookbook, even a rolling pin, which I never leave home without."

"Now, who brings a rolling pin to college?"

"It was my mother's. I just couldn't leave it behind. Brian once tried to use it as a hammer."

Cathy and Mary unpacked the wash basket, and when Cathy saw the cupcake pans, there was no further discussion about what they should bake. Cupcakes were the perfect happy food, she told Mary, and the best way to start off their new semester together. Cathy tried to apologize for breaking down, but Mary insisted she was doing great and that crying was a natural way to get the sadness out.

Mary was soon at home in the tiny kitchen, setting up the cabinets with Cathy's blessing, her mixer energetically whirling butter and sugar together.

"Do you know, I won a gift basket at some Chinese auction, two years after my mother died," Mary said, enjoying the coffee she had fixed for them both with her newly purchased coffeemaker, which prepared a full pot in three minutes. "One minute I was saying thank you, and the next I was in the bathroom sobbing. It happened so quickly. And I had to talk myself out of that bathroom."

"I remember hearing an announcement in sixth grade, that Jerome Collins's mother died," Cathy offered, licking the coffee from her spoon. "He was this unassuming kid with long black fingers and super large feet. I couldn't get him out of my mind. No, maybe I was afraid to get him out of my mind, afraid if I did, it might happen to me. I only ever had a mother," Cathy added.

"You didn't want to be left alone. I had those same fears," Mary admitted.

And if you were like Mary, who by her nature was always seeing patterns, you harbored some amount of paranoia that because your father died, your children's father might die or maybe, in Cathy's case, that she wouldn't make it much past forty, like her mother.

Mary had often envisioned herself an orphan living in an institution with the other girls, playing group games, using public bathrooms and shower stalls instead of the big claw-footed tub in their small home. She was extra kind to her aunts during their infrequent visits, and tried to look pretty to them, just in case her mother suffered the same fate as her father. But she hadn't. She had lived long enough to see her grandchildren, to keep a fresh and current image not only in Mary's mind, but in the minds of her grandsons. Matthew and Brian had witnessed her decline, watched her deteriorate from the woman who used to lift them onto her lap and swing them in the yard, to the woman they sometimes volunteered to feed applesauce. Brian had even made his grandmother a tape of Glen Miller songs and placed them in his Walkman for her to listen to, long after she seemed to be capable of hearing.

Mary attempted to help Cathy instinctively, not to substitute for her mother, just to show the same relentless compassion Ted had shown her, for she knew you couldn't let go of anyone grieving. If you held on tightly, the external world would eventually come back into focus, the bright blue and white of the sky, the happy voices in the street, the calm clouds that softened the midday sun.

"When will it go away?" Cathy asked, pulling the paper off her second frosted cupcake. Following Mary's lead, she cut the cupcake in half and added more frosting.

"You're already doing better. You go through hours, sometimes days, without crying. You're doing well, Cathy. Much better than I did."

"It hurts so much. It's stupid to say that, because the words don't even begin to describe the pain. I want my mother back, Mary. I don't know why I had to give her up. I see older women and I wonder if their daughters know how lucky they are to have them. And then I feel horrible again."

"I don't think the intensity goes away, just the frequency of the crying spells," Mary suggested. "I mean, you saw the way I broke down in your store. It was as if she'd just died. But I get through six or eight months at a time now with nothing. I think that's progress."

"I wonder all the time what would have happened to me if we hadn't met," Cathy said. "I could be completely alone."

"You're not," Mary assured her.

"Do you think about how we connected, Mary? Doesn't it amaze you? I'm so grateful."

"Yes, I know exactly what you mean. It's our lack of control, our fate being controlled by something spiritual. God, I felt powerless when I first had children. I wondered what would happen if I was driving and fainted, or shopping and had a heart attack, or if I would end up in the wrong place at the wrong time, and suddenly they'd be separated from me."

"That must be scary."

"Well, I think it was the first time I valued my own life that way, as a mother. But whenever I'd freak myself out, I'd try to remember how complex the human body is, how the heart is this thing with electrical charges, and that with any slight chemical alteration, it would all be over."

"That cheered you up?"

"Sounds stupid, I know. But it made me realize that we were more than the sum of our body parts, and that no amount of worrying could prevent anything from happening."

"I'm afraid of driving, Mary. I didn't want to tell you, but that's why I didn't offer to take a turn. I think the car took my mother, and it could take me."

"It's okay. You don't have to drive. Not now or ever."

While Cathy showered, Mary phoned Ted to let him know that she had arrived safely. At first it seemed they would have a civil conversation. Mary was tempted to justify her leaving by giving him the details of Cathy's afternoon breakdown. But then he asked what time she'd be arriving on Friday. Mary stammered and then admitted she hadn't thought she would come back as early as this weekend.

"This weekend," Ted asked accusingly, "or any weekend?"

"I thought I'd just play it by ear, Ted. You know, see how the adjustment goes."

"For whom? For you? What should I tell the boys?"

"I can't imagine that you haven't told them everything already. I guess you can continue to put things as negatively as you can, until they finally hate me."

"That's unfair, Mary."

"Is it? Well, let me ask you this. Why is it that you want me home this weekend? What would we do?"

"What we always do."

"That leaves me out of a lot, Ted."

"And is that my fault? That you don't share our interests?"

"Listen to you, our interests. The boys go with their friends and come back for occasional meals, showers, and clean clothes. Don't act like this is a group thing."

"Well, you should hear Matthew."

"I'd love to. Put him on the phone."

"He won't talk to you."

"Exactly."

"So what's your point?"

"That this is fine for now, Ted. I'm sorry you are all taking this personally. But I'm not coming home to sit in the den

and take phone messages or pick up the dry cleaning. I'm trying to resolve some issues."

"And how do you think we can do that, with the two of
us living separately?"

"You didn't have a problem with my doing it alone when
you thought I was going to a fat farm!"

"That's because that would have been for me. You would
have lost some weight, felt better about yourself, and been
more playful maybe."

"Playful? I'm taking yoga and metaphysics, Ted. If I manage to achieve a sparkling half-lotus, you'll be the first one to
know."

All hell broke loose then, yelling, accusing, demanding,
until Mary asked to speak to Brian to wish him good night.
She resigned herself to the fact that Matthew would never be
reachable by phone. Her older son would always be off somewhere, playing basketball, at the library, on a date, at the
movie theater, in the mall, and even at six in the morning, jogging. Mary considered writing him a letter explaining her position, not defending it, and wondered if he would at least
read it.

And what could she say? Mary didn't feel overweight in
her body as much as her soul. She felt dimmed, dusty, sleepy,
and solemn. She remembered how she had laughed out loud
in the car with Cathy, and how that laugh surprised her, her
voice sounding so different, so bright, as though there were
signs of her old self reemerging. She couldn't remember the
last time she had laughed out loud.

She had to forget about Ted and the boys, pretend this trip was as nonnegotiable as a hospital stay or a business venture. And whatever flickering lights of hope and health she found in her voice, her spirit, her mind, she needed to collect them and ignite them until she was as full of life as she ever remembered, and she would not return until that happened, no matter how many angry conversations she had with Ted.

~ 15 ~

*B*ut in her new home, Mary struggled through the days and found little peace at night. Sleep came late and generally ended abruptly. There were recurring vibrations in her ears, and the vibrations led to ringing, which eventually emerged as a discernible voice in her right ear. It was still barely more than a whisper, but it had unreal clarity, like an animated character in a Disney movie. It was female, strong, lovely, and it didn't say much, but for the moment when Mary hovered between sleep and consciousness, it was profoundly reassuring. "Be not afraid," it would tell her.

Mary suspected a brilliant voice like that could only belong to an angel, a saint, the Mother of God. It came to her in the early dawn, after nights that were spent darting in and out of sleep, after days that were spent in utter confusion, trying to comprehend her position in this world. As she lay there, believing it was a continuation of a pleasant dream, it was a comfort. When she awakened fully, it scared her half to death.

She meditated daily to bring herself closer to it, to ask it questions. She was confronted with the same shadowy emptiness, not the white, blank screen where plentiful images were supposed to float up into her consciousness, not even the spelled-out phrases some classmates had described. If there were vibrations or spirits targeting her, she certainly couldn't seem to engage them in a dialogue. All was quiet and still, her breath coming and going, slowly and deeply, with and without cigarette smoke tainting it, all her questions seemingly ignored by a deaf universe.

As a side effect of these whispers, she was now even more uncomfortably aware of the reality of the next world, like noticing boards creaking or wild winds blowing shortly after having watched a horror movie. While her mother couldn't resist seeing the scariest motion picture, staying up late for any showing of a Hitchcock film, watching *Chiller Theatre, The Outer Limits,* and *The Twilight Zone,* young Mary always hid under the covers, her fingers stuffed into her ears, trying not to hear the discordant music. In truth, even the cinematic stories of Jesus and the saints frightened her. She remembered a series of nightmares after seeing *The Ten Commandments;* she could not shake the feeling of powerlessness, of being watched, judged, possibly even rebuked by a holy spirit.

Living with Cathy, in an apartment constructed of wallboard so thin she could break through it, was a big adjustment. The other night, as she attempted to hang the single, framed family photo she brought along, the nail disappeared into the wall as she hammered it with the heel of her shoe. Cathy laughed, remembering how often that had happened to her during her freshman year, and Mary for the moment couldn't stop apologizing, knowing how Ted would have reacted if she had put an unnecessary hole in a wall. Mary said she hoped it wasn't an omen, it being a family picture and all.

"Even if it is, Mary"—Cathy had laughed—"at least we're finally getting some feedback."

Mary had laughed then, both of them admitting how absolutely boring it was sometimes to meditate. Mary occasionally alluded to the whispering, but never actually admitted to hearing what she couldn't prove she heard. They laughed about feeling for vibrations and confessed how their minds sometimes veered off. Cathy's thoughts had recently been to the runway of the Miss America Pageant. Mary's had been to the one-day sale at Macy's. But at Cathy's urging, they were going forward with their plans to contact their mothers.

"Don't you feel as though the dead are always with us?" Cathy had asked instantly upon shaking hands with the psychic who asked that they call him Luke. This was a characteristic of Cathy's personality that took Mary some getting used to, that she spoke what she felt with such ease, that she took action without much deliberation. It was a form of freedom Mary had previously admired in others.

"More accessible sometimes than the living" was his answer. His smile was kind and compassionate, and his graying hair made him seem more like the learned professor than the sorcerer Mary had imagined. Still, the idea of someone unbuttoning her soul was a bit unnerving.

"Mary, I'll read for you first, okay?" he asked, his blue eyes warm and inviting.

"Yes, certainly," she smiled, feigning courage, feeling her legs wobble just a little as she followed her new psychic counselor to a private room.

As Dr. Lucas Petros lit a votive candle, Mary shuffled tarot cards, believing in the afterlife, acknowledging the oneness of the universe, twice as fearful of paranormal happenings as she ever was, but hoping, with every last fragment of her broken heart, that at least if she couldn't dredge up enough positive imagery to share with Luke, Cathy would be able to hear her mother, maybe the two mothers would talk, and Deborah would pass on a meaningful message.

In the dim, cozy room, at a card table, over a vanilla-scented candle, Luke took Mary Sullivan's shaky, sweaty hand. She had given up trying to manipulate the large deck of cards, and cut them three times with her left hand as much to be rid of them as to pronounce them ready. Luke took the cards in his hands, held them, and closed his eyes for a moment. The first thing he told her was she had made the right decision to follow Cathy, that this was exactly what she should be doing, despite the strain on her marriage. She could feel her face nervous and unnatural.

"Try to relax," he told her. "You don't think the dead are really accessible, do you?"

"No, I guess I don't," Mary answered. "I mean, certainly not in a good way."

"You just think they're more important than you."

Mary said she wasn't sure she understood, and then apologized, as was her nature. Nothing in her head seemed to contain any focus, and the thought of someone probing there amid the disorderly dust balls and graying gray matter was unnerving. But she held on to the notion that somehow, according to the books she had begun reading, her subconscious energy could be transferred, across space and time to someone like Luke who knew what to make of it.

"There's an enormous sense of loss here," he told her. And Mary, forgetting now that this was exactly why she had come to be here, not just her loss but that of Cathy's, worried instantly that this was from some future event. Her vibes must have screamed out her fear so loudly and distinctly for the safety of the husband and sons she had abandoned, that Luke immediately responded, "No, no, this does not pertain to your family. In fact, you think it has something to do with your mother, but it doesn't. This is not from the loss of your mother, but rather from someone else."

Mary felt like objecting, as if a physician had misdiagnosed her, although she had never had this feeling before, of someone gazing into her being with her permission. Feeling vulnerable, Mary crossed her arms at her chest and sat back against the soft, worn cushion of the chair, her eyes gathering enough information from the room to know this man had not gotten wealthy from this line of work. For all her open-mindedness, Mary could not help thinking that a really good psychic would know where to place his bets, which stocks to pick, when to buy lottery tickets, how to make his own life easier—assuming the gift of prophecy and love of material things were not mutually exclusive.

"Uncross your arms and legs please," he instructed, sounding slightly frustrated.

Mary obeyed and continued to watch him, trying to discern any sense of what was going on, trying to hear non-noises, trying to gather imagery, trying her best to appear relaxed.

"You've been so lonely, Mary. Why is that? I see you telling yourself, I have this, I have that, I'm fine, I'm fine, but the tears are so close. I love my family. I love my home."

In an instant, Mary remembered thinking those exact things, saying them out loud to God, to her mother, to herself as early as nine-thirty in the morning, when everyone in her household had gone on their way.

He continued. "I feel so sad, it must be because of Stella."

"Stella was my mother," Mary said, sitting forward with a lurch.

Luke paused with his eyes firmly shut. Mary glanced at him now in complete awe. Talking about her dead mother was one thing, referring to her by name got her attention.

"She said she's glad you came here. And that you don't

need a fat farm. Cousin Josie could use one, though," Luke told her, mimicking the timing of the chuckle Stella would have offered had she really been in the room. "She's got a good sense of humor, Mary," Luke commented.

Mary let out loud a nervous, frightened giggle, which turned into tears, and then she stood and backed away from the table, just as certain that her legs would surely go out from under her if she stayed one more moment in a room where her mother and this odd man were so casually conversing.

"Where are you going?" Luke asked.

Tears were rolling down her face, and she felt as though she had been able to see through a crack in the sky, a world that belonged to someone else, and as curious as she was, she was that much more frightened.

"I'm not sure I'm ready for this," Mary admitted. "I was never brave enough to use the Ouija board. My mother used to love watching horror movies. And even when I closed my eyes and hid under my covers, I could still hear the music. I have to leave this room now," Mary said, nodding, "before I start to hear that music. I have to get back to earth, out there, you know, I really think that I'm going to fall right down if I don't—"

"Okay, sure, step outside and drink some tea. I'll read for Cathy," he told her. He had the warm, understanding smile of a minister, a tinkerer of extremely private places. His kindness, his love of humanity were blasting out of him so effortlessly, Mary felt drawn to him but frightened of the strange power he seemed to possess.

"Next time, Mary, you'll know what to expect," he said, forgiving her. "But let me leave you with this. Those issues, that loss, it will get worse before it gets better. And once it's out in the open, you'll heal."

"Yes," Mary said, apologetically, backing out. "I'm sorry for your trouble."

"It happens often enough. It's unnerving, Mary. I see your past and future colliding, and it all revolves around Cathy."

Mary just nodded solemnly, feeling instinctively he was right, but not knowing or maybe not wanting to know how all the pieces fit. As Mary stepped out, Cathy zoomed to the room in a flash, and Mary could soon hear tones of her happy voice filling the room.

In the light, everything began to return to normal. Luke in retrospect seemed an ordinary man, not the voice of dead Stella Sarcowski. Luke poked his head out to check on her. Mary was no longer embarrassed; he was that easy to be around.

"There's a pound cake in the kitchen," he told her. "Why don't you help yourself, and you can turn some more lights on if you like."

"Thank you. I'll do that."

"Mary, don't be upset. You'll be fine next time," he told her, with practiced reassurance.

Cathy poked her head out for a second. "Have a cigarette," Cathy encouraged, comforting her friend. "Are you sure you're okay?"

"I'm fine," Mary said. "Go. He's authentic. Please," she encouraged the young girl.

Mary eagerly pulled a cigarette and some matches from her purse. She dragged long and hard, and had her first thought in the light, of going home, of running right back to Schenectady, to Ted, the boys, the supermarket, and the PTA. She didn't want anything to worsen, even in order to get better. She lacked courage. She lacked emotional strength. And Cathy, well, Cathy would be fine.

Cathy had wonderfully bright moments when no one was aware of her pain, when perhaps even she wasn't aware of it. Mary would notice her on campus, a bright yellow bow wrapped around her ponytail, her walk confident and carefree, men trailing her after class, trying to get to know her. Mary knew it would turn out all right for Cathy. She would get through this and be the same happy person she once was, as Mary had been after her father died.

Mary thought of her mother. In her imagined conversation, she heard a typical admonishment, "I don't understand where the sorrow comes from, Mary. I'm here. I'm fine. I'm telling you, I never left you. You're going to have to let go of this grief, Mary. Get on with your life. Even if Ted and the boys don't seem to need you as much, you've still got work to do out there. Look what you did for Cathy. She has someone now. She has a house for Thanksgiving and Christmas. Mary, are you listening? Don't go home, Mary. Not yet," Stella insisted.

Mary heard laughing from Cathy and Luke and considered pressing her ear to the door. Some things were always easier for other people. But of course, Cathy's mother had died a totally different death—alone and suddenly. Not those endless days of agonizing decisions. Not the way Mary's mother had left, as if everyone was too tired to hold on tight anymore, as if they had all just opened their hands and let go, the way you see it in the movies, people reaching over cliffs, over the sides of buildings, finally losing the strength to hold any more body weight than their own and losing their grip. Always, the camera zooms in on the face of the person falling, the shock, disappointment, helplessness.

The door opened and Cathy and Luke emerged, arm in arm, laughing and chatting about the reading. Whatever messages Cathy had received had cheered her up considerably.

"Oh, Mary, it's wonderful, isn't it? It's great to know those things we feel are so real, that our mothers are always with us, watching," she finished cheerfully.

Mary couldn't think of a more frightening thought than being trailed by dead people, even ones who loved her.

~ 16 ~

Back in the vicinity of Peace Hill Cemetery, in the dimension of the not-quite-dead-yet, Agnes Morrison, age eighty-two, had arranged an outing with her lady friends to call upon the Sullivan men Saturday afternoon at four o'clock sharp. She was suspicious about what had happened in that household to drive such a dependable woman as Mary to up and leave town as though she were being chased. Agnes put on her first blazer of the season. She centered her brown, rayon skirt before fastening its accompanying safety pin, to keep her seams where they belonged. She would continue to grow thinner with Mary gone, without those luscious desserts the seniors looked forward to, which Mary dropped off weekly at the center. She sighed. She stepped into her Easy Spirit oxfords, ready, with ten minutes to spare.

Gertie, Shirley, and Margaret were already in the van, early as always for the few social engagements that still kept them circulating locally. Beatrice decided to leave her favorite chair and join them, eager to do whatever she could for Mary. Agnes asked about Penelope, but learned she wasn't coming, that she felt it was more productive to nap away this part of the afternoon than visit the house without Mary in it. Agnes was pleased to take her place up front next to the driver.

In the short miles between the center and the Sullivan house, the ladies testified to Mary's generosity, her skill as a baker, the warmth of her home. She had unselfishly gone to help the orphan girl, everyone decided, unwilling to make any accusations against Ted Sullivan that were yet unsubstantiated.

When Agnes found none of the boys at home, she proceeded undeterred to the back porch where Mary had confided to her that a secret key was hidden, should she ever find herself out in the rain or in need of shelter. The driver helped the other passengers out.

Having gained access to the house, Agnes picked her way through the appalling puddles of clothing, newspapers, pizza boxes, and other trash. She unlocked the front door to let the others in, cautioning them about the immediate danger of breaking a hip should they step upon a haphazardly discarded paper plate.

When the seniors had been safely transferred inside, Agnes announced to her friends that she had never before encountered such a disaster and that, perhaps, whoever was still capable of ascending the staircase to the bedrooms should inspect the premises for bodies. But it was the driver, Yolanda, who reassured Agnes that death itself was much neater as a rule, if not less harsh on the nose. What they smelled was the stench of old syrup and oregano—not, thank goodness, that of decaying human flesh. Yolanda, having driven football teams around on occasion, was quick to attribute the disaster of Mary's home to its sole occupation by males.

In a matter of moments, the ladies had unpinned their hats, surveyed the living and dining rooms, and decided their cake and cookie boxes should be returned to the car. They could see, even with their own poor vision, that Mary had been gone for some time. Should the men decide to return to such a slovenly habitat, they would not be rewarded with one more bite of food until the place had been completely restored to order. The ladies meant to do at least that much.

Gertie, taking a liberty or two to locate cleaning supplies, was quick to organize a caddie and a crew, convinced that between all of the ladies, they could manage the polishing, sweeping, and sanitizing. One of them would gather and scrape the crusted plates and cups piled everywhere and load the dishwasher. Another would disinfect the counters and bleach the sink. Those who could see well enough, like Margaret, would take on the dust. Those who couldn't bend would sweep, and Yolanda, at least a decade or two away from her first attack of lumbago, would scoop up the trash from room to room and deposit it elsewhere before anyone took a catastrophic step and, God forbid, ended up down in the mess.

Shirley, who could not bend, stoop, or wring a sponge,

was positioned near the door as a lookout for the men, to avoid any surprise entries. So it was she who screamed first when Brian burst into the living room and inadvertently wakened her, followed by Matthew, and the three women working nearby. Ted walked in last, carrying fishing poles, nearly screaming himself, hamburgers leaping about within his full and fidgety stomach.

"I'm Ted Sullivan," Ted announced, not knowing what else to say as Agnes stared at him from above her bifocals. The other ladies chatted among themselves for a moment, whispering, pointing, and tsking at the Sullivan men who collectively were beginning to feel like apes in an unkempt zoo.

"I know who you are," Agnes said. "I am Agnes Morrison from the center. We came to see about Mary."

"Well, as I told you on the phone two days ago, Agnes, Mary is away for a while," Ted repeated, trying to sound more patient than embarrassed.

"It's a pity she couldn't take the house with her. Do you know poor Shirley could have broken a hip on this floor?"

"I could have broken a hip," Shirley repeated.

"Young man, how old are you?" Agnes asked, addressing Matthew, commanding his attention.

"Seventeen," he answered.

"And do you drive?"

"Yes, Ma'am."

"Then is there any reason why you couldn't take yourself down to the supermarket and buy me a nice thick sponge? The one in the sink is moldy."

Matthew looked at his dad for help.

"Agnes, that won't be necessary. We were just planning to clean up a little—"

"Mr. Sullivan, with all due respect, this place is a profound ruin. I've been here when Mary was here. I've seen the sparkle on the windows, the perked pile on the rug, the sheen on your wood furniture. She filled the place with the smells of lemon and bread," she paused momentarily.

Shirley was quick to jump in. "Her raisin bread is my favorite," she told Ted.

Agnes redirected her attention to Matthew. "Young man, hurry off then! When you're my age, you take time very seriously."

"I'll go with you," Brian volunteered.

"No, you won't. He's a big boy. He can buy a sponge. You can do the toilets."

"What? Dad!" Brian whined.

Ted shrugged helplessly.

"Start with the downstairs, that's the one everyone sees. My lady friends are afraid to use it in its present abominable condition. Why are you looking at me? Have you never cleaned a toilet?"

"Not yet."

"Gert, teach this boy about cleaning the bathroom. Ted and I are about to have a chat."

"And you, young driver, what time are you let out from school during the week?"

"Four," Matthew replied.

"Would you be averse to transporting a few of the seniors to some appointments?"

"What appointments?"

"Some of us have left our walking days behind us. If it's too much trouble, we'll find another way. It seems to me our help with the housework might warrant a ride or two."

"Well, I guess I could drive you. But I stay late at school on Wednesdays," Matthew warned.

"Good. We need you only on Thursday and Friday afternoons, and just until your mother returns. Seems to me from the look of things, you and this house would be a whole lot healthier if you spent more time out," Agnes grumbled.

"But I don't have a car," Matthew protested.

"We'll use our van. Yolanda only drives us on the weekends."

"Cool," Matthew responded.

"I'll give you a set of keys at church tomorrow. I assume you'll all be there at the service?" Agnes asked Ted, probing.

"I guess," he stammered. It had been a long time since Ted Sullivan had attended church. Mary took care of all that, all those social, spiritual things that interfered with Sunday newspaper reading and football. Mary always cooked a tremendously aromatic roast, with boiled and browned potatoes, green salad, and fresh garlic bread. They ate around three and he picked at the leftovers until approximately seven when he was treated to the pie he had been swooning over for two hours, apple, cherry, or, if Mary was thinking about the holidays, pumpkin. Sundays were the best family days. If the

televised games were boring, he and the boys would play basketball in the driveway. He'd mow the lawn during halftime.
It had all gone along smoothly. What was happening to his
life?

"Now, please," Ted began, sitting across from Agnes at
his cleaned and polished dining table. "I appreciate what
you're trying to do here, but there's really no need. I'm sure
Mary will be back soon—"

"And then what! Shame on you, Ted Sullivan. Bringing
up your boys to be helpless and sloppy. That's a short walk
away from being lazy and stupid."

"Now, just a minute—"

"I know what I'm talking about. I raised six boys, and
they raised two boys each. Not a girl in the bunch. And never
once did any of their homes look like this. Running a home is
supposed to be a cooperative effort."

"Well, with all due respect, we weren't expecting visitors,
and I have my own set of house things—"

"Don't care," Agnes interrupted. "I've seen your lawn. I
know you can work. A family ought to have a house clean
enough to turn inside out at a moment's notice. Your wife has
helped all of us. The least we can do is save her home from being condemned by the Board of Health, and check up on her
family, such as it is. We didn't come to clean, you know. We
came to visit. We have a cake box out in the car. But if cleaning is what's needed, we'll do it, and do it well."

"It's not as bad as it looks."

"Is that so? Is your mother still alive?"

"Yes."

"God bless her. Call her up. Invite her over. We'll get her opinion."

That would make Ted even more uncomfortable.

Oh, he had wanted to call his mother, even before Mary had packed her bag and left home. He had wanted to ask for help with the house, with the boys. But he conceded Agnes's point. He would be horrified if his mother had seen how he had let things slide. Mothers in any form were to be shielded from such a mess.

"We came to have tea and cake with you. A man can get lonely without his wife. We came to bring you and your boys some female companionship. And it's nothing to be ashamed of, for you to accept it. It's what a community should do, what your wife does so naturally."

"What would you like me to do?" he asked, resigned to receiving the help and criticism of these intrusive, good-hearted old women.

"First, you can put on the teakettle, but only if it's clean. If not, boil a lemon in it first. And then you can learn to clean up after yourself, and teach your boys to do the same. If you can't manage it, then we will. Never saw anything like this before today. And let me tell you something else," she continued as though nothing on earth or heaven would dare interrupt her. "Those boys miss their mother, and you're just making it worse for them by allowing their home to disappear too. Don't you understand, their home is their mother. They're one and the same. You lose one, you cling to the other. Now, I don't want to appear like I'm blaming you, because I don't know both sides of the story, and I don't care to know either. It's none of my business. We know something had to do with the poor orphan girl Mary was helping. The point is, if you ever want Mary to come back, you'd better take care of things."

~ 17 ~

Ted was not prone to sulking. But he had endured hours of unsolicited advice on how to run his household from Agnes Morrison, a woman who had barged her way into his home uninvited—at least he assumed she was uninvited, not dispatched by his wife from afar, on this, his fifth weekend alone. And just last night he had resisted the urge to be sarcastic on the telephone, had been polite enough to only roll his eyes in silence, as Mary told him about the classes she was taking, about Cathy's latest art project, sounding ever so much more like a roommate than a wife.

He sat upon the fluffed-up cushions of his sofa in his polished, vacuumed den, listening to the tired whine of the washing machine from afar. His muscles and his mind were weary from the drudgery of forced housework, his boys were beyond mad at him, and his wife, God only knew. He really felt like calling his own mother, but knew in a flash that her presence would only serve to compound his problems. If she took Mary's side, he'd further resent Mary for driving a wedge between him and his mother. Worse yet, his mother could take his side, forcing him to defend his wife even as he was mentally prosecuting her, something he found even more distasteful than subsequent rounds of lecturing from Agnes.

Agnes had actually said, "Shame on you, Ted Sullivan." He didn't think anyone had spoken to him like that since he was five years old. And she did it in front of his sons.

What had brought that reprimand down on him? It was as if some invisible signal announced that his house was without its female essence, causing a van full of women like homing pigeons to swoop down and restore the balance. Ted understood little of the society Mary had recently ditched, except for the sincere care and concern the seniors had for her health and well-being. They were all mothers and grandmothers, some of them even great-grandmothers whose arthritic kneecaps had once passed through Ellis Island, and they had filled his home and impressionable sons with stories of childbirth induced and accomplished in kitchens, hand-designed quilts, shared loaves of bread during the Depression, brothers and sisters with polio, and the greatness of our country's resources. They had preached lessons in history, geography, religion, science, and home economics simultaneously, pouring out buckets of names and dates and graphic details, along with their soap suds, working with vigor and pride, even while assembling an abundance of casseroles for the boys to bake at a later date.

It finally occurred to Ted that Matthew was right; Ted was in deep denial. Only when a SWAT team of elderly women had taken over his home did he actually understand that Mary had really gone. He was honestly stunned that she had left, knowing how angry he was, without so much as a farewell romantic evening, as if saying, in that respect, he was to be left to his own devices. "Play lots of tennis," she had teased, when he first acknowledged the impracticality and inconvenience of this ludicrous, one-sided separation.

Tomorrow was Sunday, and now they had to go to church where the most holy name of Mary Sullivan was revered by parishioners for her charity work, her baked beans, her lemon chiffon cake, her selfless and indefatigable baking for the aged and wheelchaired masses. Agnes explained that the whole congregation presumed she had gone to help the young, motherless college girl from town. That was Mary. Kind-hearted. Giving. No sacrifice, not even separation from her family, was too great for her compassionate nature to endure. Perhaps that was all there was to it, and Ted should accept the temporary disarrangement as concrete evidence of her good heart.

Now that he was admitting her absence, he could swear he noticed her nature beginning to change before she departed, the piled-up towels, the haphazard dinners, the forgetting to leave messages, her eagerness to be off the phone with him, her needing more time free to wander the mall, to pack up the orphan's condo, to plant another set of burgundy or yellow chrysanthemums again at her sanctuary, Peace Hill.

He gulped from his beer bottle, taking little consolation in the cool, familiar taste, noticing even what he previously considered to be enjoyable and relaxing was now only at best mechanical in his wife's absence. As the dryer buzzed, he yelled down for his boys, determined to enlist their help in developing some strategy. One look at his older son's annoyed face had him abandoning any remote concepts such as teamwork. This was not the family he once had.

"Now what?" Matthew accused, hands barely able to drop flat at his sides due to his overdeveloped arms. Ted couldn't help but notice he was shaping himself into an admirable, perfect V. Before all this, they occasionally worked out together, ran, played ball. Before they had begun a steady diet of fast food and cereal.

"Sit down," Ted barked, waving his beer bottle to the many free seats.

Matthew sat across from him, leaning forward, father and son locked in a standoff until Brian, the last to arrive, bounced through the doorway and whirled to protect his imaginary basketball. He dropped to the floor, the day's events having little effect upon his perpetually easygoing temperament.

"What's up?" he asked, still unable to sit motionless, his foot tapping energetically.

"It's time to take some action," Ted began.

"Oh goody. Is it my turn to fluff the wash?" Matthew mouthed off sarcastically.

"There's no need to be like that, Son. We're all on the same team here."

"Correction, we have become pacifists in our own home," Matthew continued.

"What?" Brian inquired, shooting a confused look back and forth from his father to his brother. "Did I miss something?"

"Flower-power, peace-loving, casserole-cooking guys who get bossed around by very old women," Matthew continued.

"They scared the heck out of me," Brian agreed. "I mean, I don't know what was worse, having to scrub the toilet or worrying that one of them was going to keel over if you didn't do whatever they said. And did you hear about that one who gave birth to the twins and sewed six coat linings the same day? I'm telling you, those women are not human."

"I don't know what you're complaining about. I'm the one who has to drive them around," Matthew growled.

"So why didn't you say no?" Brian taunted.

"Say no! Right," Matthew laughed with contempt.

"Well, you could have," Ted interjected.

"No I couldn't," Matthew insisted.

"Why not?" Brian asked.

"Because she reminded me of Grandma. And I kept thinking when Mom and Dad get that old, I don't want them out on the street alone," Matthew explained.

Brian howled with laughter. "Come on. I think Agnes got to you with those sunken brown eyes."

"Yeah, well, you were cleaning toilets for them!"

"That's different. That kind of work could have killed them."

"Well, I'm just trying to protect the lives of innocent people. If one of those old bats drives and has a heart attack, an innocent teen could be hurt!"

"Are we through with this yet?" Ted said, peeling the label from his beer bottle. "I mean, can I get a word in here?"

"Sure, Dad," Brian said. "But use a coaster," he added, slipping one under his father's beer bottle. "I worked hard on that shine."

"This is so completely pathetic," Matthew moaned. "In my senior year—"

"The point is," Ted yelled, "tomorrow, right after church, I'm going to see your mother. Don't wreck the place. Meeting adjourned. And thank you, Matthew, for remembering to fluff the wash," Ted finished.

"I'm going with you," Matthew announced.

"Me too," Brian added.

"I'm not so sure that's a good idea, boys. I mean, your mother and I are bound to have a few words. What would be the point?"

"To let her know I'm on your team," Matthew offered.

All eyes moved to Brian. "I've always wanted to see a dorm room. I just never expected it would be my mother's."

he Sullivan men made a handsome team. They knew it,
but never said it, and when they gave dressing half an
effort, matching ironed button-downs to the pants Mary
coaxed them to wear on family outings, they looked exceptionally good. All three of them arrived on campus in wrinkle-
free shirts, looking intolerant, confrontational, and well
rehearsed in their blocking. Their muscular arms bulged, and
Cathy, who had gotten her first unmemorable glance of
Matthew the night her mother passed, now was reminded as
she opened the door to him that even under the heaviness of
his indignation, he was devastatingly cute. His father, having
coached his offspring during their three-hour ride to appear
irrevocably offended, looked like an unbendable plastic sol-
dier, even with his kind eyes and down-turned smile that still
acknowledged Cathy's tragedy.

"Come on in," Cathy smiled with effortless welcome.

"Sit, Mr. S," she offered, inviting him to sit on the sofa balanced on blocks.

Matthew lost his breath at the sight of her in her silk shirt and black jeans. He tried to remain unaffected by the smell of her citrus perfume, and steeled himself to look irritated and keep his eyes from pausing on any of her body parts. He was on a mission to retrieve his mother from this immoral orphan who had stolen her away. This doe-eyed, silken-haired beauty with the fullest, rosiest lips he'd ever seen—that was the difference, he hadn't seen her smile until now. He could ignore her attractiveness under her mask of sorrow, but with that wide, inviting, spectacular grin, she was nothing less than mesmerizing.

"Where's Mary?" the Sullivan patriarch asked.

"Down at the bookstore," Cathy offered. "She won't be long. It's the one place there are hardly ever lines—except for the first week of the semester when everyone is trying to sell back old books."

"How are you feeling?" Brian inquired, eager to at least behave in a manner he found personally acceptable, revived into humanity by his impending proximity to his mother.

"Better," she said with determination, raising up her head for emphasis. "At the very least, calmer," she added. "Your mom's been awesome," she answered.

There was that smile again, that set of brilliant white teeth, those pronounced, pink lips moistened from translucent gloss or perhaps her own tongue. Matthew fought to break his stare.

"Do you have a roommate?" Ted asked anxiously, peering around the corner of the kitchen wall, not wanting to be taken by surprise. "I mean, other than my wife?"

Matthew's eyes instantly swung back to hear her answer, excited and terrified that there could be others like her within arms' reach, for a moment considering nothing less than complete defection from his father.

"No, I don't. Just me and Mary." And there it was again, a flicker of pleasure, that sweet tempting mouth.

"Cool," Brian responded, eyes widening, automatically reverting to teen mode, nodding his head in approving admiration.

"You have the whole apartment?" Matthew repeated, not wanting to appear even mildly friendly enough to chat, but unable to restrain his curious and lusting eyes from roaming the digs.

"I'll give you the tour," she offered, bouncing effortlessly forward and up, her corn-colored ponytail swishing.

Matthew abruptly cleared his throat and objected, catching himself on the brink of accepting such corrupting cordiality. "No thanks, I'll wait for my mom."

"Well, you can show me around," Brian volunteered, looking at his older brother like he was truly insane, jumping up to have a look. He was now much more himself since emerging from the car ride of relentless mother-bashing, the influence of his humorless father and brother fading in the presence of Cathy's lighthearted feminine nature.

Brian was in exceptionally good humor considering he

had the harsher assignments from the blue-haired ladies, not the least of which was cleaning all three toilets and vacuuming drapes while his brother of driving age got to pick up this and return that, food shopping for "wholesomes," as Beatrice called vegetables and fruits, before being delegated the title of cook. Brian, unlike his father and brother, was still young enough to have fun despite anyone's agenda.

Ted and Matthew shot betrayed looks at Brian, which he responded to with a casual shrug of his shoulders, for it wasn't every day he got to inspect a college apartment. Boys his age fell away from honor and promise at the first whiff of a pizza.

Matthew, already choking with desire for Cathy, vowed to remain loyal to his father. He retreated into some corner of his mind, a beaten boxer on a stool in a ring, listening to some inane voice, his or his father's encouraging him to stay firm in the fight, despite the heat in his loins. For this discomfort alone, he could have deeply resented his mother. But he could suck it up for one afternoon and take a mental snapshot of Cathy, perhaps as some yardstick for the future women in his life.

Ted noticed his older son staring with longing and re-straint in the direction of Cathy's bedroom. Hearing Brian's charm exacting trills of melodious laughter from the attractive young woman who had robbed him of his wife, Ted felt mo-mentary pity and abundant guilt for the position he had inad-vertently thrust upon Matthew in this, his senior year in high school.

And that wasn't the worst of it. Even jogging didn't tire

Ted out. He just couldn't sleep, couldn't seem to sink into his pillow the right way. Overnight television was horrid, his beer tasteless. He didn't even feel like mowing the damn lawn anymore. Nothing was right, nothing was the way it should be. And his wife was to blame.

Cathy and Brian offered Matthew and Ted a cold can of Coke from the refrigerator, like a polite, young married couple entertaining family for the first time. Brian made sure to hand one to his irate brother, wiggling his eyebrows in acknowledgment of Cathy's appeal, aware of the amount of salt he was purposely flicking into his brother's wounds. Cathy, draping her invisibly sweet aroma upon the three of them as she walked by, touched Ted's shoulder with appalling familiarity as she asked if he'd rather have a glass.

Matthew—a tick about to pop, his instincts all on overload, no longer able to remain still, wanting to claim Cathy, wanting to kill Brian, wanting with all his will to support his temporarily inept Dad in this wife-retrieving endeavor—asked to use the bathroom to at least gather composure enough to unclench his teeth. His mind, what was left of it, mercilessly repeated Cathy's name as though he were sick with fever.

He would never survive college with even one of these profusely sexual sorceresses conjuring up such yearning within him. He saw himself slamming his limbs through the next few hours, in whatever way possible, picking fights with college punks twice his size if need be, drinking goblets of foaming colas, throwing bricks through windows, burping long and hard, spiking basketballs—just to be rid of the energy.

He sat on the toilet with his hands folded almost in prayer. Who knew that a single trip to a college campus would have such an effect? He wanted to learn to joust. He could feel fire in his veins, while sweet, unsuspecting Cathy laughed at his brother's wit on the other side of the bathroom door.

Mary arrived, quickly deposited her books, and put a smile on her shocked face. To hide a mixture of guilt and fear, she excused herself for a moment. Matthew accidentally accepted a kiss from her as they bumped into each other by the bathroom.

Mary washed her face and brushed her teeth, wondering if they could pick up the scent of her resumed cigarette habit, concocting all sorts of excuses that would buy her time if anyone accused, and then considered lighting up in front of all of them if they gave her even a slightly hard time.

"So, isn't this a nice surprise?" she said, trying to begin on a pleasant footing, hoping that the men in her life had the best of intentions in visiting her.

Brian immediately stood and gave his mother the seat next to his father, sitting on the arm of her chair, a politically incorrect move that brought a deeper look of disdain from his older brother.

"I miss you, darling," Mary told Brian, hugging him with gratitude.

"Well, I thought perhaps if we visited, we might come to some terms with your return," Ted began.

"Oh," Mary replied, looking from one to the other. She nodded and wandered off to the refrigerator for a Coke of her own.

"Perhaps I should go for a walk?" Cathy offered, eager to give the family some space.

"Maybe we should go with you?" Brian astutely volunteered.

"That's a good idea, dear," Mary agreed. "Cathy, would you mind showing them around?"

"Not at all," she replied, grabbing a denim purse. "Coming, Matt?"

Matthew looked at his father, but Ted nodded that he should go. Feeling incredulous, he raised an eyebrow to his father, but Ted shot him a look that said he should go, and fast. Matthew Sullivan sensed it would be a long afternoon.

"Where are we going?" he demanded of Cathy.

"It depends on what's happening out there," she told him with nonchalance.

"We'll get you back by curfew," Brian taunted.

Matthew shot him a look of pure contempt and fired a flaming arrow through the back of his hollow head.

Brian, having felt the assault psychically, responded to his brother, "Excuse me!"

"There's no need to hurry," Ted assured them. "Enjoy your visit, boys."

Brian opened the door for Cathy while Matthew shot his father one last look to let him know he would never forgive him for allowing these women to divide and conquer.

~ 19 ~

Ted and Mary sat across from each other, Mary on the denim chair with the hole in the cushion, Ted on the three-legged sofa, out of place, out of patience, out of his own time period.

"How have you been?" he asked, restrained and polite.

"Just fine, thank you. And you?" she answered in kind.

"Good. Good. Just great."

"Good."

Silence. Mary, feeling the negative vibes as though they were puncturing her aspiring-toward-enlightenment spirit, shut her eyes for a brief moment, attempting to relax. She breathed in deeply, slowly, audibly.

"What are you doing?" her husband asked.

"I'm picturing orange daylilies. They're waist high, and growing in a flat field near a white farmhouse with a porch swing, and blowing ever so gently."

"Mary, honey, is that space ship you're on ever going to land?"

"Ted, that's a very judgmental statement. Just because you don't possess the capacity to understand something doesn't mean it has no value."

"Mary, you're living in a college dorm with a girl young enough to be our daughter, while the boys and I are fending for ourselves—"

"Please, Ted, you are not incapable of surviving without me for a little while. Cathy and I are kindred spirits. It's been a long while since any of you even noticed I've been living along-side of you. I'm tired of being the person who gets everything set and then steps out of the way so all the fun can happen."

"What are you talking about?"

"My life, Ted. It's got to be about more than you three. Anyway, it's certainly not your fault. But I'm always left out," she admitted.

"Mary, how can you be left out if you're always there?" Ted asked, confused.

"Ask Matthew how his day was, he'll say it was fine. Ask Brian who he's thinking of asking to the fall dance, he'll say a girl. Ask you what's going on at work, you'll say the usual. I'm tired of it. I'm tired of just going through the motions. I'm tired of the mall. I'm tired of the news. I'm tired of talk-ing myself into being content, and falling asleep earlier and earlier each night, with or without our predictable sex. Do you know what time I went to bed last night?"

"Obviously not. Nor do I now know with whom."

"Don't be ridiculous, Ted. Two-thirty. I went to bed at two-thirty. I'm forty-five and I stayed up half the night. And it felt wonderful. I wasn't even tired."

"And what were you doing until then?"

"Communicating."

"With the living?"

"For the most part."

Ted crossed his arms at his chest and remained silent. He could smell the cigarette smoke, the coconut candles, the beginning of fall through the open window. Inside, he could hear himself objecting. After all, he had been the primary breadwinner, the one who had allowed for all this luxurious boredom to surface within their perfect little home. His eyes wandered around the college suite. There were posters of rock musicians, candles, bookshelves made of milk crates, wooden planks and concrete blocks, a clock shaped like a cat whose eyes and tail moved eerily back and forth.

"And just for fun, would you like to know what we were doing, what I went home to last night?" Ted couldn't resist telling her.

"Sure," Mary replied, interested.

"Agnes Morrison and her pack of seniors invaded our house, Mary. Can you imagine? There were half a dozen of them at least," he freely exaggerated, "ordering us around, sending Matthew to the store, teaching Brian to clean toilets. In my house, they were actually cleaning my house!"

"And why would they need to clean your house?" Mary asked.

"That's not the point!"

"But I think that is the point!"

"The point is, if you really want to know, that they wouldn't have come like that, uninvited unless—"

"Ted, just what's been going on? I mean, you are three energetic males. Don't tell me you can't figure out some way to keep things neat. I mean, with the least amount of effort—"

"Neat? Is that what's important here?"

"No, not to me. Not anymore," Mary answered, sighing. "Maybe, not ever again. But it sure used to be."

"So what are you saying, Mary? Is this what you want? To live in a campus apartment? To revisit the poverty of college life? To stay up past your bedtime? To pretend you're not really forty-five?"

"No," she answered firmly, knowing he couldn't possibly understand, but giving him the benefit of the doubt for having driven all the way here to see her. "I want to get some things resolved. I want to stop feeling so sad and so empty. I have to figure out what to do next. All I know is I want to do more with my life than drop worms into everyone's mouth and put out the pumpkins for Halloween. There's a reason I met Cathy. Call it fate or God or just a coincidence, but I want to know why. Maybe I'm supposed to help her get through the loss of her mother. Maybe helping her is helping me. I don't know. Maybe my life is supposed to change now, along with my body, and that's why women get a little mixed up, because they ignore it."

"Ignore what?"

"The need to change along with your body. I mean when it happens as a teenager, you know instinctively what to do, you pursue it, you don't fight it or try to fight it. You just go after sex—"

"Sex! Now you've lost me. Unless you're trying to tell me you came here to pursue sex?"

"Don't be ridiculous, Ted. That's not what I'm saying. Although the sex was definitely part of the energy when we went to college, don't you think? I mean, what happens to men at middle age, they have issues, they have adjustments—"

"The middle-aged men I know have jobs and children and houses and wives—"

"And young lovers! Don't insult me by acting like you're not even aware of such a thing."

"Of course I'm aware of it. I'm not blind. Half the men in my department have already tasted the fruits of their labors—"

"Fruits? Is that what you call it? Like an executive perk? A fruit makes it sound so wholesome."

"Will you tell me what you're talking about?"

"I'm talking about truth. Just the truth. I want us to be honest, that's all. There's life and death and just a small patch of time in between. I have to figure out how to use mine. I want us to talk about things, get to the heart of what's going on between us."

"My God, how did we get here? Is this between us now?"

"What?"

"This thing you need to get resolved? Am I it?"

"Well, I don't know. I don't know. I feel as though I've been away and at home at the same time. I don't know where I am, who I am, what I am—"

"And just where do I fit in?" he demanded.

"Well, maybe you're supposed to keep things at home running until I get it all worked out. Maybe you miss me terribly or maybe not at all. I don't know. The winter is coming. It gets dark so early at night. I know every corner of that house, how things look from every pane of window. Damn it, do you think this is easy for me?"

He looked at her, and as sad as her answer seemed, he listened to her with equal amounts of curiosity and fright, considering for the first time the possibility that he was losing her.

Tears were falling now, and she felt for the first time in touch with the enormous distance she had fallen from him.

"I don't miss who I was in that house, Ted. I can't even say I miss who we were, not when I left."

Matthew had tried to warn him, but since he always looked at things as darkly as possible, Ted had ignored his opinion. But Matthew was right, some horrible, uncontrollable circumstance was happening to his marriage. He stiffened.

"Mary, if this is about that comment I made about the spa—"

"Fat farm!" she corrected, crossing her arms at the mere reminder of it.

"Mary, I am truly sorry if I hurt your feelings. But that's

no reason to abandon us. What kind of example are you setting for our sons?"

"You really are amazing. Do you ever see anything beyond
your own perceptions, Ted?"

"Now, what kind of antagonistic comment is that?"

"My leaving is not about you. I'm not one-dimensional.
My being here is not as trite as moving away from your insen-
sitive comments. I could have done that ages ago. It's about
me! You don't even know there's a real person inside here,
someone who doesn't hang on your every praise and criticism."

"I just don't understand," he yelled, crushing his Coke
can in his hand, and slamming it into the trash basket.

Watching him, Mary felt spontaneously erotic. She allowed her mind to fill with as many delightful impressions of
her husband as she could recall, igniting her hide-and-seek li-
bido. She stepped up to him, before him, moved his face with
her hands, and kissed him, really, truly kissed him for all she
was worth, and it felt glorious, as though she had reached far
down inside him, found his heart through all that anger and,
for the moment, connected.

"Would you like to take a walk, Mary?" he asked, in a tone
sounding so much like Matthew on the telephone with a
teenage girl, trying to get a date.

"What?" she said, surprised.

"Show me around," he said, shrugging his shoulders, feeling the depth of his potential loss in the pit of his stomach,
knowing that now, despite all of his well-rehearsed condem-

nations about what she was doing to the family, he just
wanted to be with her while he could.

"I'll write a note to let Cathy and the boys know where
we'll be," Mary replied.

She grew nervous, for there had been many times when
Ted had feigned interest and accompanied her somewhere,
only to growl the whole time and take the very joy out of her
outing. But this time she knew she had his attention. Maybe
outdoors, their passion would be ignited by the splendor of
the fall afternoon, and it would all be salvageable.

*A*t the student center, Brian wandered off in search of *Ultimate Mortal Kombat 3,* while Cathy and Matthew sat at a table with a view of sugar maple, oak, and birch trees. Matthew gazed out the window memorizing the sight, so he could picture Cathy with her wide, blue eyes, her sexy lips, her enticing body there in the future.

"Give me your hand, Matthew," she suggested, after staring into his eyes for a good minute.

"Why?"

"I want to gather impressions. You know, your mom and I have been studying this intuitive stuff. I just want to see what I get," she explained.

"You don't really believe in all that hooey, do you?" he asked, knowing full well what the answer was, but finding it necessary to state his position, in the event that she did stumble upon the truth of his designs on her, to ease his way toward categorical denial.

"You tell me," she said, putting out her hand to receive his.

Matthew let his hand lay, palm up, in the most vibrant and warm flesh he had ever encountered. It was enough. It was more than enough. It was the dawn and the darkness, pleasure that bordered on the painful.

"Okay, you're a little uptight. Move in closer," she instructed, sliding her chair nearer.

With their heads nearly touching he was lost in the smell of her.

"I guess I was wrong about you," she said, looking up now into his attentive eyes.

"What?" he managed to speak.

"I thought maybe you were recovering from a bad relationship. But actually, none of the girls at school understand you. You're pretty intense," she remarked, diagnosing his palm.

"Where do you see that?" he wondered. And how much more could she see? That he had wrapped her in his favorite bath towel after having run her bubble bath, and scrubbed her back with the softest of sponges? That he had fed her strawberries with his teeth? That he had slowly undone the buttons of that silk shirt, and forbidden her to ever leave their cave in it. That he had slung her over his horse and run his spear through the five hundred worthy noblemen who had challenged him for her hand.

"I see you're on the verge of falling in love," she announced. "And the feelings you're having—now, why are you angry with Brian? He's just having fun."

"Brian's an idiot," Matthew confided.

"You don't really think that. You're a little jealous," she accused.

Matthew drew his hand back in defense. "I wouldn't quit my day job," he told her curtly. Five minutes, he thought to himself. He could ravage her so completely, and she'd forget all this psychic nonsense. He'd pin her down to the very crust of the earth until he took that one kiss, and then she'd submit all.

"Okay, so what else do you want to do?" she asked Matthew, wondering what would make him suffer the least. "Want to see the gym?"

"Why not the science lab?" he taunted.

"Sure, there are some pig cadavers I think you'd enjoy," she giggled.

"Now, what's that supposed to mean?"

"It was a joke, Matthew. You know, girls like fun. You might try to lighten up. You could have more dates if you'd smile every now and then."

"And I suppose you have a guy?"

Anyone he could kill would do. Just point him in the direction and he'd triumph. Give him one twice his size. A scholar, a dweeb, a rich or holy man.

"No, I don't have time for that right now. I'm trying to focus on my inner growth. Not that I don't miss the sex."

"What!"

"I'm sorry, does talking about sex make you uncomfortable?"

"No," Matthew lied, listening intently for a name or a house he could lay his flaming torch to.

"I haven't had a boyfriend for six months. Luke tells me I could have a relationship if I want one."

"Who's Luke?" Matthew asked, gleeful for the opportunity to pound someone's unfortunate skull into the gutter.

"Luke, Dr. Petros, the psychic. I'm sure your mom's mentioned him."

"No," Matthew replied, feeling betrayed, for a moment forgetting he had yet to have a conversation with his mother since she left home.

"We're both under his guidance," she explained.

"So which of you is he tutoring the most?" Matthew almost accused, already sure of the answer.

"Both," she replied.

"I'll be sure to tell my dad about this," he growled.

Cathy slapped his arm. Matthew was nearly grateful, but feigned disapproval.

"Who do you think you are, anyway? Your mom has every right to pursue knowledge in whatever way she wants to. I can't believe you'd act like an elementary school tattletale."

"It's none of your business," he advised her.

"It's none of your business," she told him back.

"Does this psychic ask you out?" he demanded.

Cathy laughed. "No, of course not."

"Watch out for him. Guys like that have one-track minds."

"Not psychics. They have multidimensional minds. And why do I get that angry vibe again?"

"You know what I think? I think you shouldn't be seeing this guy. I think you should let your dead mother rest in peace and get on with your life. I think you should stop filling my mother's head with all this supernatural nonsense. She belongs with my father. He needs her."

"And what do you need?"

Matthew, in his mind's eye, stood quickly and took her arm, bending his neck down to meet her lips. He kissed her forever in that one moment. Life images, love images, sinful, romantic images went through his thirsty mind, and he hungered still for more of her, even though he could feel her coming at him, strong and sure of herself, meeting his desire with her own.

"Another Coke," he answered dryly.

The October air was cool in the shade but warm in the sunny patches, and when the breeze grew stronger, Ted placed his arm around Mary under the guise of protecting her from the cold. He rubbed his hands up and down her arms, as if to generate warmth against the wind. Mary didn't care why. She only knew that what she felt from him was as refreshing as the fall wind itself. She led him to sit at her favorite place, near the stream she had found earlier in the week, and she sat against him listening to the water roll by, looking up at the plentiful white clouds floating through the blue sky, noticing the mist that still hung on the trees from the early morning rain.

"You don't look the same," Ted announced, touching her face the way he had twenty years before. "Your face, your hair. It's different," he told her, caressing her cheek.

"I'm not the same here," Mary confirmed. And she kissed his hand, slowly at first, not to frighten him away. But as she followed the trail up his arm to his neck, she could not keep the pace slow enough for him not to notice just how much she really had changed.

For a second, it didn't seem to matter that this Mary wasn't the Mary he had come to see. He recognized in her eyes the look of desire, and appeased it, kissing her deep and deliberately, this woman who suddenly seemed to have so much more to bring to him than he had ever been aware of. His desire increased, until he noticed her hands moving a little too aggressively.

"You're not suggesting we do anything here?" he asked, perplexed.

"Oh, yes, I am," she insisted.

"Out here?" he asked again, his eyes watching out for passersby.

"We can't go to my place. I have a roommate," she told him.

"Mary—"

"Shh. Ted, it'll be all right."

"You know, we could get arrested."

"Only if we get caught."

"Matthew would never—"

"Matthew is with Cathy and Brian. There's no one watching, Ted. And there's a big pile of leaves we can dive into if anyone walks by."

"Who is this woman?" he laughed, his confusion struggling with some locked-up sense of adventure.

Mary put her hands out, and Ted withdrew from his logical self, lying next to his wife on the cool ground. In a second they were kissing, ignoring any of the routines they had fallen into, Mary watching her lover's brown eyes shine in the bright afternoon sun, Ted amazed by the transformation of this churchgoing, crisply dressed, whispering lover, to this borderline exhibitionist.

Even her laugh was different, deeper, earthier. She laughed with wild abandon now, laughed as the wind delivered a fresh blanket of leaves upon them, laughed with delight as Ted acknowledged the cigarette smoking, a teen caught in a lie, a teen with her pants to her knees, defiant and strong in her wayward conviction, now expressing herself loud enough for the neighbors' children to hear, an untamable entity that Ted could get so used to—if she were anyone else.

He opened his eyes. He glimpsed her pink cheeks, there in the shadow of his arms, with her hair spilled over the fallen maple leaves, her smile showing contentment. He wanted her. But on what terms?

"Mary, this isn't you," Ted accused, abruptly recovering, sitting up sharply.

"It is," she declared. "I don't know what happened, or

how it happened, but I was in a very dark place at home. I attributed it all to grief over my mother's death, but according to Luke, it's not so."

"Who?" Ted asked, inhaling as he sat up, raising one eyebrow as he and Matthew could, suspiciously.

"Luke, Dr. Petros, the psychic," she said, smoothing her clothing. Her mother always told her not to kiss in public.

All desire sped away on the wind, traveling from the uptight Sullivans to the next lucky couple.

Ted was silent, but calculating the possibility that this Luke had designs on his wife, and therefore was encouraging her to remain in this place. That it was Luke she was imagining, Luke here on the public lawn of a college campus, Luke inside her, not him.

"So what does he suggest?"

"Meditation, journal writing, dream interpretation, all those things associated with self-growth."

"And how often do you meet with him?"

"Right now, once a week. But once I get a handle on things, I suppose less."

"And where do you meet with him?"

"His home mostly."

"And Cathy's with you?"

"Yes. Well, no, not in the room if that's what you're asking. You can't possibly do readings if anyone else is present. You pick up their vibes."

"I see. So your visits to this man are private?"

"You'd be surprised how alike his manner is to a psychologist's."

"Daytime or nighttime?"

"At night mostly. His place isn't far from—"

"Damn it, Mary. Are you fooling around with this guy!" he yelled, angry at the idea of it.

"What?" she exclaimed, inadvertently laughing. "Are you serious?" she continued, now digging in her purse for a tissue, for her laughter was making her cry.

"How dare you laugh!" he scolded, standing up angrily. "Of course, why didn't I see it? This explains why we're out here like this! It's not you I'm touching. It's you and him! And if you're not actually sleeping with him, you're sure as hell wishing you could! I can feel it. Nothing is the same. You're not the same."

Mary rose, but continued to laugh, unable to believe that her husband of so many years thought she could possibly be involved with another man.

"I'm sorry for laughing," she managed. "But it's just so foolish."

"Is it? You meet with this psycho-navigating guru each and every week, stay up until two in the morning under the guise of contacting your dead mother, smoke cigarettes, and God only knows what else here at college, and tell me you hate our predictable sex. What do you think this guy can do, levitate the bed!"

Mary howled now in uncontrollable laughter at the absurd image Ted had drawn. But she was delighted that he thought she was still attractive enough to have an affair.

"This is great, just great! What am I supposed to do with this information, Mary, except tell you that I will not allow this relationship to continue!"

"Oh, Ted, please, hear me out," Mary begged, trying her best to compose herself. "Don't you see, you went from seeing me as a woman in need of a fat farm to an adulterer? And I must say, I prefer the latter, even though one is just as absurd as the other. I wouldn't have to leave town to have an affair. I don't even notice other men that way. Everyone from the butcher to the newsboy is invisible to me."

~ 21 ~

On the way home, Ted and Matthew yielded the conversation over to Brian, who, having mastered at least one technique in video battle, was eager to explain the strategy his new college buddies taught him. This irrelevant chatter rained down upon the disinterested Sullivans in the front seat, men who were still very much at work turning over in their minds the events and conversations of the day.

An hour into the drive, they had yet to determine whether they had fought a slick and subtle battle with their respective coeds or lost a major war. Men who were rock-hard in their bodies and belief systems were destined to be unsteady in their interpretation of women. It was the unalterable way of things.

Brian yipped like a toy poodle, happy for his meaningless victory over his animated enemies. Ted, desperate for a quieter ride, stopped for burgers and fries, hoping Brian would drift to sleep on a full stomach.

Matthew noticed his father had bypassed all of the avail-able sports stations and tuned the radio to a music channel; he didn't make an issue of it, since he couldn't yet bear to be dis-tracted into real conversation. That suited Ted just fine. Nei-ther of them cared to talk about anything, let alone the women on their minds. Ted, having had every intention of chastising his wife for leaving, found that the outdoor es-capade only confused him. Perhaps this was Mary's intention. Or maybe he was imagining a plot where none existed. Per-haps he was always this confused when he thought about Mary's motives, and he'd just forgotten. It had been so long since she had done anything new—longer still since she re-quired any energetic thought.

Ted caught the smell of wood smoke in the air. They passed cabins at the last exit. No doubt a family was enjoying a fireplace on this cold night. Ted was jealous. Even a camp-fire would have been a lot of fun, the sky was loaded with clus-ters of stars, and Mary loved autumn. She was all he could think about, that sunny, crunchy campus where she walked, the student center where she shopped for notebooks, the bo-hemian apartment she shared with Cathy, where she had gone to dust off her wings.

Ted glanced over at Matthew who was obviously suffer-ing. A spell had been cast over both of them, Ted decided. Neither of them was immune to supernatural elements, al-though they swore they were, wanted to be, pretended not to notice the strange vibes in the air. Why else were they no longer angry? They had planned to exact some kind of justice, and were now riding ever so pleasantly in the opposite direction, as though they had earned some sense of accomplishment.

It was inconceivable. They were somehow returning without the wife, duly reprimanded, in the passenger's seat. Without the nubile instigator, Cathy, whom Ted had decided would benefit greatly from some fatherly discipline, which he would deliver with his usual compassionate and authoritarian demeanor, to rerail her sauntering little caboose onto more practical intellectual pursuits than chasing the dead about. He had rehearsed it all with such conviction.

Somehow, the Sullivan men were on their way home, without even an apology and an estimated time of return, without even a schedule of an upcoming semester break. But even this perceived failure was readily accepted, in fact eagerly exchanged for the fresh, October flurry of erotic imagery blowing through Ted's revived, boyish brain. He also deduced that Matthew was A-OK with all of this too, with abandoning the mission.

They were victims, the two of them, the third spared only by his innocence and youth, in combination with his rapid expenditure of energy and quarters, and his skill in slaying imaginary beasts. Father and firstborn son were retreating without so much as a consolation prize.

Ted determined the silence needed to be broken, the issues addressed, and the explanation of their lack of conquests and progress—perhaps delivered on a need-to-know basis.

"Did you have a nice talk with Cathy?" he asked softly. To

Ted's surprise, this son who offered no more than a five-word vocabulary most days seemed in the mood to converse.

"Well, I think she got the message loud and clear," he began, swallowing back his vision of Cathy in the student center, doing his best to maintain a coherent conversation.

"Oh, you do? Good. Good work," Ted responded, recognizing the presence of abject pride taking the round.

"What did you tell Mom?" Matthew asked, deflecting the subject before more details were required of him.

"I laid it out for her," Ted began in similar form, nearly choking at his choice of words. "I mean, she does have these issues, but I can't have you two suffering indefinitely," he concluded.

"So how long will she be staying with Cathy?" Matthew asked, and at the mention of her name, Cathy resurfaced in bright and brilliant detail, the gold-spun highlights of her hair, the rounded, script-sketched *M* of her upper lip, the orange-peel smell of her—Matthew nearly groaned out loud.

"It's complicated. She's determined to see this through," Ted heard himself rationalize. "Now, of course, I could demand that she return, but I think the lesson here can be much bigger, if we give her enough rope." Ted nodded confidently, certain that by alluding to powers greater than his, to some expectation of justice from a universe that pretty well ignored his occasional heartfelt commands, Matthew would believe there actually might be a strategy at work.

"You're just going to let them stay!" Matthew reacted,

having long ago decided that his mother and Cathy both would return, that his dad had at least accomplished that much. "You can't!" he insisted. The details shot out of him. "There's this professor, this psychic guy, and I think he might be after her. He calls himself a doctor," Matthew laughed sarcastically. "Ha, I think he's hitting on her."

"I knew it!" Ted yelled, banging the steering wheel. His theory confirmed, he swung his head around to nod at Matthew to continue. "Did Cathy tell you anything about it? I hope Mom at least admitted it to her."

"Admitted what?"

"That the guy's after her."

"After Mom? What are you talking about? I meant after Cathy. She's vulnerable after losing her mother. We have to stop this."

"After Cathy? No way, I know those old con-artist, academic types. Your mother had a run-in with one at our school. Didn't even know what was happening until I pointed it out," Ted bragged.

"Dad, get a grip. Cathy looks like one of those fashion models," Matthew taunted. "I mean really, Mom's practically fifty!"

"Forty-five! And I hate to tell you this, Sport, but Cathy can't hold a candle to your mom," Ted argued. "I'm telling you I know what these bookworm types go for. They prey on the generosity of a woman's heart."

"Yeah, right. This guy's not after a heart! He's after sex. I know about these things, Dad. They count on tricking their young impressionable students. Especially ones without a family. Cathy's an orphan. How appealing is that?"

"You don't know what you're talking about, Matthew! I'm telling you, I know what's going on. I could see the change in your mother."

"What change? She looks exactly the same. Maternal, respectable. Did you see the difference in Cathy? Cathy looked really hot."

"You know something, your generation has no concept of beauty. You have no clue what you're talking about! You wouldn't know hot from holy."

"Oh no? Wasn't it you who said Mom needed a fat farm?"

The head popped up from behind then, jarred abruptly from its French fried bliss and Big Mac slumber, to add its two cents. "So, how much will you two pay me to destroy this videotape of your conversation?" Brian asked, flashing the camera he hadn't even charged, much less turned on.

"Pull over, Dad, so I can beat him up."

"I'll beat him, it's my right," the father reminded his son, still competing.

"You both are so pathetic. I'm embarrassed for you, really. It's no wonder you can't hold on to your women."

"Shut up, Brian," his older brother told him. "You don't understand crap."

"I understand I just witnessed a conversation that involved two of the most love-sick saps ever. Arguing over who's more attractive. In the meantime, that psychic guy is laughing his guts out. In fact, he can probably even hear you," Brian howled, falling against the backseat of the car in explosive, antagonistic laughter.

"Shut up, Brian," his father told him. "The last thing we need is your absurd perspective," Ted warned, conscious now of this eavesdropper.

"Fine. I'll keep my information to myself."

"What information?" Matthew bit, spinning around.

Brian went back to singing over his Walkman.

"Okay, Dad. Either you pull over now or I'm jumping the seat to beat him."

Ted pulled onto the shoulder and tapped Brian on the head. Brian winked tormentingly.

"Now you've got our attention, Son," Ted smiled with intense restraint.

"Mom told me how this psychic stuff happens. I just think instead of arguing over who he's after, you ought to see for yourself what's going on. Spy on them."

"And we're supposed to go back and forth to Potsdam?" Matthew objected, secretly delighted.

"No," Ted pronounced, pulling back into the traffic. "You guys have school to worry about. I'll do it myself. I can handle it."

"No way, Dad. If you go, I go. I'm a straight-A senior. Nothing will happen to my grades," Matthew vowed.

"Okay, but that's it. Brian, you'll stay behind. I'll get someone to check in on you."

"Great. Good idea. Leave me alone all those hours with

the phone. Maybe Mom will call so I'll have someone to talk to. Maybe the seniors will stop by and feed me. Maybe Pastor Hadley will invite me to stay with his family until you return. I can't guarantee your confidentiality. Not without some cold hard cash."

"When did he get to be such a pain in the ass?" Ted demanded of Matthew.

"On his mall trips with Mom," Matthew pronounced with infinite disgust. "We'd better take him with us, Dad. I don't trust him."

"Great. Now I'm responsible for contributing to the delinquency of two teens," Ted complained.

"Relax, Dad," Matthew comforted. "We're all just protecting our interests."

"Not me. I'm just in it for the fun. I'd do anything to see you lovesick saps suffer," Brian joked.

"How is it no one at school has beaten him?" Ted asked Matthew, moving back into highway traffic.

"I have Mom's charm," Brian added. "Students love me, teachers love me, other people's parents love me. It's all in the attitude. You get a lot more information out of people when you're acting nice. You two should try it sometime."

"Shut up, Brian," Matthew concluded.

"This week, get your assignments. We'll stay somewhere close by."

"Cool," Brian responded, popping his head out of his Walkman once more. "Should I call forward the phone or just program my computer to pick it up."

"Can he do that?" Ted asked Matthew.

"Anybody who's taken the nerd-computer course can do that," Matthew taunted.

"No way," Brian defended. "I figured it out last winter during one of the four hundred blizzards we had. Remember, you and Matthew were amusing yourselves with Sega games."

"Well, that's very industrious, Son. I'm grateful for your technical ability. Now, let's cut to the chase. Can we make it seem like we're still there?"

"Just rent me a laptop, and I'll see what I can do."

Ted looked suspiciously at Matthew, who shrugged his shoulders in defeat. "It couldn't hurt," he told his father.

"This whole situation is really out of hand," Ted growled.

"I told you this would happen," Matthew added. "Just don't let me forget I have to drive back Thursday afternoon."

"You have a test?" Ted inquired.

"No, but Agnes has an appointment with the chiropodist, Gert has to get a perm, and Shirley just wants to ride around in the van."

"I can't believe your mother has done this to us," Ted grumbled.

"Done what?" Brian asked.

"Forced us into the community."

Mary and Cathy braced themselves against a powerful October wind that bent branches and scattered leaves as it roared through the trees proclaiming its might. The women huddled against each other, attempting to walk. Mary locked her arm protectively on Cathy's to keep her from taking flight. They felt compelled to walk to Luke's, head out into the pre-Halloween fall evening to admire the decorations on porches, in windows, in the local stores.

"Not the best idea ever," Mary yelled, tightening her grip on her companion, bending her knees as if getting lower would help keep her balance. She could feel her ears burning, and suspected her lips would soon be chapped.

"Could be worse," Cathy answered, momentarily yanking the scarf down from her mouth. "It could be sleeting."

"No chance of that," Mary answered, pointing out the full moon flanked by two picturesque clouds.

"Nothing scary about that," Cathy remarked, pulling her green scarf up over her nose again, until her eyes appeared to change over from ocean blue to evergreen.

"Of course not," Mary answered. "But why don't we take a bus home anyway, because of the wind? It sounds like it could snap a tree in half."

Cathy nodded vigorously.

The stars were just becoming visible when they reached Luke's. He greeted the women cordially, taking their coats, offering tea and butter cookies, making sure to put out ashtrays. They both sank into his sofa as though they had just run a marathon.

"What would bring you out on foot on such a windy night?" Luke asked.

"You tell us," Mary teased, biting into an almond crescent.

Luke raised his eyebrows, wondering if Mary meant to challenge him.

"I keep having these dreams where I'm walking around campus," she confessed. "Except I don't think it's this campus, at least nothing that I recognize."

"So you're wandering around to find the setting?" Luke was nodding now. "That's a positive step. But if you don't think it's this campus you're dreaming about, why don't you trust that much and work through the dream?"

Mary realized he was right, although it seemed like a good idea at home, in their warm, sunny kitchen.

Cathy offered, "We thought we might stumble upon something familiar. You know, sort of intuitively."

Luke was finishing his tea, smiling approvingly at Cathy. "You know that's always good, to put physical energy behind your intent."

"Except for the wind," Mary interjected.

"Except for the wind," Luke agreed.

He stood and led Mary to the candlelit room and table where he performed the readings. She was somehow soothed by his voice, relaxed by his calm demeanor, able to let go of her preconceived notions and keep an open mind about whatever information he delivered.

As Mary shuffled the cards, Luke asked her what she'd like him to focus on, what was troubling her. Mary knew better than to deny anything to a psychic. She looked into his compassionate eyes and spoke honestly.

"More than anything, I'd really like to know what I'm doing here—I mean, what I'm supposed to be doing here. My husband is upset, my kids are upset, and when I think about them I am too. I'd like to be able to explain myself." Mary sighed.

Luke held the oversized cards in both hands as Mary relinquished them and, after a few moments staring off in concentration, he began to turn them faceup.

"You are supposed to be here," he reassured her. "You were to have come with Cathy, just as you have." He nodded as though convinced, still listening or watching whoever was passing on these insights. There were an equal amount of pauses as words coming from Luke, and Mary couldn't help but feel left out of the conversation.

He flipped over a few more cards, stopping at the King of Pentacles. "Your husband is very confused. He feels like he woke up one day, and everything had changed. But he's rising to the challenge. He's begun a process of change. He's thinking of you differently. He's thinking of you constantly, where before, well, he was just kind of taking you for granted. Have I got that right?"

"Well, I don't know," Mary stammered, reluctant to criticize Ted for anything, especially in front of another man. After all, he was the one still at home. She was the one who had run off.

"Trust me, this is good for him. It will probably be good for you both. He's learning things about your sons that he never knew. They're bonding."

"They needed me gone to do that?" Mary asked, temporarily offended.

"Well, when the energy shifts, it fosters change. You either go with it or it will be something like what you and Cathy experienced walking against that wind out there. It will take more out of you than it should."

"So what do you mean, *probably* be good for us both?" Mary asked.

"He's there. He's changing. But you're the wild card right now. They're growing their relationships. And Brian is fine, by the way. He'll always be fine. He's got a wonderful disposition. People love him."

"Well, that's a comfort."

"Look, it's not going to be easy for you, Mary. It will be

hard work. I've told you already, it's going to get worse before it gets better."

"Yes, but what does that mean?" Mary was horrified. "I don't understand. Can't you try and elaborate, give me something to go on?"

"The sorrow, it surrounds you. In this card I see swords piercing your heart. But it's an old wound."

"My mother. Losing my mother?"

"No, not that. It's not female energy."

"My father then. It would have to be him. That was a very old wound. I remember talking myself out of hurting when he died. Maybe I never dealt with that. Maybe I'm substituting the grief over my mother for my father."

"No. This is something sewn up so tightly, it's just going to explode. I can't even see it, it's buried so deep."

Mary was unnerved. The thought of anything exploding made her terrified. Perhaps it was her heart. Perhaps all that late-night palpitating would lead to a cardiac infarction, just as she suspected. Perhaps the hot flashing was the beginning of death by stroke, and her mind was so terrified, it had hidden the truth from her psyche and her psychic.

"You're not going to die," Luke offered, butting into her terror fest, patting her hand. "It's not that at all. It's some kind of emotional shock."

"An emotional shock?" Mary inquired, not nearly consoled. She would live, that was good news. But this—

"In fact, I see your legs going out from under you. It's powerful. It hits you hard like a thunderbolt."

"How do I avoid it?" Mary demanded. Dear God, what was worse, knowing something bad was coming or not knowing? Hearing in advance that you were going to fall down, or tripping spontaneously? Why had she ever opened this door? What was she thinking? How would she ever sleep again?

"It's nothing you did or have done," Luke answered. "It's not coming from you. And I'm afraid there is no way to stop it."

"Does it affect my family, my children?" She hoped nothing bad would happen in Matthew's senior year.

"No. It's entirely about you."

Mary couldn't conceive of anything being about her and not about her family.

"I'm sorry I can't tell you more," Luke said, patting her hand.

"But that can't be all. You have to give me more to go on. Look again," she said, pointing at the cards. "Who's with me? Ask them?" Mary continued, as though these dead people Luke consulted could be held down and interviewed. She scattered the drawn cards before her, noting an empress, a king, a falling tower. "Find my mother somewhere in that pack. She'll help you."

"It doesn't work like that. In fact, we need to stop now, continue another time. You need to be calm."

"Calm?"

Luke shut his pale blue eyes and appeared to be trying to gather more impressions. Mary quieted down, her eyes studying him for any signs or signals.

"Mary, listen to me. It ends well. Whatever this storm is, it finishes beautifully. Look, right now you're like a planet that has gone retrograde. You've stopped, taken a few spins back, and when you're ready, you'll begin moving forward again. I'm afraid that's all I can give you. I can't follow this energy any further tonight. It's gone. Call me if you need me, though. Another day, another time, we'll try again."

"Okay," Mary said, standing. And being an efficient person she couldn't help asking, "Is there a time frame on this shock?"

He was nodding. "Soon."

She took a deep breath and opened the door, returning to the living room unsatisfied. Cathy sprinted past Mary toward Luke, while Mary's hands went in search of her cigarettes. She sat and she smoked and worried and wondered. How was Luke able to know so much, and yet so little? Male energy, female energy, old wounds. If only she had more information.

Cathy and her mom had a great conversation. According to Luke, Deborah had reunited with some family and friends in the afterlife, and couldn't have been happier. She sent her good wishes to her daughter, advised her to follow her instincts about school, and told her she had found a true friend in Mary. It was enough for Cathy.

"The level of detail was astounding," Cathy later told her.

Mary had made hot chocolate and defrosted a golden layer cake, and the women sat in their humble living room, after a quiet, uneventful bus ride home, finally able to talk about their sessions.

"Really?" Mary asked, slightly envious.

"He mentioned my grandparents by name, and said my grandmother was the one with the artistic ability, and that she loves seeing my crafts."

"That's wonderful," Mary chirped, her eyes momentarily wandering off to the full moon. She supposed you got what you asked for. If she didn't want to know what was about to happen, she surely shouldn't visit with psychics.

"You know, I'll help you," Cathy offered. "I mean, whatever it is, we'll get through it."

"He told you?" Mary asked, surprised. She hadn't decided whether to involve Cathy. She thought maybe Cathy had enough to cope with and could be spared.

"Well, he didn't really. My mom did."

Mary gasped. Did everyone know but her? This was a very unfair universe at times. Where were all her dead relatives, and why weren't they coming forward to shed some light?

"She said you were going to need my help now. And that it would all happen naturally."

"But did she tell you why?"

"No."

"Damn it! What good is knowing half of something?"

"She did say it would all be okay. And she also said something funny, at least Luke said she said it, but I can't imagine my mother speaking like this. 'Be not afraid.' Isn't that weird?"

The next sound was that of Mary's cup speeding across the coffee table, shattering on the floor. Cathy seemed to be moving in slow motion toward her, and Mary, of course, descended to the floor to begin picking up the glass. Was this enough of a shock, she wondered? Seeing kinetic energy up close? Watching a cup slide itself across a table and smash on the floor? Knowing there was enough wind to push it, but not being able to deny the timing had been too perfect, the movement too precise, the conversation too targeted.

Mary was so impressed by the sudden movement of her mug that she immediately confessed to Cathy she had thought she'd been hearing Deborah's voice telling her, "Be not afraid." Was this the big emotional jolt, what Luke saw, Mary down on the floor, cleaning up glass? Technically, her legs were out from under her.

Cathy didn't think so. In fact, she was thrilled her mother may have spoken to Mary. She was finally beginning to feel a sense of family, even if her relatives seemed to include both the living and dead.

After two hours of TV, Cathy had taken a shower, fixed her hair in a tight bun, and settled into her flannel pajamas, which sported stylish pink poodles. The wind had stopped its moaning, and the leaves seemed to be settling peacefully on the ground, except when someone walked through a pile. It had been hours since she heard anyone's footsteps, but it wasn't for lack of listening.

Cathy found Mary reading in bed.

"Can't sleep?"

"It's amazing," Mary admitted. "Considering I used to have trouble waiting up till eleven for the boys to come home. I guess I'm just unnerved."

"I feel bad that something so comforting to me has made you so upset. It seems like everything I do has a greater impact upon you than on me. I don't understand."

"Me either," Mary answered, throwing off her covers in frustration. She tied on her red flannel robe, with two things in mind: Ally McBeal and Cup of Soup.

"Do you regret coming here, Mary?" Cathy asked with a pinched voice.

Mary slung an arm around her friend. "Nah. It still beats watching Monday night football."

~ 23 ~

*A*s Mary lay in bed imagining the worst, she considered what she had already gained by following Cathy—her recently acquired freedom. She had longed for it through those drowsy lunches she ate in the den, plate of salad poised upon her knees, cordless phone within reach if anyone should call, the midday news of even the most vicious fire or brutal murder, delivered as regularly as the daily bread. Now from this new perspective, she could mentally revisit the Mary of the Den, the Mary who on some afternoons had dumped all the family underwear onto her bed and, in sorting the items by color and texture, by size, by wear and tear, began to feel the faint beginnings of desperation. In leaving that Mary, she felt as if she had already removed herself from her body, for it was a product of that house, that family, that lulling comfort of domestic security, the familiar geography of her town stores, the smiling faces, the outdated existence, the logic that had dominated her decisions.

It would have been easy to dismiss the discomfort as the blues, even boredom, to suppress it with a phone call, a movie, a trip to the senior center with baked goods. But honestly, there were days when that bubble of restlessness gurgled softly within her, and she pulled out the photos of her mother and purposely opened her heart to the grief. She was grateful for the pain, for it seemed that as long as she had that, she had some degree of life, some intensity of feeling, some proof of her ability to generate energy of any sort. Yes, she welcomed the pain, chased after it, perhaps needing it to feel alive.

"I always feel so much better after I cry," Cathy had once commented.

As an infant, Matthew cried every afternoon from five-thirty until seven. The pediatrician had said it was because he hadn't cried all day, it was a means of exercise, a manner of releasing energy. Now Mary wondered if that was why she needed the grief, if her life and being ensconced in sorrow was simply more vigorous than her ordinary life. She supposed she was right in reaching toward the spiritual, hoping to comprehend something of a new earthly assignment, now that the children were almost raised. But hanging over her head now was this awful threat of an emotional collapse.

Mary was on her guard all right, spooked beyond belief, even though there were no whispers, crashing cups, apparitions, or cool unexpected drafts bursting into her bedroom. Some unbreakable, invisible thread of an idea was moving her along this path, and to defy it was to consign herself to another twenty or so years of the remoteness she had only recently begun to resent. This change would undoubtedly cost her. Perhaps elements of her family life. Perhaps the daily, restored perfection of her home. Perhaps in twinkle lights for the apartment.

"You look fifteen years younger with those gold highlights," Cathy had said after they experimented with her hair. "Can I do your makeup?"

"Sure," Mary agreed, having never had a makeover of any sort. She was pleasantly surprised by the result. Her eyes had been lined in subtle navy, her lids with a smoky brown shadow, and her lips, which seemed to have gotten smaller with age, were plump, shiny, and of all things, red. She wished Ted could see her. He always complimented her when she took the time to apply eye makeup. She pushed thoughts of him away. It hurt to miss him.

Mary of the Den had gotten her hair cut an inch at a time, and, when the gray began to be visible, had it gradually turned back to its original color, not a tint or a highlight detectable. She had worn the same mix-and-match clothing from the same designers, buying two or three of the same blouses in neutral colors, black and navy sensible pumps, and drawers full of expensive makeup that did little more than darken her lips to their original shade of youthful rose, lighten the drooping, darkening circles of her eyes, and brush in the eyebrows where her hair had become sparse or gray.

Here, among the wide-eyed, smiling spirits of youth,

where energy was limitless and optimism abundant, where the world was to be conquered or saved, humanity defined and analyzed, and the God-blessed traces of childhood were still evident in a bright orange pair of sneakers, Mary was regenerating. It was as if each breath brought closer the excited buzzing or spontaneous giggling, the sweet confirmation of the heart's limitless capacity not only to love life, but to shine especially bright and brilliantly in groups.

Mary was learning she invented each and every limit upon her life: the wash, the groceries, the duty-bound, joyless movement of one activity to another, slicing vegetables for salads on Sunday, changing all sheets on Saturday, driving Agnes to the beauty parlor and staying there to read magazines, making deposits at the bank, the mother, the maid, the volunteer, the wife with the right things to say, the pliable nature—"You shouldn't have, Ted"—the going to the shore each and every year because the boys liked swimming, the inability to splurge on anything for herself but a Boston cream pie and a Hershey bar. It had been a long time since she had shared her heart with anyone who didn't require her housekeeping, driving, or cooking. What was she trying to make up for, some awful past sin? What terrible thing had she done?

"Could be a past-life thing," Cathy suggested, having read up on the subject.

Mary's life had veered off schedule while her mother was sick; the impact was immediate. In those first few seconds of crisis, as she looked for her keys, her purse, her jacket, with her own heart racing, she was wild and clawing for time, for

life, an unstoppable force ready to speed off to the emergency
room to catch perhaps the final, departing wishes from her
mother. But each heart-stopping interruption only bred more
routines, performed automatically, like checking the lights
and the door locks or making sure the stove and iron were
turned off. It didn't take long for her to adapt. Her keys, anticipating the next call, the next summoning to the hospital,
were hung above a larger purse purchased just for these trips.
Mary had a pocket for a hardcover romance novel, fruits,
sandwiches, or pretzels, to usher her through those long,
dramatic standoffs in the waiting room, while doctors were
working furiously to keep her mother alive. She carried
caffeine-free tea so she wouldn't overdose on coffee, and a
condensed version of her telephone book, emergency listings
of doctors, tables of drugs, her boys' school schedules, pictures of her young children at Disneyworld that she could
look at to temporarily stop the flow of tears, anything to distract her from the pain—the pain she later refused to give up.

Entire years had evaporated. Christmas would come, then
Easter, then July at the shore. Until it was over. Over. Quietly
finished. Her mother was gone, and she too was discharged
from the familiar hospital faces, freed from the screaming
sirens, the anticipatory fear, left to face a completely unstruc-
tured day, in a calm week, in a life that had been spent tossing
and turning at the whim of her mother's disease and utter terror of losing her. Mary was empty.

"It's like I have nothing left inside," Cathy had put it suc-
cinctly.

Mary was actually surprised to hear her thoughts echoed through Cathy, whose mother had been killed instantly. Many times she prayed life would end for her mother's sake; it was inconceivable that it ever would happen. It was dreamlike, the way it all floated by her, the way Ted touched her shoulder and told her, the way her boys hugged her, and the way it all ended for everyone eventually, with a name on a stone at a plot in Peace Hill.

Battling cancer was an extraordinary job. It transformed her, trained her to challenge death. Death was something to drive off, to argue about with a second or third physician, to deter with a new drug, an alternative therapy, anything to out-think, outplan, outmaneuver, outrun the disease. But even as the days passed and her mother lived beyond the grim predictions, death was always winning. It was taking Mary along, flexing its grip on her heart—got you, Mary. Maybe today, maybe tomorrow, maybe the next day—a bad guy hiding in a bush ready to spring out when you aren't paying attention. Better stay at the hospital—no, better go home and rest for tomorrow, better get coffee, better call the family, better not step away, not for a second, don't turn your back, it will take her.

Mary had been exhausted by the fight. And moment by moment, it worsened, until it required a hospital staff to keep her mother's breath and blood flowing, a cluster of bleeping machines, tubes to feed her, three women to roll her back and forth to change her sheets, her diapers, cleanse her goose-pimpled flesh, until she was less and less alive, less body, less mind, less flesh and blood, more like a trapped creature than the living, loving person Mary had known.

After having been at the mercy of that six-year crisis, it was no wonder she didn't know what to do with herself, how to fill her days. And the suffering she had witnessed, not just her mother's, but the others, the elderly patients who were wheeled from their rooms and lined up in the hallway near the nurses' station where they could be more closely observed. There were dying men and women who would pull at your arms, toothless and desperate like beggars in an alleyway, confused and powerless, caged in their double-sided, railed gurneys, moaning their way to death. Mary sometimes took the elevator to a different floor so she wouldn't have to pass them. She would ride down to the lobby where she could see new fathers or grandparents pass her by with bundles of pink or blue balloons.

It should have been an affirmation of sorts, Mary supposed, to know babies were being born and that it was all happening only a few floors away, but instead it made her ache. She remembered holding young Matthew and Brian for the first time and couldn't believe how the years rushed by, that precious time of high chairs, strollers, and trips to the park.

She missed her younger family. Ted, with barely enough cash to survive on street hot dog lunches, carrying home a rose that he let each of the boys take turns giving to her. Brian couldn't wait, would run all the way shouting, hand her the flower, and get the dime-store vase. Matthew would walk very slowly toward her; if she looked up he would stop moving until she looked away again, and when he had come right up, close to her, he would say nothing, tongue poking his cheek, and deliver the gift without a smile, and she'd reach down and hug him, invite him to help her put it in water, and together they'd walk to the kitchen handling the rose as if it were as precious as their love. She'd wink at Ted, who would just shrug, never understanding Matthew, who would inspect it daily, dreading the moment when its first petals had fallen and it would have to be thrown away.

Death had poisoned Mary. There could be no other explanation. She stood guard over her home and family, offered spiritual security. And when she saw the other women out there, their dangling earrings gleaming in the golden light, their bangs not quite touching the bridge of their noses, their rock-hard, gym-conditioned legs, shining and slender in their stockings, she couldn't help wondering about their days, if they had meetings, power lunches, illicit lovers, nights in small apartments, minimal possessions, like Cathy's mother, Deborah.

Mary had so much freedom now, it frightened her. She adapted to living in this apartment that required weekly plunging of its plumbing, that barely had enough counter space to slice a bagel or put up coffee, that had walls as thin as book covers. She never understood women who went on retreats, rode off on some bus trip with nothing on their minds but themselves and prayer. Mary's spiritual life had revolved around issues of safety—that of her boys, her husband, her mother, her daily prayers as she let them out into the world that they would return to her unharmed. It never occurred to her that she should have been asking something for herself.

Mary remembered her mother, always in her home, always cooking a pot of vegetable soup, always a fresh pot of coffee for visitors. It was that pleasant feeling Mary constantly tried for, the comfort of walking into her mother's home, of pouring a cup of coffee, of warming her very soul. The simplicity of seeing clay pots of mums and perfect pumpkins on the porch stairs. Finding blissfully sweetened lemonade in a sweating pitcher on a summer afternoon, cookies in the dark of winter, and coconut cake in the spring.

Perhaps, like Cathy, all she wanted was her mother back from the dead, even by re-creating her through her own life. She aimed for the smells, always stirring soup, sauce, onions, gravy. It just seemed to Mary that it all shouldn't evaporate, everything that was her mother.

As much as Mary loved the idea of communicating with discarnate beings, of having the ability to be indirectly in their company, of having her mother potentially accessible through mental discipline and meditation, she had to admit she'd rather have a hug or imagine herself a wonderful homecoming.

Like Cathy, she wondered what death actually felt like, never thinking of it as anything pleasant, despite the descriptions that came her way about warm white lights and love. She just knew she wanted to study its face, to know in her soul that she wouldn't lose anyone else to it, or at the very least to protect herself from its insidious grip on her heart.

Even though I'm spooked I can't go home. I've grown accustomed to being the oldest one on campus. No one takes my parking space. And I think that what I'm doing here is necessary, although I'm really not sure what it is. God, I don't even understand how this happened to me," Mary said, irritated with her cigarette lighter.

"What?" Cathy asked, lighting Mary's cigarette with a match.

"How did I become this ambiguous, out-of-touch, empty woman with homework? Even I don't believe it happened because my mother died. I'm inclined to blame the boys and especially Ted, but then I know that's unfair. If anything, they just let me drop down and out. You know, it's all very subtle. You don't notice the changes. But one day, you answer the phone and a pleasant female voice calls you by your first name, and she sounds happy to have found you. So you think for a moment this is a friend, or a cousin, or someone from your old high school class calling you for lunch, and the truth is, she's trying to sell you magazines. So, as quickly as you can, you get off the phone, and next thing you know, you're so disappointed, you're weeping into this elaborate salad you're making. You look at the cucumbers, the sliced tomatoes, the red onions you refrigerated hours ago so you wouldn't cry, and these little rolled-up pieces of fish, and feel absolute pity for yourself, because before that phone call, everything revolved around homemade croutons and breadsticks, but now, now that you've been reminded there's a world out there by a telemarketer, you look upon yourself with complete disdain."

"How is it possible to roll a fish?" Cathy asked with such genuine curiosity that Mary laughed, and then they both laughed.

"Oh, you see, you're so much healthier than I am. You say what you think. It comes right out of your mouth. You're so in touch with yourself," Mary said with fond appreciation.

"I think that's probably it. You don't have to stay in touch with the world, just with yourself. I think that's why the grief doesn't devastate me. I'm packed full of myself. Mothers aren't like that, I guess. I guess they're packed full of other people. Anyway, you were trying to mourn without peers. I've got lots of them. I meet them at support groups, and I go out of my way to bring up the subject. You'd be surprised at how many people are going through it."

"I'll just bet in elementary school, you were able to announce when your birthday was," Mary added, impressed by her young friend. "I never could. It always felt like I was asking for something in return."

Cathy placed her hand on Mary's shoulder, understanding the difference between them went far beyond age. "And what's so bad about that?"

"You know, I'm not sure I remember," Mary confessed.

"I found this cork board wall in the student center, sort of a bereavement wall, names and photos of people we're mourning. John Lennon is there, Martin Luther King, Rock Hudson, River Phoenix, lots of celebrities, but other people too, people no one knew, like my mother. I put her name and picture up there. People bring flowers, write notes, light candles."

"Right there in the student center?"

"My grief group started it. I never even paused before that wall last year. I never even noticed it until I lost my mother. Some days I stand there and wait for someone to talk to. I put a rose there just yesterday. It's so much better than that quiet cemetery. You should place a picture of your mom up there. I bet it will help. You can talk there, or you can cry, or just look at all those faces and know your mother's in good company. The spaces are small, so you can only fit a wallet-size photo."

Mary sat thinking and wondering how Cathy managed to seem so effortlessly astute and so innocent simultaneously. She had watched her progress from crying each night for thirty minutes in her bedroom, to going to support meetings, out with groups of friends. And this psychic stuff, while scaring the daylights out of Mary, really seemed to be helping her heal.

"It just seems like we all should be doing it, investigating the next world," Cathy added. "I mean there's life, and there's death. It doesn't hurt to acknowledge it, to grow spiritually."

"I think it's easier for most people not to think about it. And maybe the older you get, the more you'd like to avoid the subject."

"Why is that?"

"I guess because you know every day brings you one step closer, statistically speaking."

"That's depressing. But my mom was younger than you are now, Mary. And as much as I hated losing her, I love the thought of her being young and beautiful eternally. I love that she didn't lose her mind or control of her body."

"I think of my father like that too. But I don't think I'd want younger people embracing the idea of death. Young people should enjoy life."

"Until how old?"

"What?"

"Which age is the right age to focus on it? Thirty? Forty? Fifty?"

"I don't know, Cathy. I guess I always figured it magically came up, when the time was right, like love."

Mary made coffee and Cathy moved from painting her nails to painting faces on the tiny pumpkins Mary had lined up on the kitchen windowsill. Mary couldn't help but be impressed.

"You see, I would have never thought to use nail polish on those little pumpkins. Where did you learn to do that?"

"Oh, this is my first time. I was doing polka dots on my toes when I realized the brush would be a perfect size for the pumpkins. That's what I like about art. Sometimes you don't even know what you're doing until you do it. I get midway into a painting sometimes, and then I'll realize what the subject really is, where the emotion is, and I can't believe how lucky I am to have stumbled into it."

"You are lucky," Mary said.

"Why?" Cathy wondered, reaching for a third bottle of nail polish, lime green this time to dot her ghoul's cheeks. "I'm sure you do that too."

Mary bit into a marshmallow. "I don't think so. I mean, I seem always to map out things, each event, each day."

"Until you threw it all away for a second round of college," Cathy offered, lighting a cigarette.

"Well, not college so much as my curiosity of the psychic world," Mary countered. "Of course, that's assuming I'll one day master my fear of the psychic world enough to face the real reason I'm here."

"What does Luke say about that?"

"That I have the answers already, but I'm terrified to face them."

"Well, doesn't he give you any hints?"

"He tries, but then tells me I'm hiding it on him. So I eat another slice of his crumb cake," Mary admitted, pouring Cathy the remainder of the coffeepot.

"Maybe I could try for you," she suggested.

"I wouldn't turn away the help," Mary answered. "You seem to be making real progress."

"I think I am. I almost did it last night," Cathy announced. "I almost talked to my mother in my dream. She was sitting at our kitchen counter at the condo, and I saw her looking so beautiful, so happy. She was making toast and jam for me, spreading the strawberry jam so slowly, I can still hear the knife scraping. And then I could hear my own thoughts insisting that since she was so happy, she must be dead. And then I woke up."

"Oh I hate those dreams. You get so close, but not close enough."

"Mary, I'm not sure I want to stay here anymore," Cathy admitted, softly tearing up. "I think I made a mistake renting out the condo. I want to go home. No, I have no home. Where is home when your mother dies? It's so awful. I've been left behind, Mary. I have no one. I really don't think I should stay here. There's nothing for me to do but this, and I could do this anywhere. I've dropped three courses already."

"When?" Mary asked, horrified.

"Last week," Cathy admitted. "I'd have dropped the meditation one if you weren't in it. And the art, well, it doesn't really count, because I'd be doing it anyway."

"Oh, Cathy, I wish you would have talked to me first," Mary sighed.

"Mary, you would have talked me out of it. There was no point. I feel compelled to spend more and more time at the wall, looking at the names and faces, and I think, maybe, I'll being going soon too."

"Don't say that."

"But it's the truth. I want to be happy, I think I am, but then I remember I'm completely detached from everyone. I remember my mother died young, and you know how those things seem to follow families. Maybe I'm not meant to have a long life with a lot of people in it. And I'm not really so upset about it. It's only when I think about things like how much I like playing with the kids who came in the luncheonette. I think I could have been a good mother."

"It's the grief, Cathy." Mary knew it was nothing you could point to, an invisible bruise. You were its passenger, its prisoner, its victim.

"Don't you know, sometimes I just want to crawl into a warm dark place and sleep until I can see my mother's face again?" Cathy was crying now, but trying to talk through it. "I want to go to the cemetery and lie down upon the grass and wait to sink in, or wait for everything to grow up around me. I don't want to deal with the pain anymore. It's too hard. Tell me, Mary. Don't you feel it?"

"Yes, sometimes, but then I think of my family—"

"You see, you have a connection here. I have no one."

"You have me, Cathy! I don't care that you weren't born related to me. You're in my heart. We're together now. You are with me."

"My mother was my best friend. I was so much like her. I just didn't get too close to many people. I hung out with her, painted, made wreaths, and she always told me how much talent I had. I didn't need to make friends. Now I think it's just too late. I've got to go my whole life without her. I don't know how long that will be. It's not fair. I never had a family. I grew up with only her. I don't know if I can do it anymore. I see women with mothers in the mall and I think, I can never have that again. My mom was so content to lay back and let the world go on. I don't know. It makes me angry. Who's going to care if I fall in love or get engaged?"

"I care about you. You care about me. We can be together even though we're not in the same bloodline."

"It wasn't our choice, Mary. It just happened. Just like my mom's accident. It was an accident too."

"Luke would say there are no accidents."

Cathy was sobbing now, fitting the words around her breath as best she could, clawing at the tears with her fingers.

"Mary, sometimes I'm happiest when I'm thinking how close I am to death, to her. I think I can always just walk off a cliff, take a handful of pills, get rid of my body, and then it will be over. Do you know how much that cheers me up? Knowing that all I have to do is make the decision, and I never have to wake up again. Knowing that there might be a truck out there waiting to smash into me, that something may fall out of the sky and crush this body, the only thing that's separating me from my mother."

Mary was now down on the floor embracing her, holding

on for dear life. She knew Cathy had gone temporarily mad from the grief and that things no one meant to say out loud were pouring out. Mary knew she'd recover. You learned the hard way that even if you cried until there was nothing left of you, even if you made yourself sick and tired and drunk and crazy, you could not free yourself from it just by wishing it away.

"You have this precious life. You have people to love. People need your love, Cathy. People like me. And people will love you. So, you're not going anywhere. I'll stand in your way. You're not leaving me behind! I won't let go of you. I'll make sure you have a wonderful bridal shower," Mary told her, wiping tears from her own eyes.

"Mary," Cathy said, looking up with her tired, flushed out eyes, "what if it wasn't an accident? What if my mother meant to do it? What if she just let go of the wheel, or saw the truck coming, and didn't even try to get out of the way?"

"Don't think like that. What makes you think that?"

"She always needed so much rest. The more I learn, the more I think she may have been depressed for the past few years. She wouldn't talk about it, though. I think maybe she was heartbroken. I used to make all these crafts to cheer her up. She loved to watch me work."

"Cathy, you've barely begun your life. You've got to see the distinction between her choices and yours."

"I don't know. It all seems so difficult sometimes."

"It is. But then when I see you walking off with your friends, I think to myself, now there goes someone so full of life, everyone wants to be around her. You inspire me, Cathy. You're so easy with people. God, people need that so much. They need your kindness, your compassion. I can't begin to tell you how much you've helped me. And besides, you're talented. You have to use what you've been given."

"Oh, Mary, there are lots of people who have lots of different talents. No one would even miss me, I mean, other than you."

"You don't know. You have no idea just how many people you've touched, how many you will touch, how often someone will look up at you, people you don't even notice, and think, wow, she's got something, or she just smiled at me, or what a kind, beautiful heart she has. You'll be important to the people you meet. They'll notice your heart. Doesn't this world need as many kind people as it can get? I mean, look at me. I changed my entire life because I met you. I wasn't even really alive. I was somewhere in between life and death."

"Do you wonder what it's like to die? I mean I think it might feel great, like having your neck cracked by a chiropractor, you get that rush or release of energy. The freedom," Cathy said, casting her blue eyes up to the heavens.

"Never mind freedom. Freedom isn't all it's cracked up to be. It's directionless. I'll tell you what you need. A family. Love. Responsibility. Lots of it. That way you always know what you should be doing, and if you don't, everyone around you will be glad to tell you. You can have all of us, Ted, Matthew, Brian, and me. You can have my extended family of seniors to dote on. And I'll tell you what I've decided. I'm going to give you my mother's knitting needles. I'll just bet you can figure out what to do with them."

"You know, I've always wanted to knit. I've just never worked with wool before. That's something I could try, something to look forward to. Mary, I'm sorry. I just miss her," Cathy sighed, shaking her head, lighting a cigarette.

"I know. I think all of us miss our mothers, and lately, since we've started to see Luke, I also think that maybe we can miss ours less because they're dead. I mean, he's always telling me the dead are always with us, always accessible, and you can kind of communicate with them, like you would with God—my mother would like that I said that, she did think of herself as a great power. Anyway, when they were alive, you had real separation—time, miles—now it's only physical, and maybe not even that so much."

"So you think they're hanging around, listening?"

"How could they not be? I mean, even though Brian and Matthew are miles away, I always, always think of them. Do you think any family members would ever really leave us? Could you even get away from them if you tried? My mother was certainly inescapable. I can't imagine it's different with Ted, Matthew, or Brian."

"Brian's so great," Cathy said, sipping a Coke now, straight from the bottle, a nostalgic treat Mary never bought for herself at home, twelve-packs being so much more economical.

"He is incredibly easy to get along with, and just about as manipulative a person as you'll ever meet," Mary said, placing *Rubber Soul* on her turntable a second time.

"I could knit him a scarf that would compliment his personality," Cathy said. "Lots of bright colors, lots of orange and electric green. And when I'm finished, don't tell me, navy blue for Matthew?"

"Please, he hasn't worn a scarf since first grade. I think he sees it as a sign of weakness."

"Then maybe I should work on his first?"

"Absolutely," Mary smiled. "He could use a little warmth."

"So, what do you think about having a séance here?" Cathy asked, changing the subject back again. "Just maybe talking to my mother from familiar surroundings would be worth a try."

"The two of us?" Mary asked.

"And Luke. I'm sure he'd do it," Cathy assured her. "And let's face it, other than some whispers and a broken mug, we're not getting much in the way of messages."

~ 25 ~

As Luke repeatedly called on Deborah's spirit to communicate, Mary was aware of how warm Cathy's hand felt in hers and how small her hand felt in Luke's. Twice the candle flame seemed to jump toward the ceiling. Mary broke out in a cold sweat—unless that was an unseasonable outbreak of prickly heat. Against Luke's advice, she had agreed only to the daytime séance, aware as she was of her own limitations in courage. Truthfully, she was only slightly hoping for success.

"Deborah, come to us. Deborah . . ."

If the table rattled, dishes crashed on their own, or worse yet, the voice or embodiment of a ghost arrived, Mary didn't know that she could trust herself to remain seated. She had read about things being levitated and secretly prayed she wouldn't be among them.

Mary's mother frequently testified to the existence of curses, ghosts, and the dependable powers of the saints. Mary remembered the often-told stories of dying relatives who, eager to bid farewell to loved ones that for one reason or another were not present at their bedside when their detachment from earth occurred, managed synchronistically to rip a shade off a window, spin a clock backward, make an unwound music box sing, or drive a cold wind through a sealed bedroom. These kinetic good-byes were routinely accepted, at least by Mary's mother and her generation, as traditional, respectful courtesies, like greeting and departing kisses or handshakes in the earthly realm. So the thought of an apparition on a polite mission to communicate seemed more than slightly reasonable.

Because of this ethereal lore, Mary's mother always kept the statue of the Sacred Heart of Mary in full view, its manual candleholder replaced in the sixties with a blue, electric bulb the size of a Christmas light, which eerily brightened the night a shade or two. In Mary's mind, this served only to highlight the frightening darkness to a degree where shapes, which would otherwise be invisible, were now more than slightly discernible, where shadows leapt along the walls. Afraid, Mary's imagination conjured up not aunts and uncles blowing kisses, but witches' hats and monsters. Yet, in theory at least, Mother Mary, compassionate and maternal to all, full of mercy, full of love, the Queen of the rosary and promoter of peace, was plugged in and on duty. So even if a gang of mischievous spirits arrived looking to levitate a corner of a bed, a slumbering soul, or, in young Mary's worst fears, drag an innocent child kicking and screaming for a terrorizing flight into the netherworld, she, from her authoritative position on the starched bureau doily, was not without current to intervene.

"Deborah, come to us. Deborah, mother to Cathy . . ."

As Luke continued to call, Cathy seemed to swoon a moment, unless that was Mary's imagination. It was awfully hard to maintain this hand-chained circle with good posture, without leaning to one side or the other. Mary noted the good things about the room. It was remaining at a stable temperature. No inexplicable wind was evident. And in broad, sunny, daylight, if there were sinister shadows creeping along the wall, they were impossible to detect.

Mary had never even seen a ghost. There was no reason to assume Cathy's dead mother would behave impolitely. Mary's father had managed to leave the earth without any ghoulish activity twenty-eight years ago. His watch had simply stopped ticking from the crystal dish where he routinely left his valuables. Her mother had a dream of him walking toward a brightly lit garden, red roses in bloom. She could hear him whistling "Bye, Bye, Baby," which was one of their favorite songs from some Marilyn Monroe movie. Whistling was always bad luck, worse than shoes on a table, umbrellas opened inside a home, or even the number thirteen. Her mother swore she knew immediately from that dream he would die. Mary routinely thanked both the Mother of God and her prematurely departed father for never having visited her in the dark, despite her mother's insistence that he might one day appear, hazy, transparent, floating at the foot of her bed, to attempt some consoling form of a permanent good-bye.

The thought of encountering a spirit, even the spirit of a loved one, gave Mary goose bumps. Before her coma, Mary's mother had effectively managed to increase Mary's anxiety. She described how both her hands might rise up as she looked beyond everyone in the room to the apparitions who would come to collect her.

Mary remained focused on the flame, the blue, the orange, the yellow, the white, until it all seemed to blend into one color. She concentrated as best she could, until she could hear the flame blowing back and forth like a flag in the breeze. The flame seemed all there was in the room, as though it had grown brighter, larger than life, with more and more rumbling. It ruffled and rolled onto itself, until it seemed no longer to be of fire, but a wave from the ocean.

The afternoon grew brighter still, as though it had been swallowed by the flame, and Mary was transported to a place upon the sand where she could watch young Matthew swimming. As she scanned the water to see him, the light continued to grow brighter and brighter, till it no longer felt like sunlight, till it lacked the softening yellow haze and heat associated with sunlight. Instead it felt white, a true white light, no less white than the clouds or the shimmer from the water.

The day grew brighter still as Mary stared tranquilly across the water, watching Matthew swim. Her eyes didn't flinch, didn't water, didn't need to be shielded from this intense brilliance, and for a second she wondered why. Matthew looked so beautiful as he turned and smiled and waved, and Mary waved back from the shoreline, feeling her heart leap, certain that she could run and jump, spin in circles on the sand, jog a mile energetically, sing out loud in a pure voice, fall backward without apprehension. It was the absence of fear that elated her as she laughed out loud, unable to contain her joy. Feeling unafraid was a remarkable freedom, unlike anything she had ever felt. And Matthew was not only safe, but also appeared to be uninhibitedly happy. Her eyes closed as a refreshing breeze cooled her face.

Mary opened her eyes, slowly recognizing the surroundings. Cathy was gently pressing a wet towel to her face as Luke was calling her name, and Mary tumbled back reluctantly into the reality of her kitchen séance without a clue that she had even been gone from her chair.

"You're back!" Cathy exclaimed. "I wasn't sure you could hear me."

"Hear you what?" Mary wondered out loud.

"She doesn't know what happened, Cathy," Luke volunteered.

"What do you mean?" Mary asked, sitting forward.

"Do you remember anything?" Cathy asked.

"I must have fallen asleep. I was on a beach watching Matthew. It was a perfect day—"

"Mary, you channeled my mother!" Cathy shrieked.

"I what?"

"You were the voice of Deborah, Mary," Luke told her, placing one hand on her shoulder.

"How do you know?" Mary was aghast.

"The things she said," Cathy said, wiping tears away. "Oh, I wish you could have heard them too. Then you'd know how much I appreciate your doing this for me. She was so happy. I couldn't believe it. So much happier than she ever was on earth. Mary, thank you. Thank you."

"Shall we try and reach your mother now, Mary?" Luke asked.

Mary nodded, somewhat relieved to know that if ever a spirit would take over her body, at least she wouldn't be quivering in a corner shielding her eyes. She'd be on vacation at a beach where she was totally fearless, where Matthew was happy, and where it was possible to feel real joy.

～26～

It's very noisy," Luke explained to Mary and Cathy. "Your husband and sons are visiting?" he asked Mary.

"No, they were here last weekend," Mary told him, wondering if her guilty conscience was that evident, or if maybe her family did in fact miss her. She hadn't had a single conversation with Ted since he had driven back home, and Matthew had gone stone still when she kissed him good-bye. Only Brian had suggested she invest in some sort of computer so he could communicate with her privately.

"It's your boyfriend, Cathy. He's in town."

"I don't have one," Cathy told him.

"Someone who's very protective of you, of you both," Luke added. "More than one person actually," he said, shutting his eyes against the noise. He took both their hands and seemed to be trying to hear through static, but he kept coming back to the same pictures and sounds, all of them male.

Across the street from Cathy's apartment, dressed greener than a leprechaun, spying from a tree, binoculars in hand, was Mary's firstborn son, Matthew. As soon as his feet were secure, he began listening through a plastic earpiece, designed by Brian during the long drive. It operated with such ease that even he had to respect his brother's weird nerd-leanings, wondering not only from whom he had inherited his aptitude, but also why he had never chosen to use it previously.

"Come in, Mad Dog. This is the Wizard," Brian, the younger, more technically astute Sullivan son crackled from the backseat of the car.

"Moving into position, Wizard. Is the Warden online?" Matthew asked.

"Roger, Mad Dog," Ted answered. He was relieved that Brian had used all this paraphernalia for good, aware now that both his sons had admirable criminal capabilities. He supposed there were worse family outings than this one, but at the moment he couldn't imagine a single one.

"Wizard to Mad Dog. The Warden is smiling today," Brian said gleefully, noting his father couldn't help but have a little fun on his headset. Nothing felt better than having his entire family together, and under his control. It was a moment he intended to talk about, well into his twenties.

"Hold on, I'll tell him," Ted waved at Brian, eager to communicate. He loved the code name he picked for himself, and was going to get to use it at least once. Even from his hunched position in his car, he was still in charge of this operation and the only one who could give the go order. "Mad Dog, this is the Warden. Let the games begin."

"Roger that, Warden. I've got a fix on the duo. But one eye is drooping," Mad Dog said of the living room curtain that had slid free of its tieback. "I'm observing some physical contact now. Do you copy?"

"Cool, Mad Dog," Brian, the Wizard, exclaimed.

"Say again, Mad Dog. Physical contact?" the Warden asked.

"That's affirmative."

"Damn it," Warden cursed. "Describe this contact, over."

"First base, Warden, from my field of vision. Finger locks on both Jane and Bridget Fonda."

"I'm going in there to bust that guy—"

"Negative, Warden. Wizard can evacuate the building on your command," Mad Dog explained.

"What's he talking about?" Ted asked Brian, holding his hand over his mouthpiece.

"I rigged up a stink bomb. It smells like a skunk convention, lasts about twenty minutes. All I have to do is hit this key," Brian bragged, his finger poised over his portable computer.

"Don't! I'm the one who will get arrested!"

"This is Wizard to Mad Dog. Warden is waving the white panties."

"No, I'm not," Ted defended. "I'd just like to stay the hell out of jail. You know what, I'll bet there are other ways to handle this. Maybe you should get out of that tree, Mad Dog."

"Mad Dog to Wizard. Are you prepared to neutralize the Warden on my order? He's compromising the operation."

"That's affirmative, Mad Dog."

"Hold on, you guys! There'll be no neutralization unless you both want to be grounded all year."

Brian covered his mouthpiece. "Dad, people could be listening. That's embarrassing."

"Oh, sorry," Ted mumbled. Then catching what Brian said, he reacted, "What! What do you mean, listening? If I go to jail, I'm holding you responsible, and your brother, and most of all, your mother! I had a nice, uncomplicated life, now look at me. I'm in a car spying on my own wife, using my own sons. I'd like to know what she thinks she's doing with this psychic guy. This isn't what you do when you go to college. You're supposed to study, listen to music, maybe try some Thai food—"

"Warden, this is Mad Dog getting vertigo. Whenever you're done playing the Big Chill. Remember my position, over."

"Evacuate, Mad Dog," Ted grumbled.

"Wizard, confirm," Matthew requested.

"Affirmative. Warden needs a backup plan or a beer."

"Copy that. Need another few minutes before evacuating. Is the Warden stable?"

"Affirmative. But not singing at the moment."

〜 〜 〜

Luke had his eyes tightly shut. Mary wondered if what he was feeling was uncomfortable, like trying to remember a particular word, or trying to put a face with a name.

"There is this other spirit trying to communicate. The connection is very strong. Men surround you both today," he continued. "If not physically, then emotionally. It's like they're closing in on you."

"Oh my," Mary sighed.

"This man will draw Mary closer, very soon. And when it happens, you'll both be leaving here."

"It must be Ted," Mary insisted.

"No, it's not your husband," Luke insisted.

"But I don't understand. There is no one I know here."

"From your past, Mary. That's really all I can see. Except that it's a bittersweet reunion."

"I did have an uncle I was close to," Mary suggested. "Maybe he's with my mother."

Luke could neither confirm nor deny. He was apologetic as he had tea and brownies at the table where he had failed to provide Mary with any contact from her mother, despite their lit candles and earnest effort to remain psychically open. Mary was less disappointed than she was unnerved by the spirit who was, as Luke described him, "psychically and kinetically present." He explained that sometimes it's not the person you're trying to reach who shows up at all, and that the best thing he could do was go with it, and get whatever information he could. He advised Mary to continue her meditating and promised to try at another point in time, perhaps when the energy around her was less congested.

"Mad Dog to A-team. Physical contact has subsided. Now, they're smoking cigarettes and eating dessert. Over."

"Who's smoking?" the Warden asked.

"Jane, Bridget, and the gypsy. Wait, the gypsy's leaving. Take cover."

"Mad Dog, I think it's time you stepped out of that picture," the Warden whispered.

"Negative. When the Fondas leave, I'm going in."

"Negative, Mad Dog. Negative. You tell him, Wizard."

"Negative, Warden. We need the night music."

"What?"

"Off channel for a moment, Mad Dog."

"Copy that, Wizard."

"Come on, Dad. This is how it's done. Matt's got to plant the bug in their apartment. Then we can really spy," Brian whined.

"We are absolutely not planting a bug. There could be things you two shouldn't hear. And just when did you two become so adept at this?"

"Action movies, Dad. Don't worry. We'll cover you."

"No. We need to rethink this operation. I need to rethink a lot of things—"

"Mad Dog to A-team. Red alert. Red alert. Take cover,

take cover. The Fondas have left the building and are scanning the street. Wizard, Warden, keep your heads down."

"I'd just like to know how I arrived at this point in my life," the Warden sighed from under the dashboard.

"Cheer up, Dad. I could be working for the enemy," the Wizard chirped.

~ 27 ~

$\mathcal{M}$ary decided to walk over to the bereavement wall in the student center. Immediately, she felt the names and photos beckoning her and backed up to gain a full view. Her eyes scanned a few pictures until they fell upon the photo of Cathy's mother. A fair-haired woman lounging in the yard, not quite smiling, Deborah displayed nothing of her daughter's enthusiasm. In fact she seemed to manifest sorrow.

"You're welcome, Deborah," Mary told the photo. She hadn't heard the thank-you as much as she felt it. "And thank you for showing me such an incredible place. If it's like that, heaven I mean, it's no wonder you're so happy."

It seemed odd to Mary that a woman so attractive hadn't married, that she seemed to lack the stamina to seek and maintain a relationship. Mary immediately felt the presence of pain through the eyes of the photo, a skill she had always wished for, to be able to pick up more than superficial impressions from a picture. She realized she felt tired—something of her study into the spiritual world had to be taking effect, for Cathy had often described her mother as lacking vitality and, according to Luke, information from the other side could come through sounds, images, or feelings.

Mary watched as a young man in baggy blue jeans, a striped shirt with rolled-up sleeves, and a day or two's dark growth on his face, placed a bouquet of flowers on the pedestal by the wall.

Mary felt she shouldn't smile, but couldn't help looking into the young man's eyes as he turned toward her. She acknowledged his pain with a nod. But being away from her two boys, missing them, missing mothering, she couldn't keep herself from saying at least a hello. It was Mary's experience that people who were grieving didn't mind talking, so after hello, she continued the conversation and told him how pretty the flowers looked. He began to open up.

"My brother," he said with an Hispanic accent. "Today it is his birthday."

"I'm sorry," Mary said.

"He's here," he said, pointing to another young, attractive man, unable to lift his finger from the photo, rubbing his finger along the face, his eyes more than misting.

Mary noticed the date of birth, was appalled by it, only three years older than Matthew and gone from the earth. "He was very handsome," she said, not even believing she had said that, but trying to speak from her heart without getting in her own way.

"I try to make a quilt for him," he told her, "to put with the others. He liked to dance. He moved so smooth. Like the river, you know. He moved just like the river," he finished, wiping tears. "You couldn't separate the motions, one from the other. He made it look easy."

"I'm so sorry," Mary said.

"I tried to have it finished by now, but I'm not so good with the design work."

"You should meet my roommate," Mary volunteered. "She's very creative. I'll bet she could help."

The young man only nodded, unable to speak.

Mary continued. "Are you part of the grief group?"

"No," he shook his head. "I just come to class once a week. I work during the days. You have someone here?"

"No. Not yet, I mean. I was going to put up a picture of my mother. Here's my roommate's mother." Mary pointed.

"That must be terrible," the young man said sadly. "To lose your mother. You have no one to leave the light on at night."

Mary could feel the lump in her throat. "It's all terrible," she managed. "But there's nothing we can do about it except go on."

"I know," he nodded. "I just miss him."

Mary remembered when Brian was young and crying, how she always looked for something to distract him, a new rattle, a music box, a pile of empty plastic containers he could stack and knock down. But there was nothing to hand off at this bereavement wall, nothing to say, no sign of anyone else approaching.

So Mary just wrapped her arms around the young man and let him cry. It was all she had to offer, her heartbeat, her warmth, her understanding of his pain. If she were home she could make him some cocoa, cookies, a nice plate of sandwiches, and she could listen to all of his stories the way she did with the seniors. She hoped if one of her sons were hurting, another mother would share an embrace.

For a moment she thought back to her boys, fighting constantly, but never with enough anger to keep them out of each other's hair. How would one ever do without the other? It must be horrible to grow up with that big an empty space, imagining all the things that might have been.

"I'm sorry," the young man said, pulling back from her shoulder. "I made you sad."

"No," Mary said, taking a deep breath. "You just made me think a moment about my own boys, and I wondered, you know, how they would feel."

"Left," he answered. "Left behind. And with so much loneliness."

"It's the same then," Mary told him, "as for me with my mother. Left behind with so much loneliness. Except my mother had a much longer life, and even then, I kept saying it was too soon to lose her. I think if she lived another hundred years, I'd have felt the same way."

"But I feel cheated. I know he's better off now, but I'm the one who must learn to live with it."

"Well you certainly don't have to do it alone," Mary said forcefully. The young man just looked up at her. "I mean, do you have to be anywhere? We could have lunch together. You could tell me about him. Or I could show you where the grief group meets. They've been great with my roommate."

"You have a family and a roommate?"

"Yes, well, my family is three hours away."

"Then why are you here?"

"That seems to be the million-dollar question. I thought it was to help Cathy, my roommate. Her mother died suddenly in August. There are times she helps me much more than I help her. My mom died five years ago, and I'm still not over it. I don't know. I take classes, but I don't have one for a few hours. I was on my way to the library when I detoured here. My name is Mary Sullivan."

"Julio Orta."

"Lunch, Julio?"

"I don't mean to be trouble."

"No trouble. I don't like to eat alone."

Mary had a favorite table at the student center, the one overlooking the campus trees, now so brilliant with color, which reminded her of Candyland, where flowers were made of candy cane stems, and all was well unless you got stuck in gooey-gooey gumdrops. She remembered Brian howling, "Mom's stuck in gooey-gooey gumdrops," and Matthew trying to discreetly cheat, and pass her the card she needed to be free.

She couldn't imagine Julio's pain, didn't want to imagine

it, because the mere thought of having to bear the loss of someone so young was too painful. They got cheeseburgers and Cokes and exchanged details about their families. Eventually, Julio spoke again of his brother, this time with even more emotion.

"Do you know what it's like, Mary, to see someone suffer, and then to have people who don't even know him judge him?"

Mary frowned. "I don't understand."

"My brother had AIDS, Mary. And we had to keep it quiet so we didn't scare the people in our building. And sometimes at work when the people took lunch hours, when it was in the news, I could hear them talking about it, like it was something he deserved. Well, what about the babies who suffer with it? Did they do something too? Sometimes I think my brother was too good for this world. You know, once he died, he became like a saint to me. I can't remember any of the fights we used to have, only that now he's up there with God and the angels, like a saint."

"My mother, too, seems so much bigger now that she's gone. And she was pretty big here on earth. Lately she's on my mind more often than not."

"That's my problem. I can't forget about my brother. I can't forget, even for an hour. It's like he's moved from outside of me to inside of me."

"That's so true." Mary nodded. "I never thought of it that way before."

"He tried to comfort me before he died," he continued.

"He said to look for him in the sky, in the flowers, in the wind. I look and look, but I don't find him."

"I know exactly what you mean. I can't seem to find my mother out there either."

"But you can hear me," Mary's mother gently reminded her.

"I can hear her sometimes," Mary added naturally to the conversation. And it suddenly occurred to her that she had been pushing her mother's voice away by attaching so much pain to it. Mary hoped she remembered to run that by Luke.

"She speaks to you?" Julio asked. "Out loud?"

"I'm sure no one else can hear her, if that's what you mean. She's in my head," Mary tried to explain. "The voice, her voice, sometimes breaks into my thoughts, and it's exactly what she would have said if she were here."

Mary waved at Cathy from across the room. She explained to Julio that this was her roommate, the artistic one she had told him about, and that if anyone could help him with the quilt, it was Cathy. As Cathy walked toward Mary's table, one of her plastic containers popped open, spilling hundreds of tiny, multicolored glass and wooden beads all over the cafeteria floor. Cathy put her books down on a neighboring table, rolled her eyes at Mary, and began crawling about.

Mary and Julio automatically began retrieving the beads under tables, chasing a stream of them as they rolled in one direction, then divided into several. It rapidly became a group effort. Students and cafeteria attendants were smiling as they crawled under their own tables, captured a handful of beads, lost some in delivering them to Cathy, but got right back down on the floor again. Another eight or so students entering the room were quick to join in and chase the shiny objects under and around the table legs and chairs, laughing, carrying them by hand and pocket, to Cathy who was doing her best to scrape them into her container before losing any more. Cathy giggled and apologized, introducing herself to her helpers as they dropped off their finds, promising to return the favor someday.

Julio couldn't help but joke, "You sure know how to make an entrance."

"If you ever want to see the best of human nature, you only have to drop something and look completely helpless," Cathy offered, putting out her hand to seal their introduction.

Mary excused herself to go to class, and Cathy sat at the table with Julio, spreading out her sketchbook as though nothing at all had embarrassed her.

*E*ven though Mary was fearful of Luke's prediction, she took his advice to search her soul. First, she went to the library where she checked out more of her favorite albums from the seventies. She had tried to wring details out of Luke's impressions, an establishing year, an event, a building to focus upon, perhaps to validate him or dispute him. But Luke just smiled, reminding her that the doorway to her soul was only hers to open, and while he could sense something was amiss, she had all but buried that treasure chest.

Treasure, Mary thought, encouraged. A matter of digging it up. She recalled her college days. A quick rub of strawberry lip gloss, a squirt of Charlie perfume, and she was out the door of her dorm room, braless in pale gauze blouses that barely met up with her hip-hugger jeans, a look completed by long, straight brown hair the color of her earth shoes. Music was essential. Along with classic rock bands, there were folk songs—Judy Collins's "Since You've Asked," playing in a candlelit suite where students like Mary practiced their amateur drinking with cheap wine or beer. Long drags on cigarettes, towels stuffed under the bathroom doors where joints were covertly passed from hand to hand, coconut incense, and long nights typing her papers at the dinette set where she would watch the sunrise, loving the adventure, the freedom, the independence that was college.

She ate dark Red Delicious apples and slice-and-bake sugar cookies, Clark bars, bubble gum, hot dogs, and tuna fish, finally free from the well-balanced meals that had left her too full in the evenings, but that she couldn't refuse without hurting her mother's feelings. At first she dated infrequently, even though her young, smooth body protruded and dipped where it should, long before anyone threw around the word *aerobic*. No one was trying to shrink, Mary recalled, because freshmen already felt too small.

But Mary was a good sport, open to new experiences. She could laugh at herself. She arrived at school unattached, unlike many freshmen who had hopes of keeping their high school boyfriends. Her mother, that constant voice in her mind, always inserted herself as Mary made decisions, but she expected that to take time to overcome. Little did she know, at forty-five, she was still trying to put that voice in perspective.

Mary clearly remembered how much she looked forward to being away from her mother. It hurt her to confess that even now, when all she wanted to do was have a reunion. But just to be away from that person who had sustained her, to think for herself, make her own wrong decisions, was blissful. Could her relationship with Ted be like that, a bond that had to be broken to allow her to grow?

Mary opened the curtains over the wobbly small table she and Cathy had pushed against the kitchen window, where she felt most comfortable. She poured a fresh cup of coffee and collected her cigarettes. She lit a candle as Luke had taught her, to solicit help from beyond, to increase her focus. She put on Electric Light Orchestra, a band she hadn't listened to in decades. If she had forgotten something that her meditation, her walks in the woods, her psychic healer, and her dead mother couldn't bring back, then maybe the music would.

Yes, there was a tender spot there, something that could have elicited tears of sorrow, tears of loss, so long before the death of her mother. Mary began writing words in a circle as Luke had instructed her: grief, mother, woman, Ted, loss, Cathy, children, college, sex. She waited for revelation, reflection, any breakthrough imagery. But Mary's present-day concerns kept pushing through her concentration, until all Mary could see was that bereavement board on the wall in the student center. She wondered who was there at this moment, if Julio had returned, and if there were any new flowers.

She turned off the music and listened hard through the silence for anything that would present itself: an image, a voice, a feeling, a color. But it was becoming an obsession, thinking about the wall, visualizing herself attaching her mother's photo, wondering about the other photographs and the mourners who stopped by sometimes in between classes to leave their flowers. She told herself she'd give it a half hour, and if her meditation didn't progress, she'd give in and go. And having decided that much, having felt the flow of energetic excitement at the thought of being at that place, she knew she had to go immediately.

Cathy had encouraged her often enough to go, for it was there that she had become part of a group, not mourners exactly, but a support group. Every week, each member was assigned to organize something fun to do. This week had been Cathy's turn, and their field trip had been to the mall to look for babies in strollers. When Mary seemed puzzled, Cathy had reminded her that babies are always cute, and out there for everyone to see. "They smile at you if you wave, they wave back, and they look so sweet sleeping," she had explained. Since her involvement with this grief group, Cathy had taken the position that if you looked for cheering up, it was there. A past field trip had been to the pet shop, which had yielded two goldfish for the apartment.

"The world can't be too bad if you have goldfish," Cathy told Mary.

Another outing had been to a late-night showing of the Marx Brothers' *Duck Soup*. When Cathy asked Mary for ideas, she had said a walk under the stars, in the dark, for after her babies were born and she had given herself over to the scheduling of baths and bedtimes, she hardly ever went out in the night for the sheer joy of it.

Mary blew out her candle and grabbed her things, taking

the picture of her mother and the label she had printed, practically running toward the student center building.

Mary couldn't help noticing how clear the sky seemed, how the wind, so mild and refreshing, carried the smells of someone's pipe, of freshly dug earth, of a passerby's perfume. She felt lighter on her feet than she had in years, and actually ran a few steps, her hair bouncing on her shoulders.

She remembered her mom on her two-inch heels chasing Brian around the church parking lot, her mom in her sixties, running still on those heels, throwing a scarf up in the air when the boys' ball sailed too far out of the yard, throwing anything that would momentarily crest upon the air—paper, string, baseball cards, throwing all her cares, it seemed, as high up as she could get them, watching the boys dashing about, drawing in their laughter, clapping and cheering for them.

Mary ran now, finally on a mission, half breathless, half possessed. Attaching the photo of her mother would relieve her of the greatest burden of her life. She had told the stale story of her mother's departure to anyone who would listen. Each detail had become a thick and twisted rope so tightly strung around her, she constantly tried to talk each knot away, express each image loose. She felt as though she had lugged about the enormous degree and dimension that was death itself, and she had finally completed her penalty to carry the soul-crushing weight. Until Cathy, escape was impossible.

From the far end of the corridor in the student center, Mary could see she was alone. Her heart pounded as she approached the wall, and she looked around again, down the narrow hallway. Seeing that no one was approaching, that no one would be there to witness this onetime, all-important rite, she felt strangely disappointed. She would have liked to talk to someone about her mother, to describe the day the photo was taken, to share the blessing of her life.

Having Cathy present would have been wonderful. Having her young, perpetually optimistic friend there to cheer her on, to encourage her to bring an end to this mourning, would have been comforting. Yet, on a college campus, it seemed only fitting to be independent. Mary had withdrawn from her family, her home, her image of herself as always being a good and available mother, to come to this place. She had come here to heal, to rise up from the cloud of grief that inhabited her, to take back whatever of her life was left, and to live it without sorrow. It wasn't any one answer that she desired, only to trigger some release from the sinking feeling in her heart. She took the stapler from the shelf and, drawing a deep, reflective breath, attached her mother's photo to the remembrance wall.

Mary sighed, admiring the wallet-sized picture of her mother as though she had just hung a decoration on her wall at home. Her mother was smiling, always smiled so much more than Mary, who had to be reminded to be happy. Brian was just like his grandmother with his light heart and easy charm, so quick to run out the door and talk to a neighbor he saw walking a dog, while Mary just peered from behind the curtains, arguing with herself about starting a conversation, worrying if she'd be imposing.

Mary looked at the celebrities' pictures and thought how sad it was they'd died before their work had been finished. She liked seeing her mother with them: Martin Luther King Jr., the Kennedy brothers, Elvis, and, of course, her mom's favorite, Marilyn Monroe. As she began to scan the rows and rows of ordinary people, she noticed these were mostly the faces of young men and women. She was stung by their beauty and youth. It could have been a college yearbook, they looked that young and vital. She looked closely at the victims, their enthusiastic eyes, their soft pink lips, their hair, rich with abundant color, no gray shadow of illness, of death, of despair. Nothing like the elderly people she remembered from her days and nights with her mother at the hospital.

There were fair-skinned and dark-skinned alike on the wall, all attractive, appealing, young, bright lives. Mary could not even bring herself to think about the sorrow they left behind, but she would tend to agree with Julio that they had all inadvertently achieved the peaceful look of saints.

As Mary looked at the young faces, it amazed her that she left her boys alone, without those last calls to buckle their seat belts, drive safely, be home at a decent hour, hold the door open for their dates, not go swimming alone, order only well-done hamburger. Mary always felt that as long as Matthew and Brian were safe, she was safe. She paused for a moment to find Julio's brother again, and then one face stopped her cold.

Young like the others, with inviting eyes that were so tender and open and then, all at once, so horribly familiar. The face seemed to be smiling hello at her from twenty or more years ago. Mary stared at the name, the birthday, and then her mind shut down. Alexander Thomas Wyatt had died on July 12, 1995.

29

*A*lex? Oh God. She dropped to her knees to get closer to the photo. Time snapped her backward as though she were roped around the ankles and yanked from her feet. Now she could see his ever-present grin, head cocked to the side, golden strands of hair falling into his face.

She could hear him, "Mary, Mary, quite contrary," the way he played when she argued, the way he was both man and boy, lover and child, the way he gave himself to her, the way his very soul seemed rooted in her flesh.

"Do you believe in love, Mary? The kind of love that is so deep, it could destroy you absolutely, and you wouldn't even mind?"

Mary's shaky hands reached toward the picture and touched the smiling face of Alex Wyatt, her first love, her first lover. It was becoming more real each second, more horrifying. Mary felt her heart melting, grief dragging her away from the reality of the student center as surely as if she were clamped within the jaws of a wild animal, away from the photo of her mother—the reason she thought she had come here.

Alex, sweet Alex.

He couldn't really be gone. She thought for sure they'd cross paths at a party, a reunion; that they'd have a chance meeting in a crowded theater, a restaurant; that there'd be a letter, a phone call. He'd appear, his sheepish grin sketched with creases, his beckoning eyes, his long, pale fingers, his body perhaps a pound or two heavier, his attitude a little less intense, mellowed by whatever portion of the good life he'd finally granted himself. They'd chat. They'd walk. They'd exchange those sweetly polite air-kisses. He'd tell her she looked good. She'd deny it. She'd tell him how she missed him— maybe not how much.

But Alex had died. Before his hair had lost its luster. Before his eyes had lost their boyish curiosity. Before his mind had dulled or his heart grown cold. Before Mary could find him, talk to him, thank him.

Mary knew now that this discovery was what Luke had predicted, that she would come upon this truth, this death, this departure. That she would slam back, face-first into the pain. Death seemed to be taking her heart away in pieces, one loved one at a time. Freeing herself from grief seemed impossible, like running for her life, hearing the predator's breath behind her—better not look over your shoulder, don't take the time to wonder just how close it is, just keep running until you can run no more. This psychically engineered nightmare had shattered Mary's peace, yet she was incapable of making a sound.

She remembered the first time she mourned for Alex. Ted, her future husband, watching from the doorway at a spring dance as Mary, helpless to steer Alex across the room, dropped him into a chair, laughing, stumbling, trying to get him to drink a Coke, wondering what had been in that pipe he had been smoking. Those green eyes had looked upon her hungrily as he took the straw on his tongue, mischievously flirting, conscious of the spectacle they had become, but never ever diverting his attention from her.

Mary had automatically smoothed her blouse, brushed nonexistent wrinkles as though brushing his touch away, her mother never approved of public displays of affection, wiping off his grip upon her in such a busy place. He had, even in his stoned state, taken note of her discomfort and reacted, whispering an obscene intention in her ear, making her blush, reminding her just how quickly he could arouse her. She was conscious of Ted's eyes upon her, of the crowded hall, and kept Alex's hands from roaming any farther than her shoulders.

Whenever he was angry with her, unlike any other man who might sulk, pace, argue, or even curse, Alex recited. "For beauty, starved with her severity, Cuts beauty off from all posterity."

"Never mind that," she had said, impatient, the adult, the mother, the caretaker. "Drink it, please."

"O true apothecary!" he responded, pulling her onto his lap.

Ted had come to her assistance.

"Is everything all right, Mary?" Ted asked, judging Alex with that paternal look.

Mary and Ted stood together like a handsome, responsible couple. Grown-ups who could own a home, make children, retrieve a Christmas tree with a sled. Adults who would buy insurance, plan sensible vacations, save for college for their offspring, walk dogs, eat well-balanced meals, take care of each other's parents.

Alex had struggled to his feet, slung an arm around Mary, and, even through his sly, drunken haze, had managed to evaluate Ted, in fact found him a worthy and honorable man, and introduced himself jovially as Romeo. He was always equally charming to men and women. Ted later admitted he was surprised by the firm and hearty handshake, enough to have reconsidered his assessment of Alex as a self-indulgent pseudo-intellectual.

"Allow me to see you both home?" Ted had offered, ever so casually, the polite, gentlemanly thing to do, under the awkward circumstances. Mary had winced with embarrassment, and it seemed that was all it took for Alex to make up his mind to discard her once and for all, to send her off to a solid, stable future with this caring, decent man.

"The lady is in need of an escort, noble, fine gent," Alex had answered impressed, nearly sad. But recovering quickly, or pretending to, he added, "I have business elsewhere."

"Alex, don't be foolish, you need to get home and to bed," Mary had cautioned.

"Never a truer word was spoken, my lady," Alex had teased. He leaned over to kiss her, shutting his eyes first, a good-bye kiss Mary couldn't help but recognize, his fingers pressed tightly into her neck—go, he was telling her—go, it's okay, get married, have children, love and live without me, I love you, I'll always love you, we are forever, now go."

He held on to her even after he had pulled his lips away, and smiled. He placed her hand firmly in Ted's for safe and sober keeping, nodding to Mary to go, to Ted to take her.

"Away with you both," he had told them so casually. And Ted, so effortlessly chivalrous, seeing the look of devastation on Mary's face, pulled her out of the dance.

She had wept it seemed for days, right upon Ted's shirt, sobbed, just the way she would when, years later, she had lost her mother. Through it all, there were days and nights, but they were tasteless, colorless, void of life, empty of passion. She slept long. She lost weight. She stopped attending campus dances. Ted, refusing to give up on her, eventually talked her out of her apartment for a day trip to the country, where finally, the smells of the earth, the heat of the sun, the sounds of a brook invited her back to life. He had somehow managed to resurrect enough of her to love. They were pre-engaged within six months, and married the winter after graduation.

Alex would pass Mary on campus, never without another woman or a line from Shakespeare, whose works had been dumped into the bottom of a box she sometimes had the urge to open, but dared never. It was a pain worth running from, worth burying. As Ted ushered her away from Alex that night at the dance, after two and a half years of codependent, inexplicable rapture with a man who could turn her head right around on her body, she followed the man who could share her home and desire for children, knowing Ted would never send her away. Ted would never hurt her.

And now she suspected she had never forgiven Ted for taking her away from him, even though she knew Alex would have left her anyway, for the signs and signals were already in place. Alex often told her that she had a "handle with care" characteristic about her, one which he could honor in his quiet, rational moments, but not be trusted to respect over time. He warned her he could never be relied upon to do the decent, right thing—although he had done it, hadn't he? He had let her go.

~ 30 ~

The afternoon sunlight fell in geometric slices on the red carpeting. It brightened the baby roses Julio had left, and created a small, circular reflection on the wall from Mary's watch. Mary was inside out on the rug of the student center, captured tightly in the funnel of grief, the grim truth of Alex's death rebounding within her relentlessly.

Mary's ears buzzed and her eyes remained half open as she noticed the young faces, circles of light, like flashlights poking through a thick wet fog. They drew her up from her knees, embraced her, encircled her, and walked her to a chair. They were strangers, beautiful, sweet, and kind like Cathy, their hearts wide-open, their skin soft and warm. They didn't ask Mary to speak or explain. They didn't care who she was, where she belonged, how she had come to crash down upon the floor. They didn't tell her who they were. They simply scooped her into their arms and led her to a cafeteria table.

They moved chairs, notebooks, napkins, and cups, and helped her sit. One brought her hot tea while another one held her hand. Mary tasted the tea they set before her—too much milk, too much sugar, too light and sweet, as her mother would have given her when she was sick with the flu.

"Drink this, you'll feel better, have a cookie, pamper yourself, tomorrow will be better, each day a little better, struggle up off the bed, fluff your hair, smile a little each hour, this too shall pass." Her mother's words seemed more and more accessible.

One young man, slightly older than Matthew, squeezed her hand to comfort her. For a moment, she felt she could tell him everything. He was a stranger who felt like a friend. His eyes were the color of Ted's, his arms looked as strong as Matthew's, and his smile had a flicker of the jokester, so like her son Brian.

"You okay now?" he asked.

Mary noticed his sweatshirt was maroon, one of the few colors Matthew wore, a shirt bearing wrinkles—signs of an absent mother. The others were watching, waiting for her to answer. Leave it to Alex to surround her with the collective human heart in all its resilience, alive and well, beating beautifully in this young group.

Mary answered, "Yes," and she began to weep.

"Go ahead and cry," he encouraged her. "It's better to get it all out."

Mary wept almost obediently at first, for Alex's death wasn't even real yet. Maybe she wept out of fear of this pain, which had barely presented itself. This was the beginning of actual grief, not what she had been walking around with, which now seemed like nothing more than emptiness—until Cathy. That connection had nourished her and given Mary the courage to leave her den.

The students gathered around her. They were mercy divers in a deep, dark sea, retrieving her against her will, so much like Ted, so much like her boys whose demands wrested her from the obsessive image of her mother's casket descending into the earth. They drew her back to the light, just as Cathy had.

Cathy acknowledged her own and Mary's losses, but would never let them keep her from enjoying life, the wind's soft voice through the trees, the perfect curling ribbon for her wreath. She didn't retreat into denial, for that would have meant it hadn't happened, hadn't hurt. No matter what, Cathy's outlook stayed positive.

"Did you ever wish that trees and flowers had eyes?"

"What?" Mary had laughed.

"So you always knew they were alive. So you could look at them and tell them just how pretty they were," Cathy had said.

"I guess I never really thought about it."

"Craig had the best idea yet at the grief group. He brought out these records at the meeting, and we all began dancing the polka. Have you ever danced the polka, Mary? It's like flying. How can you mourn when you're flying?"

Mary was in awe of such conscious determination to be

happy, to live as though life could be improved instantly through an upbeat tune on an accordion. But Mary had lived in bondage to herself, licking her own wounds, hiding her crying spells to keep her weaknesses secret, making sure there were stamps in the house, the rugs were cleaned every six months, and Ted always had his umbrella handy. Mary wondered what mindless activity she was engaged in the day or night Alex slipped away.

Oh, it didn't seem possible . . .

There was a chance before she felt any worse, Mary could make it back to the apartment, lie on her bed and wait for the sun to die out, to try to reach Alex in the darkness. She struggled to move. She felt heaviness from her neck to her thighs, as though she had sustained a blow. Only fierce determination could raise her back to her feet. But the loss was so immediate and profound, she was left with barely any energy at all.

She sat there in blinding sunlight, listening to small talk. Students came and left the student center. It was an ordinary autumn afternoon still rolling along in rhythm. The sounds of human traffic continued, backpacks dropped, binders snapped closed, plates clacked from the cafeteria. But Mary wasn't part of it. All she could hear were the phrases Alex whispered against her ear as he lay upon her, quivering.

And now, the brightest of all lights was coming toward her, her walk light and carefree, carrying a chocolate doughnut and a bottle of Coke on a turquoise tray. Her young friend in a ponytail, her blue denim jumper and white T-shirt immediately recognizable, her crystal earrings, green and gleaming in the sun. The life and kindness in Cathy's eyes had been enough to force Mary to chase her own life.

"Mary, what happened?" she heard Cathy ask.

"I found a friend of mine on the wall," Mary said, voice trembling. "I didn't realize he was dead. It was a shock."

"Oh no," Cathy said, tossing her backpack on the table, flopping down in the chair as though she, too, had been taken by surprise. She offered Mary the first sip of her Coke. Mary declined.

She ripped the doughnut in half and took a bite, offering the other half. Mary shook her head.

"We were close," Mary continued. "Very close."

"Close in the sense of," Cathy paused, taking a swig of her Coke.

"Intimate," Mary said, sipping her tea, laughing, crying, confessing all to everyone within earshot.

"I'm sorry. I'm so sorry," Cathy offered.

"I just can't believe it," Mary managed. Cathy hugged her tightly. Mary cried uninhibitedly upon her friend, wishing she could have said good-bye, or have had one more chance to speak to Alex, even if just to remind him that he was loved.

The grief group laughed and chatted. Mary smiled insincerely; she couldn't help it. Chocolate doughnuts. Positive outings. Unconditional compassion. Death was maturing these students. Mary wondered what exactly it was doing to her.

If only she had begun her paranormal study sooner, perhaps she would have been able to predict this tragedy. She could have hunted Alex down to warn him—no, he would never have listened. Whenever she tried to convince him to drive more slowly, he would wink and recite a line from "Thanatopsis." He was at peace now, she consoled herself. His mind was quiet, relieved, free.

But questions raced through Mary's mind. How did it happen? Did he lie suffering alone? Was he weakened progressively? There was no explanatory caption on the wall. Did he quietly slip into a coma the way her mother had? Was he even in a hospital?

Oh, she would have gone to him, read to him, broken into that taped-up basement box and let out the Shakespeare, read from every book he had given her, bought all the new ones and read those too, page by page, phrase after phrase, instead of making dinner at eight-thirty in the morning, instead of driving seniors to get their blue hair bluer, instead of always indulging Ted and the boys with her presence. She could have brought him movies to watch, comedies, musicals, old black-and-white romances. And it might have kept him an extra hour, an extra day, long enough for her to summon up another mind worth exploring, some company for his sick and weakened soul.

Ted and the boys would have objected. My God, how were they doing? She hadn't thought of them in the past few hours, hadn't wondered about their lives, their inconveniences, hadn't felt connected with them since Alex had stepped back into her life, dead.

In Alex's bedroom it was all she could do to rise again from the tangled sheets, stumble into the shower, so drained she felt drunk, smell at last the reviving soap upon her face and hair before he lifted her, bubbles running down her front and back, and returned her to the bed, a full head of shampoo bubbles, which he played with, moving himself upon and within her slippery body until she forgot about the time and the mess and the homework, and the inclination to do anything else but love and be loved by him. Loving him had almost been an illness. She knew it, but she willingly submitted to it.

Was there ever a way to let go of someone who had actually existed inside of you?

When Mary saw the news stories of mothers losing their children, she wondered how they kept their sanity. Now she feared for her own. Her mother's death somehow fit into the logical progression of life. She had ripened and died. But Alex was still in her blood, parts of him moving within her. Alex had transformed her body from its virginal state. Alex occasionally intruded in her kisses with Ted. Was this why she needed to follow Cathy, to finally put this relationship to rest?

Mary excused herself from Cathy and her group in the student center to go walking, even though, moments ago, it was all she could do to breathe. Now she needed to be out, unbound, in motion, confronting her true feelings about this tragic news.

It hurt. God, it hurt. That much she verified again and again like a tongue revisiting an exposed nerve. She looked at the slow-moving clouds, the blue and steady peace of the sky, the leaves that let go of their branches and twirled downward, the sight of freshly dug soil. She didn't know where to go. She didn't know what to do. She began to run as if she could escape the pain, quiet her rambling mind. Mary could pass only a few buildings before she was winded. Smoking had its consequences. She sat on a bench to catch her breath.

Why hadn't it been her instead? Such a predictable question for such an ordinary life. The world could live without another carrot cake, another mother yelling cheers on the basketball court, another seasonal mall walker. But Alex was a shooting star, inflamed and bursting all the way down, committed to living all of his life, every day on the edge. What had been strong enough to kill him?

Just when she thought her pain was too much to bear, she saw children entering the fenced-in playground across the campus, little boys in all their glory. She never even knew what Alex looked like as a boy, probably lanky and thin, but suddenly she needed photographs of him at all ages, playing happily as a boy, grown and sullen, pictures that she could hold in her hands and cradle against her now broken heart. She needed to study his eyes for any signals or symptoms of tragedy. After all, she still had her own sons to look out for. Was that why she felt so anguished, because it wasn't just the pain of his leaving, it was her perspective as a mother that made his death seem so wrongly premature?

A young blond boy made an awesome catch as Mary watched from afar. She missed watching Matthew and Brian play with Ted, even those inane basketball games during Sunday football halftimes. She missed the stupid sock folding, the phone calls that were never for her, the sound of Matthew's car rolling into the driveway at midnight. And Brian, the light and laughter of her life, always with a story to cheer her up or a completely absurd suggestion to keep everyone entertained.

Mary walked into town and sat at the diner. She ordered coffee and smoked, her stomach too upset to eat. This indulgence would have been impossible at home. The mourning. But she had a right to it. This man had been in her most intimate places, and though she couldn't hold on to him, part of her believed she had been possessed by him for all time, had understood him, had matured differently because of him, and part of her was always determined to find him.

The suddenness of Cathy's mother's death made it all seem so haphazard, and yet so perfectly planned. Encountering Alex as she hung up the photo of her mother, almost an exchange, relief for pain. Mary had her religious conviction, but it didn't offer her much in the way of enlightenment or insight at the moment.

She was convinced of one thing, that she had been led to this place to encounter Alex's death. It was what Luke was referring to. Yet it was what she was supposed to do with the information that completely confused her.

~ 31 ~

Cathy was waiting for Mary at the apartment with chicken noodle soup heating on the stove, a loaf of French bread warming in the oven, and a tube of slice-and-bake cookies hand cut into shapes of leaves. Mary couldn't help but smile. She saw Cathy's artistic streak asserting itself in the elaborate feathering of the cookie leaves, embellished with colored sugar.

"I know what you're thinking," Cathy said, nodding. "That none of this will help, that you can't eat a bite, that this is all too simple. But I remember you saying if you went through the motions, sooner or later, it would all get better."

Mary, crying and laughing, answered, "I don't think I ever saw myself in anyone before. I look ridiculous."

"I know," Cathy agreed, laughing along. "But you have to admit, the place smells good, sugar cookies, soup, and bread. And let's not forget the coffee. How about it?"

"Coffee I'll take," Mary concluded, sliding off her sweater. "And maybe some soup."

"You see, it really does work," Cathy added, cheerfully.

"What?" Mary asked.

"These concrete forms of compassion. I think you were right. You only have to meet the world halfway, Mary."

"When did I say that? It seems to me I should be the last person on earth giving advice. I haven't a clue what to make of any of this, our bizarre connection, your mother's death, my friend's death."

Mary sipped her soup, tried a heel of the toasted bread Cathy had buttered for her, and inhaled deeply, feeling better.

"You're trying to make it make sense. It doesn't have to make sense," Cathy insisted. "When we met, you were upset. You insisted you wandered in the store and impulsively chose peppermints. I don't think the connection between us is a logical one. It's heart to heart. Like your mother, my mother, my grief group, maybe even your friend."

They sat at the rocky table with cigarettes, coffee, and tissues, not knowing what to make of what seemed to be the force of death's presence, its need for attention in the form of parents and ex-lovers.

"You know what? I have absolutely no idea what to do now," Mary admitted.

"That's because you're at the acute stage." Cathy comforted her. "I feel I'm at the next stage. I've decided to go back to my old job at the luncheonette. I figure I can live in the area, work on my crafts, and see nice people every day."

Mary frowned but realized it was difficult to find fault with anyone who knew her own heart and mind so well, and followed their call.

"It could just be a reaction to your mother's death, Cathy," Mary offered.

"Maybe. But I know it's time for me to get out of this place. I need to get back to the soda counter. That's where I'm happy. Maybe it's just the wrong time for school, or maybe I'm not a school person," Cathy offered, placing a dish of glittering sugar cookies in front of Mary that were almost too pretty to eat.

"As a mother I find it almost impossible to not try and talk you out of leaving school," Mary admitted. "But as your friend I have to tell you how much I admire your decisiveness and your courage."

"Really? It's just not that complicated to me. You know, it's all so overrated. I'm not one of those people who need a degree to feel smart. Studying, theorizing, memorizing, none of that comes naturally to me. I like being behind the counter. I like selling ice-cream sundaes. I like to work with my hands. And it's not like I need to leave home to be on my own."

Mary thought of Alex, the most intellectual person she had ever known, now gone, despite his brilliance. The world definitely needed people like Cathy who were brave enough to admit life could flourish outside the covers of books. They should dot the earth like sprinkles on a cookie: happy, nice, easy, hugging, open-hearted souls, so like children in their capacity to love life and experience joy.

"I know my mom fought hard to see that I had an education. But if I continued here, it would only be because she died, and I felt I had to," Cathy announced.

"I think that's the most honest thing I've ever heard," Mary told her, tears now streaming down her cheeks. "You're right. Pack. Run. Don't waste one more second of your precious life. Get where the public can have access to you, where your smile can brighten other people's days."

"Oh, Mary. That's so sweet," Cathy said, hugging her. "I feel so bad, though. I mean I did drag you away, and now I'm the one who's leaving."

"Don't be silly. I finally believe my coming here was inevitable. Now I only have to decide where to go."

The sun was setting earlier these days. Mary moved to the sofa, and Cathy began to make a new pot of coffee. Mary was going to tell Cathy about Alex, their relationship, and the strangeness of finding out about his death in the student center. Mary had planned to confess all about him, how deep her feelings were for him, but then Cathy noticed the flashlights, the car, and the young man in the trees.

"Oh, I don't believe it," she gasped, quickly moving away from the window before she could be spotted.

"What is it?" Mary responded, jumping up.

"Don't come! Sit!" Cathy told her. "Act normal."

Mary had already figured out that it wasn't a what but a who, and ordinarily she could have deduced that her family had descended on her, but she was mostly under the impression that Cathy had seen a disembodied someone, having spent the day walking around with a few in her head.

"Now I know what Luke meant. It's your family. Matthew is in the tree, spying. Your husband and Brian are in the car shining flashlights. This is so funny, Mary."

"Oh, no!" Mary gasped, panicking.

"Look at them. They are so cute. Should I invite them up? I could put a sign in the window," Cathy chuckled.

"Yes," Mary responded. "Tell them to help you box your things. Give them cookies, Cokes, pizza, just as soon as I'm packed and the hell out of here."

"What? You can't go off by yourself! You've just had an emotional shock."

"I really need to go. I'm not ready to see my family. I need to work this out. I can't see them yet. I can't see Ted. Cover for me. I want to talk to my friend."

"But Mary, your friend is dead."

"And since when is that an obstacle? Oh, I cannot believe Ted would take the boys out of school to come and spy on me. You know, he thinks Luke has interest in me."

"And Matthew thinks the same thing about me."

"Forgive him, he's his father's son," Mary said, jamming shirts, underwear, and toiletries into her canvas bag.

"I think it's kind of cute. Should we tell them about Luke's fiancée?"

"Well, jealousy isn't pretty but if it took that to get them to climb a tree on our behalf, I guess we can't fault it. Cathy,

I hate to leave you like this. But I have to stop at my house before I even decide where I'm going. I have to look through my things, get something of my friend's belongings to hold on to. And they're in a box in the basement—which means this family needs to stay here at least a few hours."

"Mary, what are you doing? Do you even know?"

"I don't. I really don't. Imagine that? Well, I guess I know I have to find his letters. I have to spend some time with my dead friend before I can see my husband again. Am I crazy?"

"Look who you're asking, Mary. I know. I'll call Luke. He'll come, they'll be watching us, and you can sneak away. I'll tell them—what will I tell them?"

"That I had a group project to work on. Or maybe that I went somewhere to clear my mind, cleanse my aura, as Luke would say. And tell them you're going back with them. I know Ted. He'll invite you to stay. Take care of each other."

"Promise me you won't make any big decisions, that you'll call me if you need to. I don't like you wandering off out there while you're in the throes of grief. You told me that wasn't good."

"I know. But I wasn't always right. I know I can't go back with them now. I need to mourn. How can I do that in front of my husband?" she finished, breaking down.

Cathy put her arms around her friend and felt her sob against her.

"I'm so sorry for you, Mary. I wish I could do something. Let me come with you. I'll take my polka cassettes and we can sing 'Roll Out the Barrel.' "

"No, I have to be alone. I'm not ready for accordion music yet."

"Are you sure about this?"

"Not at all. All I know is I feel like I'm drowning. I've got to get to him, or near him, or near where he was, or, at the very least, hear from him. Oh, God, I know I'd feel so much better if I could just talk to him for five minutes . . ."

32

Mary drove to Schenectady as though she were being chased, her heart thumping, her head sore, all four car doors locked and checked at least twice before she began. Cathy's apartment at school had provided her with privacy, and even that much had been taken away.

She had this overwhelming feeling of being spied upon, not only by the living but also by the dead: her father, her mother, great-aunts, uncles, grandparents, and now Alex. Her husband and sons were in the trees, at least that much was established, but where were the others? Were they the ones manipulating the day-to-day events that brought Cathy and Mary to each other, that brought Mary to a college campus where she would learn that a man she had loved enough to mourn excessively over their college breakup had died?

Mary pulled her car deep into her driveway. She scanned the street to make sure no neighbors would approach her. She took the back staircase directly to the basement. Matthew's varsity jacket was slung on the handlebar of his weight bench; it stopped her in her tracks. She touched the leather sleeve, remembering how proud he was the first time he wore it to school. It occurred to Mary to write the boys a note telling them how much she missed them, but she knew if she didn't stay focused, she wouldn't be able to leave at all.

In minutes, she pulled out the cardboard box that contained Alex's letters, books, even an old sweatshirt she had saved all these years. She placed everything in the trunk of her car. It never occurred to her while she was sorting through her mother's old possessions to even open up that box, much less part with the contents.

She got back in her car and drove south, as close as she could get to Alex's hometown, without actually crossing into it. She checked into a nearby hotel. She ordered toast, coffee, and eggs, ate quickly, her hands shaking, refueling, so as not to allow one more minute of her life go by without holding and touching his possessions.

Mary sat at the polished desk with her coffee and cigarettes and began to read Alex's letters. They weren't all love letters, some were humorous, some more poetic, some despairing, some cautioning her about the world's propensity to hurt an open heart such as hers. And by the fifth or so dusty page, she could recognize the voice of death in the dark imagery of Alex's writing. She wondered if he'd taken his own life, or had done something so reckless, it killed him.

Mary dug deeper and deeper, despite her own sorrow. She

kept digging, until digging became her life's work, as if she would find him immortalized, glorious, and bright, in all that was left of him, his words.

Mary allowed herself to remember Alex dashing into traffic, crossing a highway on foot the day his car had run out of gas. She had watched from the shoulder of the road, praying, trying to stop the horrible mental picture of his being hit by a speeding truck, trying to convince herself he could make it, but knowing his curiosity could be the very thing that affected his judgment for that one split second, that he might just want to know how the impact would feel. She nearly passed out from terror, hating herself for ever letting him out of her grasp, wondering what she would do, how she would ever be able to go on without him. She was exactly that panicked the first time she let Matthew out in the street with his bike. In fact, she was even worse when Matthew began driving, terrified for his safety.

Mary realized she had never forgiven Alex. She secretly remained angry with him all these years for not taking her along with him. She had sealed him up good and tight in her basement box. Even if rationally she could understand that she might one day be grateful, she didn't know why he had taken the liberty of deciding for her that her heart was not strong enough to endure life and death with him.

She wondered which patch of land he had been sunk beneath. Undoubtedly another plane of lawns somewhere, another perfect grass suburbia mowed down on schedule. Now she was desperate for the details. How did it happen? Did it hurt him? What did it feel like? Was it like fainting? Did he think of her, even for a second, even if just to say good-bye? If she shut her eyes now, would he come to her? Would he come in her dreams as her mother did, unreachable? Or, when she opened her eyes, would some recognizable form of him be there, standing, shining, full of mercy, full of grace, a visible prayer of a man who had been to heaven and back again to tell her it would all be all right, that he was all right, safe now, full of heavenly white twinkle lights and joy.

She had battled so to remove him from her heart, and now could not seem to scrape up enough of him from her memory to satisfy her hunger. When had she told him she was in love with him? It was sometime in the fall. Before Thanksgiving? After Halloween? They had celebrated with Chinese food at some BYOB restaurant. The cooking smells were enticing, and she was starving by the time the food came out through the swinging doors. They had taken the train so they could drink wine and not worry about driving home. There was ice on the city street. There was some gray snow at the curbs. The wine was red. The walls were yellow. The place was down three steps, in a cellar off a side street. The waitress spoke quickly. She had a scar on her face, as if from a burn. Alex kept filling Mary's wineglass. They talked and talked.

They kissed the whole way home on the train. Mary's conscience, lulled by the wine, forgot about her mother's rule about kissing in public. He enjoyed her more when she drank a little. She was a little more herself, he would tell her. Perhaps a little less her mother. She drank sometimes to make him happy.

They went to his apartment, which was wall-to-wall books, a table where he studied, a mattress on the floor, a stereo in a bare corner, a guitar, a stark white and black bathroom—so like the one she now occupied with Cathy. He lit candles. Mary was cold. The bed was a dismal twin with few covers.

They kissed for hours, it had seemed to Mary, who grew impatient to make love. She remembered his fingers on her buttons, his hands upon her face and within her hair. She could recall the intent in his eyes, their alternating positions that night, how he kissed her breasts, how he bent her legs, how she eventually rested in his arms, warm and excited still as he slept peacefully.

It had been so long ago. Stamps were thirteen cents. He sometimes had pot. He hated birth control. He loved the risk, the adventure. She fought with him about birth control, not wanting to risk pregnancy. He campaigned for risk. He lived in the present. Mary couldn't help but be concerned about the future, about getting a job after school, about getting married, about creating a stable home for children.

It was all coming back to her. Every sight, every sound, every precious touch from him. Their dissimilar natures. He was a genius at finding ways to beckon death, as he swayed across the train tracks whistling, fascinated, sometimes frightened, but always with a wink and a poem to comfort Mary.

"Come on, love, don't be afraid," Alex told her when she

would try and stay angry with him, never understanding his fascination with danger. "The worst is only death," he would laugh.

Each day took Alex a little closer to unleashing his own ghost. Alex had found his way out of this world without her help, while she rolled Penelope into and out of church, or baked banana breads for Christmas brunch, or sang her sons into a brand-new birthday, or watered and clipped her red geraniums, all the while trying her best not to admit his presence in her blood, his absence in her heart.

Dates floated in and out of her reach as she lay there not sleeping. She could remember her first real date with Ted, her engagement to Ted, even the days her kids had the chicken pox, but she never thought about Alex's birthday. It had been buried beneath her life.

Mary almost heard him, getting closer with every memory.

"Take the cotton out of your ears, baby."

It was madness she was courting, coming away from everyone at this moment, coming away to be with a dead man. But she couldn't help herself. Mary could almost feel Alex next to her as she lay sleepless. She concentrated. Five minutes would do it. Just the sight of him. Just a glimpse.

Luke had encouraged her to do a form of self-hypnosis before sleeping, to enable her to direct her dreams. She tried her best to conjure up an image of Alex, but each time she tried to picture him, his face remained unclear. She tried not to force it, to remove all distractions, to see a blank screen as she did her best to relax every part of her body, from her toes to her head, slowly, deliberately.

As she was drifting into sleep, she began to hear that reassuring sound of waves. A flame appeared in her mind's eye, and Mary felt herself floating toward it. The color remained yellow at first, but then, just as it had during the séance, it lightened, until it was white, whiter than sunlight, whiter than the bright clouds of the beach she was suddenly walking on again, whiter than any earthly light she had ever seen.

All her fear dissipated. Mary was back at that wonderful shore, and Matthew was swimming in the ocean. She was no longer full of sorrow. She immediately began calling to him, as she could see his firm stroke against the ocean waves. She stared out over the shimmering water, waiting for him, breathing in the refreshing air, loving the feeling, loving the place, feeling no sense of urgency or foreboding, no trace of pain.

At last, he turned around and waved, just as he had before, this time flexing his muscles, clowning around so Mary couldn't help but recognize the antics—it was Alex, not Matthew, and the shock of seeing him immediately snapped her out of her reverie and sat her up in bed.

Spirits were elusive, that much she had learned from questioning Luke when he had seen her mother's image, and when that image had abruptly evaporated. Mary considered what she had seen, the joking, happy Alex, the Alex she had mistaken for Matthew. It was a relief. She could accept that he was happy and, better still, that she was getting closer to him.

A frustrated Ted Sullivan, with a full-blown headache and a truly missing-in-action wife, tried his best to reason with her stubborn, young roommate.

"I understand that you want to keep Mary's confidence. That's admirable, really. But I could help. Instead of shouldering all this responsibility for her, you could trust me. I'm her husband," Ted told Cathy for the third and, perhaps, final time.

"I don't have any specifics, Mr. S," Cathy said. "And I really don't think she would approve. Maybe we could all just give it some time," she suggested, pouring a second round of sodas.

"Cathy, I really think it's time you and I had a talk," Matthew intervened.

"Mom's fine," Brian piped up, going for his fourth slice of pizza. "I mean, none of us knew what she did every day at home, and she was always fine. I think you should cut her some slack, Dad," he finished. "After all, this is the first time she's run away."

"Well, thank you, Son, for your concern," Ted admonished. "I'm sure your mother would be proud to know you took her side."

"She would! See, that's the problem. You guys didn't hang out with her. I did. I'm the one who wandered around the mall with her, or hung out on Friday nights, watching her paint smiley faces on cookies for the seniors. I'm the one who knew her best," Brian defended.

"I've been with your mother forever. And, need I repeat, I am her husband," Ted insisted.

"Yeah, but what's that?" Brian argued. "A legal contract. So what?"

"So what?" Matthew asked, appalled.

"Yeah, that just means you're married," Brian continued, picking up a piece of pepperoni from his plate.

"And marriage is now incidental?" Ted challenged, finishing his third piece of pizza. "You know, you are your mother's son. You argue like her. Absurdly!"

"All I'm trying to say is lots of married people have these communication problems from time to time."

"What the heck is this now, *Oprah*?" Matthew chided. "And the only communication problem Mom has is that she's spending more time talking to the dead than the living."

"I thought you were going to talk to Cathy!" Brian yelled. "She'll explain it."

"Explain what?" Matthew demanded.

"You guys. You just don't understand women," Brian said, shaking his head sadly.

"Listen to this!" Ted yelled. "My son, the expert on female relationships."

"Actually, Brian's right. I don't think either of you is looking at these things from Mary's point of view. Is this the first time you've been separated, Mr. S?"

"Is that what I am?" Ted asked his boys. "Separated? Is that what Mom said?"

"Of course not," Brian answered. "You and Mom are just living in two different places. You're not separated in the sense of being—heck, how do I know? Maybe you are."

"Isn't this just great?" Ted growled.

"Look who you're listening to, Dad! Weren't you guys going out for ice cream?" Matthew cued his father.

Ted nodded to Brian, who stood up to leave. Feeling the need to leave Cathy with advice, Brian teased, "If he touches you, scream."

"Dad, see what you can do to get him to stop talking," Matthew pleaded.

"Baskin Robbins?" Ted asked Brian.

"Cool," he said agreeably.

"Well, are you going to sit down?" Cathy asked, dropping onto her bed as a confused Matthew trailed after her. "You know it's really been a long day for me."

"You mean—on the bed?" Matthew blurted, his attention taken by all the pretty wall decorations, the painted mirrors, the hanging wreaths, the watercolors.

"Or on the floor, your choice. But if you're on the floor and I'm on the bed, you'll lose your strategic advantage."

"How's that?"

"I'll be taller."

"In that case, I'll stand."

"Whatever makes you comfortable."

"I don't appreciate your manner with my father."

"You mean telling him the truth? It would be better for you if I just said, yes sir, no sir."

"He's not stupid. He'd see through that."

"Of course. Would you hand me my cigarettes?"

"Absolutely not."

"Really, Matthew, even in lockup they give you cigarettes," Cathy groaned.

"And do you know about that too? Prison?" Matthew accused, half afraid of the answer, trying not to be distracted by her lovely, shimmering green eyes—he'd sworn they were blue. He'd known they were blue. He'd had dreams of their blueness. "What color are your eyes?"

"It depends on what I wear," she answered. "Sometimes they look real blue, but if I wear green, they change over. Usually I don't wear green but I ran out of clean clothes today. Look, if I can't have a cigarette, would you mind if I had more pizza?" Cathy asked, walking back to the other room.

"More pizza? Haven't you already had three?" her keeper exclaimed, blocking her exit.

"I eat four. What's it to you? I ordered two boxes."

"What kind of girl eats four slices of pizza?"

"A healthy, hungry one."

"You know what I mean. Most girls I know—"

"Yadda, yadda, yadda. In the meantime, the cheese is glazing over."

"Fine, I'll have another slice with you," he decided, slamming through the door, grumbling about girls who ate more pizza than he did. He had learned grumbling from his father. He had watched him when his mother had him all tied up in knots. He'd learned that grumbling was always an option. Matthew was full already, but he wasn't about to let Cathy outeat him.

"I just love pepperoni," she told him, taking a big bite. "I have a big appetite."

"But you're so petite."

"I know. I have eyes that change color and I eat like a horse. Not everything makes sense all the time. So what would you like to talk about, Matty? I don't want to monopolize the conversation."

"I'd like to know where my mother is."

"Look, I'm not going over the same stuff over and over again. I could suggest something, but none of you, except maybe Brian, would listen. I keep trying to search for images but none of you will keep quiet long enough for me to try to get a sense of where she is."

"I knew it. You knew all along."

"No. But I could ask Luke to come help."

"Luke! He's the reason she disappeared in the first place."

"He wasn't the one spying in the tree."

"Well, there's no way I'm putting that gypsy in the same room with the rest of my family. God knows what he'll do to Brian. He's impressionable and immensely stupid."

"Aren't you just afraid of being tricked? Like Brian might fake a trance and embarrass you."

"Of course not," Matthew said, amazed that she seemed to have the ability to look right through to his deepest fears.

"Then what have you got to lose?"

"There's my father to think about."

"Fine. You and I could go to see Luke. You might actually learn something," she offered.

Matthew thought, allowing the possibility that if this guy could read his mind, he might also talk about what he found out. After all, it wasn't like these psychics had to sign confidentiality agreements. He didn't like anyone knowing his business, not even his family. Not that he had anything to hide. He just preferred to keep his thoughts private.

"No, I can't do it," Matthew snapped, like a door blown shut by a wind.

"Okay, have it your way. Say good night to your family and make yourself at home. There are blankets in the hallway closet. I'm going to see Luke."

"That's it?"

"No. Your mom said you wouldn't mind helping me pack some of my things. I'm dropping out."

"You're what!"

"You heard me. The energy is all wrong for me here. I want to go back to the luncheonette. I'm already signed out of my courses. Now, try not to worry. I'll see you later." Cathy picked up her jacket, her purse, and never looked back as she headed toward the door.

Matthew took a deep breath and yelled, "Wait up."

"Really?" Cathy asked, spinning around, surprised but pleased.

Matthew's mother was more important to him than any secrets this alleged psychic could expose, and one thing was for sure in the meantime, he wasn't letting her roommate out of his sight. He grabbed his sweatshirt and took his first, giant leap into the unknown.

*L*uke greeted Cathy and Matthew at the door. He wore a white sweatshirt and jeans, and Matthew had to admit to himself that the guy didn't look overtly slimy. Luke offered hot chocolate, which Cathy accepted and Matthew declined, and they sat around the coffee table in the modest living room listening to nothing more horrifying than some oldies playing on the radio. Luke apologized for not having cake.

"Mr. Petros," Matthew began, leaning forward from the plaid sofa he occupied with Cathy.

"Dr. Petros," Cathy corrected.

"Luke," Luke insisted, shaking his head at his title.

Matthew flinched at allowing any informality between himself and this man who possibly encouraged his mother's departure, but squeezed out, "Luke," before taking the conversation exactly where he wanted it to go. "We have a situation with my mother."

"Yes, I see you're upset. Come on. Let me read for you," Luke offered, standing.

"Read?" Matthew repeated. "I'm not sure that will help."

"Well, that is what I do," Luke explained, without pushing further. He looked directly into Matthew's eyes and waited calmly, as if he had all the time in the world, as if opening the door to the spirit world was as natural to him as making a phone call.

Cathy nudged Matthew with her elbow. He sat still and quiet for a moment, his back teeth grinding hard enough to make his jaw ache, his nostrils flaring. But he stood up and followed Luke, happy Brian was not in the room, only in his head, rolling on the floor laughing.

Matthew Sullivan sat in the small room and watched Luke as he eased into the chair beside him, and lit a candle at the card table separating them. He gave Matthew the oversized deck of tarot cards, instructing him how to shuffle and cut them, making piles to the left. Matthew did his best to remove Cathy from his mind and focus on his mother.

Luke picked up the entire deck of cards and held them, closing his eyes momentarily. Matthew could feel cold sweat trickling down his back, although Luke didn't look like he was doing anything more than praying.

The first card Matthew saw leave Luke's hand was some guy on a horse, which seemed to suit his mood. He hoped the horse would soon lead him out of this room and back to the sanity he'd left in Schenectady.

"Who's that guy on the horse?" he asked Luke, not having any knowledge of how this hooey was supposed to work.

"A knight," Luke answered through closed eyes.

Knights were cool, Matthew thought as he shifted in his seat, watching Luke place four or five different cards rapidly on the table. One of them looked like a joker, and he immediately thought it was part of some prank meant to embarrass him further, but then he read upside-down it was labeled "The Fool," and presumed the card was an accurate representation of his idiot brother Brian. He hoped Luke could give him some dirt on his brother that he could use at a later date.

Instead, Luke began by asking, "Who is Leila?"

"You got me," Matthew answered with a condescending snort, certain this guy was beginning to fish and coming up dry. Matthew wasn't about to give him any information at all.

"I'm sorry. Laura. She's blond and petite—" Luke corrected.

At the sound of her name, Matthew blurted out the details. "Laura and I go to school together. She's in my AP math class," he added, confessing way too much.

"She certainly loves to wear pink," Luke added.

"That's amazing," Matthew accidentally blurted out, staring at the cards for color codes, any hint of where Luke could have gotten such information.

Matthew had admired Laura in many, many shades of that wonderful color across the years, and in grammar school had even chosen the pinkest Valentine out of his Peanuts boxed set, hoping she would notice. She didn't.

"She is definitely interested in you—"

"In me? Hell no. She's going out with someone," Matthew admitted, again breaking his rule about giving up any facts. But when Luke spoke that name, referenced that girl, described her physically down to her favorite color, he had inadvertently let down his guard.

"She's already started pulling away from him. But it's going to take time, probably another season."

"Really?" Matthew asked, hoping against hope Luke was right. The prom wasn't until the spring. Wouldn't that end high school in the ultimate triumph? Matthew remained guarded. He hadn't started any other relationships because there simply was no comparison between Laura and the others. Was Luke telling him only what he wanted to hear?

"Listen," Luke continued. "You should be careful not to confuse your feelings about this girl. I know Cathy looks a lot like her—"

"What?"

"It's okay. It happens," Luke offered softly. "Psychically, we're attracted to people who have the same physical appeal or even sometimes the same mannerisms as people we have some chemistry with—"

"Chemistry? You're probably confused because I was in chemistry class with Laura," Matthew suggested, as if he could possibly understand how this information was reaching Luke enough to make excuses for his erroneous interpretation.

"No, this has nothing to do with a class. This is just the way you two get each other. But since I can see she looks quite a bit like Cathy, you need to understand the misplacement of your feelings," Luke cautioned. "It's not your fault. And you would have realized it eventually."

Matthew wondered how he had ever missed such an obvious clue, even as Luke continued to comfort him for inadvertently desiring Cathy. Laura always wore pink, so when Cathy wore those darker colors, it was like seeing a much sexier version of the girl he had always wanted to date.

"It's completely understandable why you would have these transferred feelings, especially since Laura's already started to send you some signals."

Matthew thought back to the last time he had seen Laura. She had told him which party she was going to for the homecoming game. He assumed she had meant with Rocky, her boyfriend for the past two years, and Matthew, not wanting to have his nose rubbed in it, purposely avoided going.

"I'll keep that in mind," Matthew told him.

"You should. She's trying to figure out if you're interested."

"I am!" Matthew admitted freely.

"Okay, so just communicate that and you'll be fine."

Luke placed some cards bearing numbers, wands, swords, queens, kings, and other odd characters down upon each other as he spoke. Matthew thought he saw a Magician card. He wondered if that's how Luke appeared in readings.

"I see you're thinking of math as a college major," Luke went on.

"Engineering," Matthew corrected, staring now at a Hermit card, and wondering how in the world he could discern such information—unless his mother had told him during one of her visits. It was common knowledge in the family.

"It's something you should reconsider," Luke continued. "You're just talking yourself into it. You think because the math comes easy, it will be a good fit. I hear you say, 'I can do that stuff, make a good living,' but you won't really like the work. Your heart's just not in it."

Matthew's mouth was now hanging open, because he could remember thinking those very same thoughts, having those very same concerns last week as he was shaving. Without encouragement, Luke continued nonchalantly.

"You love history. You should start with that, because I think you're going to end up practicing law. I see you've got a very strong sense of right and wrong, you've got the analytical side down, and, like your mother, you like to help people. With your love of tradition, it seems like you could really enjoy those ethics classes. Engineering is just too technical for you. You'd be lonely."

Ah-ha! Matthew knew those school assessment tests were wrong! Sure, they pushed him toward engineering because of his math ability. He could wipe the floor with the competition at high school. But those tests didn't take into account his love of reading, or his solid character, or his boredom with being a human calculator. But law? Matthew didn't exactly embrace the idea of signing up for so many years of school.

Luke held Matthew's attention with every strange-looking person, place, or thing he flipped from the deck of tarot cards. Matthew saw a devil, a guy in a boat, a hanging man, a party. There were towers falling and Luke said the word *conflict,* just as he put that one on the pile. Matthew was relieved to make some connection between the cards and the conversation, even if it was only through logic.

Part of Matthew wanted to know everything about the process, how these very private thoughts were escaping from his being only to be captured and articulated so precisely by Luke, but he dared not interrupt the process. In fact, it took great self-control to not ask questions about his mother, the reason he had come here in the first place. But when he saw a card called Empress, he wondered where she was, missed her, and felt guilty for the way he had treated her before she left. Luke was ahead of his thoughts, already deep into the subject.

"Your mom is healing. She needs time alone. She tried to do that at Cathy's place, but you guys ended up in the trees."

Matthew hated hearing that out loud. He hated even more knowing Luke could play that mental footage of him at will.

"She wouldn't want you to be sad. In fact, she worries that you are too serious, that she may have encouraged that in you," Luke added.

"It's not her fault," Matthew defended. "And I'm not exactly sad."

"But you don't listen to your heart enough," Luke told him. "It's okay to be strong *and* happy."

"Sure," Matthew added, like he knew it all along. He regretted the way he had reacted to this psychic stuff and to his mother's leaving.

"So, I know it's hard, but just be patient. It will all end well for all of you," Luke added.

"But where is she?" Matthew pressed. Surely Luke could see her in the cards, and they could go and talk to her. He was obviously good at this stuff. Matthew knew he wouldn't even have to apologize. His mother would know from one look that he was sorry.

"Mary's hiding. Physically and psychically. I can't see her. It's the way she wants it. This just has to run its course. When the time comes, she'll come out from the clouds."

Matthew nodded. He tried to think of a proper way to ask if his parents would be divorcing, but Luke had already stood up and was offering Matthew his final bit of advice.

"You channel that intensity, young man," Luke offered. "And have a little fun. Don't worry about the rest. You have a very promising future."

Cathy had to look twice when Luke walked Matthew through the door. There was Matthew putting out his hand to Luke, with a flattering "Dude" escaping with an all too infrequent smile.

"So you got a little something out of that?" Cathy asked, settling into the window seat of the shuttle bus.

"Just that my mom doesn't want us to find her. Not yet anyway," Matthew answered, calmer.

"And what about you?"

"It's possible the man has some talent," Matthew offered. "He's given me a few things to think about."

Cathy smiled and sat back, satisfied with herself. Matthew took a good look at her green eyes, the nose that was a little too thin, the lips that were far too round, and the total absence of pink, and knew Luke was capable of discerning truth through all the jumbled images and feelings in his being. And even though he didn't have a clue how it was done, he knew he had to respect the accuracy, hell, the downright precision of his conclusions. Matthew didn't belong in engineering, any more than he belonged with Cathy.

~ 35 ~

*M*atthew and Cathy returned to the apartment and got
looks of disbelief when they told Ted and Brian where
they had been. Matthew told his father what Luke said about
Mary, and that he should try not to worry while she works
through her issues privately. Ted, who knew Matthew was
never one to underreact, sat quietly panicked. Mary had never
gone underground before. What if she needed him? The more
Ted thought, the more upset he became. What if Mary didn't
know how much he needed her?

Brian wouldn't stop whining that it wasn't fair he didn't
get to meet the gypsy, and how dare they go without him,
sending him off for ice cream like a little kid when he was a
technical wizard in his own right, and could easily spot a
fraud.

"You know I could have recorded the entire conversation," Brian reminded Matthew.

"Look, it's not like that. He doesn't let anyone else in the room when he does a reading," Matthew explained. "It's just you and the deck of cards."

"We were a team. If you needed me to distract Dad, you just should have told me. I could have wired you up. Did you forget I have devices?"

"What devices?" Cathy asked.

"I've got a bunch of stuff from Radio Shack. Earpieces, microphones. Stuff that's good enough to spy on our mother, just not some fortune-teller."

"We can't spy on strangers, Brian," Ted offered. "That's against the law, Son."

"You're kidding me, right? This is the guy who listens in on other people's personal, private thoughts. He gets paid to talk to ghosts, and I'm the bad guy?"

"He was pretty good at it," Matthew confessed.

"If he was that good he would have his own TV show," Brian argued. "Was he rich? I bet he wasn't even on *Montel*. He was probably just good at jerking you around."

"Let it go, Brian," Ted advised, having had enough for one day. He had finally gotten rid of his headache. He should have known better than to let Brian have caffeine and sugar after nine. Mary always remembered not to feed him this late.

"Look, Bro, I didn't mean to leave you out," Matthew apologized.

"Yeah, well," Brian huffed. "I guess you forgot it was my idea to come here."

"Brian!" Cathy gasped. "I never would have suspected you."

"Hey, it got me out of school for a few days," Brian said with a grin.

"Look, the next time we have a day off, I'll drive you back here so you can meet Luke," Matthew promised. "He can read for you and tell you how annoying you are."

"That's crap. I want stuff I can use."

"You're scaring me, Brian," Ted sung.

"Relax, Dad. I'll just sell enough information to buy an ocean-blue Lamborghini. Can you see me driving that babe to school? I wonder how many seniors will want to date me. Does this guy predict horse races, or should I stick with the lottery? How much should I charge? Dad, how old do I have to be before I can buy stocks? Matty, you want to be my partner? I'll even let you drive my car."

Matthew and Brian had finally fallen asleep on the floor when Ted knocked on Cathy's bedroom door, offering her dough nuts and conversation at her kitchen table. She looked young and fragile, like any other college girl in pajamas, except she had absolutely no one, now that his wife had run off. He felt strangely paternal toward her.

They sat at the table, the soft lace curtain blowing in the mild wind, which Ted tried to shield the young woman from, for women always seemed to be cold.

"Matthew told me you signed out of your courses," he began.

"Yeah, I was never really into college. I like working at the luncheonette. I like doing crafts. I know I won't get rich from it, but for now I think it will make me feel better."

Suddenly he felt pity for Cathy, even though she lured his wife away.

"It must be awful, what you're going through. I mean, I remember when Mary lost her mother. She was in an enormous amount of pain. I wasn't sure she'd ever come around."

"She told me how you helped her, how you all helped her," Cathy added, feeling as though she should confide in this man that his wife had sustained yet another blow to her heart, and was wandering around hurt, God knows where.

"Well, we're her family."

Cathy bit into a jelly doughnut and coughed until powdered sugar sprayed across the table.

"Let me get you some water," Ted offered, pouring a glass and handing it to her.

Cathy drank and started to laugh. "That's never happened to me before. Did I get you?" she asked, wiping the sugar with her napkin.

"No, I ducked," Ted answered.

"I'm not very neat sometimes," Cathy confessed.

"Neither are any of us, except Mary. You'd fit right in," Ted told her. And then, thinking only of tomorrow, of what would become of this girl when they all returned to their home, he asked, "Why don't you come home with us?"

"Well, actually, I do need the ride."

"No, I meant to stay for a while. We could fix up the basement for you and your projects. I mean, where else would you go? Did you have something in mind?"

"I'm not much of a planner actually. I just figured it would all work out," she admitted.

"You know, as a father I find that kind of thinking just a little too impractical. I insist that you join us. If you don't like it, then we could find you an alternative. But you just can't rush off and get the first apartment you see."

Cathy giggled. "You sound so—"

"Now, if you say old, I'm really going to be offended."

"Parental," she finished. "I don't know, Mr. S, I really don't think your sons would appreciate—"

"You mean Matthew? Don't worry about him. Besides, being part of a family is fraught with conflict."

"It's fine with me," Matthew grumbled from the floor.

"I can't believe he's still eavesdropping. An entire day of spying wasn't enough," Cathy commented. "Well, I'll take your offer then, and hope I don't drive you crazier than you already are," she said. "Except maybe Matthew," she added.

"Very funny," he tossed from the floor.

"Thanks, Mr. S." She smiled, putting out her hand. "Mary said you would invite me. I thought I was imposing enough for the ride home."

"But you have to call me Ted," he added, shaking her hand.

Ted felt something in his stomach as he caught the gleam in the young girl's eyes, combined with the warmth of her handshake. It was a hint of the familiar, like a song you're not even aware you're listening to, until you begin to hum along.

∿ 36 ∾

When Mary awoke in unfamiliar surroundings, her first
thoughts were of Alex. She had fallen asleep with his
letters nearby, having read every page, something she had
never done since their breakup. She found the strength to get
up, to shower, to continue searching for a glimpse of him,
perhaps through some crack in the sky. She didn't need much,
just a whisper in a dark dream, a short conversation, the tini-
est remainder of him, a wave from a familiar beach   perhaps
he would come to her like that again.

Mary checked out of the hotel and began to drive through
Alex's town, looking for landmarks he may have told her
about, anything that would hint at a family residence. She followed railroad tracks to an old train station, remembering
how he always noticed train whistles.

There were banks and convenience stores, a hardware
shop, a florist. Across the street, a young mother pushed a

baby stroller into a small park. Mary struggled to keep from crying. She pictured Alex at six, a boy in a pack of boys, not quite leading, not quite following, wide-eyed and curious. Perhaps he stood patiently as his mother bought her packs of Wrigley's gum and Winstons, and, unable to resist his silent, pleading eyes, bought him a Hershey bar. Having listened throughout the night for cries and coughs, applauded his awards and grades, wiped away tears at the sight of him in his prom tuxedo, heard his voice crack before it matured and deepened, watched him begin to shave, begin to drive—to have witnessed the descent of her child into a grave, Mary could not begin to imagine that kind of pain.

There was Alex's gentleness, the boyishness that Mary was now acquainted with through her own boys, and the mother in her was appalled for his mother, for that poor woman who nurtured him, sat him in a highchair with crackers and juice, pushed him giggling and begging, probably way too high for his own good on the park swings. How was she coping? Considering Alex at a young age was so much worse than thinking of him college age, or twenty, thirty, or forty.

Alex was always so generous with affection. Mary was sure his mother had loved him so achingly, that each little kiss bestowed upon his head had to be almost disguised as a pat on the head, not to let the young boy know he was being kissed, that there was so much love aimed at him. Mary's boys wanted love and affection when they were young, but only if you could learn not to draw attention to it, not make them aware that you were swooping down to feel the softness of their hair or cheeks, never distract them from making those rumbling noises with their toy trucks.

A sign for the *Middletown Herald* came into view. Mary was elated. She thought for sure she'd have to begin at the library.

She was breathless. Impulsively, she parked the car, grabbed her purse, and checked her makeup. She was through crying. It was time to get some answers. There had to be more than a photo on the wall. There had to be survivors in his family.

Mary always made a good first impression. She showed her college ID and explained that she was taking a communication course, biting back the half-truth, the word *psychic*. Could she please have access to their obituary archive?

She was shepherded from reception to research, and finally allowed to sit at a microfiche machine, scanning years to her heart's content. There were many Wyatts in the area, but finally, only one Alexander Thomas Wyatt matching the month, day, and year of death noted on the photo in the student center.

Interment was at East Hillside Cemetery. But of course the most important information wasn't there—how he died, whether by cancer, AIDS, heart attack, accident, suicide. In fact it seemed a painfully short obituary for someone who had meant so much to her. No charity was listed for donations. She did learn he was survived by a brother and sister who were from different California towns, who were married with families. Mary was relieved to learn that his parents had predeceased him, particularly his mother.

Mary scribbled down the information about Alex's sib-
lings, to research later. In the meantime, she asked for directions to the cemetery, and walked down the block to the
florist.

Minutes later, she drove around the cemetery, keenly
aware of the sounds in her car, her deepening breath, the
rustling of her clothes, the rising hair on the back of her neck.
She remembered her panic at not being able to keep Alex safe.
There was nothing left to be afraid of.

Alex was not to be found. Despite her intuition, the directions, and the lot number, she couldn't locate his plot. Mary
drove around slowly, never sure if she were on a road or a trail.
The paths were so narrow, she finally felt an awful panic
welling up, that she would never get to say good-bye to him,
that he didn't want her to leave, that she was meant to be in
this cemetery circling endlessly, surrounded by dead strangers,
hearing his voice forever joking in her head, "Mary, Mary
quite contrary . . . gravestones all in a row."

Now, she couldn't even find her way out of this place. She
closed her eyes and hoped for those impressions Luke was always raving about. But all she could see were the living: Brian
leaping up to hit the top of the doorway and yelling, "Score."
Matthew subtly peering into the kitchen, trying to find out if
a phone call was for him. Ted slipping his arm around her
waist as she folded clothes on the laundry room counter, then
dragging her into an open space to dance the fox-trot, dip-
ping her when she'd least expected it. Cathy showing her the
latest of her knotted necklace creations. Penelope Miller all

dressed and ready to be driven to Sunday church service. Agnes Morrison sipping tea. Thanksgiving decorations in the attic crawl space. Christmas presents she already had wrapped and stored under her bed. She missed them. She missed the chaos and the motion that kept her moving through the hours at home. She missed the comings and goings and the phone calls that were never for her. She missed her family. She missed her life.

Mary seemed to be circling the same six or seven hundred graves. How hard could it be to find an exit? Every time she turned she found another dead end. And there weren't any people she could see walking around to ask for directions. The stones and names looked way too familiar, and she now realized how much she would have appreciated finding a picture of a lighthouse on a stone, if only just to serve as a landmark.

Inadvertently, although Mary no longer believed in accidents, she was caught in a funeral procession, unable to pass or get around, unable to sit in the car and offer an explanation when the usher opened her door to lead her to the burial site. She should be polite, after all, especially in these surroundings. He offered her a pink carnation, but Mary took the single unopened rose she had bought at the florist, not knowing what else to do but follow along, to live in the moment.

Any funeral would do, she supposed. As the family of the newly deceased gathered around the casket, Mary silently dedicated her personal mourning to Alex, vowing never to forget him. When her turn came for dropping the flower, she kissed the burgundy bud, and threw her perfect rose upon a stranger's coffin, knowing Alex would understand.

On the way back to her car, her thoughts returned to Matthew and how sullen he was at times, how unlike Ted and Brian. Brian, always with a snappy comeback, was a grinning combination of Ted, Mary, and Mary's mother. Was Matthew's moodiness her doing? Oh, God, had she turned Matthew into Alex? He was too smart, too serious. Had she done that to him? She had been alone with him in those early years, reading poetry of all things, reading *Howl,* reading Whitman, reading all the classics she hadn't the time to read before, reading aloud from all of them as he sat beside her drawing small deliberate people against dark purple skies. She hadn't done that with Brian. She had let him watch television—Big Bird, Ernie and Bert, and even Daffy Duck. She had spared him the opera records from the library and gone with Broadway and the Beach Boys.

So what was she doing chasing ghosts when she had boys to raise? If the loss of her mother was so completely overwhelming to Mary as she turned forty, her sons must be feeling some amount of pain from their separation. And then there was Ted. Ted with his physical strength and emotional boundaries. Ted who left right-side-out alone, and respected the nature of things. Ted who was always her best friend. She couldn't wait to see him.

Now, it was all Mary could do to keep from advancing upon all living creatures, eager to reengage her heart, to look for all the others she had ever loved and tell them, hold them,

remind them how the minutes were passing in skipped heart-
beats and radiant fall afternoons. She wanted to find the
grammar school girls she walked home with, the cousins she
hadn't seen since the reunion five years ago, the librarians and
salesclerks from Schenectady.

Mary followed the funeral cars. As soon as she could see
an exit, she pulled away to a more private spot in the cemetery and checked the map for the quickest route home. Her
older son would soon be leaving home. Now she was sobbing
fervently. What would happen to Matthew? Had she raised
him well enough to protect himself? How was one supposed
to raise a son to have a heart, to have passion without being
too aggressive, to have tenderness without allowing the sensi-
tivity to make him too prone to unhappiness? Was she supposed to assume the heart would grow in proportionally, the
way his feet and hands did? Mary was now terrified that she
had concentrated too much energy on Matthew's brain, and
that the intellect was such a huge haunted house, so full of
dark places, her son might never grow up to be happy. Instead
of the damn spider and the waterspout, she had taught him
the Pledge of Allegiance, he had won a prize in kindergarten
for his flawless recitation. Brian of course had gotten in trouble for his Batman version of "Jingle Bells," and instantly become a class hero.

And then, the moment came, not a sound in the sky, not
a breeze brushing a leaf, not a rumor of movement anywhere,
just the all-encompassing feeling that she was not alone.

Mary slowly inhaled. She felt unafraid, calm, at peace. She

looked into her rearview mirror expecting to see his smile, but since spirits seemed not to present themselves visually to her, she shut her eyes and focused, until she could hear his voice through the strange tones and the white noise that surrounded it.

"It ends beautifully."

And then, the feeling evaporated as quickly as it had descended, and she was alone in the cemetery again. Or so she thought. Mary was conscious of a rapping noise, and raised her head out of her hands to see Cathy's brilliant smile, there in the bright fall day. Through her tears, she giggled as she stepped out of the car and into the arms of her friend.

ell, this is about what I expected," Cathy told her. "You hanging out with dead people on such a nice day."

"What?" Mary asked, stunned.

"I think I'm finally getting the hang of this intuition thing. I just closed my eyes and there you were, driving through a cemetery in Middletown," Cathy said, hugging her.

Mary blew her nose for what seemed like the hundredth time. "You know, I was thinking about doing a shot of whiskey or scotch, even though I can't imagine what that must feel like going down, and I didn't have a bottle. It just seemed an appropriate thing to do."

"If you ask me, your understanding of appropriate has changed a lot since I met you."

"I know, I know," Mary agreed, laughing at herself, sitting on a hill near the road. "So how in the world did you get here? I know you don't drive. How did you find me?"

"That's not really the question," Cathy answered, sitting beside her. "Why did I find you?"

Mary thought a moment and panic engulfed her. Something horrible had happened to her family while she was combing the gravesite for her dead lover. Something unthinkable, she was certain. And as suddenly as Cathy's mother, they would be missing.

"Tell me," she said, gripping both Cathy's hands. "Oh, God, what?"

"It's your son's birthday."

"Matthew." Mary knew immediately. "How could I forget? I remember dates. That's what I do. I write things down months in advance. I send cards for every occasion. How could I do this?"

"It's the company you keep," Cathy joked, waving her hand toward the markers. "They all had good memories once upon a time," she laughed. "Listen, Mary, I don't want to tell you what to do, but you know he's awfully mopey, and it is his last year home," she finished.

Mary seemed to understand so much in that seemingly innocuous statement of fact. Her son, her firstborn, would be leaving home for college and would return periodically, but in reality he would be grown and gone.

"Oh, my baby," Mary sighed with relief.

"Well, your baby is eighteen today. Your husband is a little nuts with anxiety over you, and frankly, I could use a good party, or at the very least a piece of cake."

"Yes, yes," Mary agreed, wiping her eyes. "We'll get hats, noisemakers, and presents."

"Now that's the spirit. My grief group sometimes has birthday parties for themselves at all different ages. Like we had a sweet sixteen party for Doreen. We did her hair and Billy asked her to dance. Her best friend had died the week of her birthday, so she never had the party she wanted."

"That's so sweet. You're wonderful for coming here. I would have felt awful if I'd missed this birthday. You can't know what it's like to hold your first baby, and then to know he's leaving."

"You know, I'd like to take all the credit for coming to you, but really, it was that man," Cathy said, pointing down the hill to that someone leaning against his car.

"Ted?"

"Yes."

"He knows?"

"I had to tell him something. I told him it was some friend from college. I never said male or female."

At the bottom of the hill, Mary saw Ted's familiar brown eyes, his soft graying hair, and athletic body. Tears rode down her face. She had married the kindest person she'd ever known. She saw Matthew and Brian in him, his parents, and even herself reflected back. Mary put her arms around him and hugged him, a friend she had missed.

"I'm sorry, Mary. Cathy never told me who. Was it him?"

"Yes."

"Then, I'm sorry about Alex," he said, ever the gentleman. "After all, I owe him."

"I suppose," Mary sighed, shutting her eyes.

"I know it's awkward," Ted admitted. "But I wouldn't expect you to feel any differently. I mean, I know you really loved him."

"Thank you."

"Mary, I never told you this. I went to Alex a few months after you had broken up, and I told him you were still in love with him."

"What?"

"I could see it in your eyes, honey. You liked me, or even loved me somewhat, but you were in love with him, and I wanted you to be happy. But he said you would never be happy with him. He was certain he'd hurt you. And he told me he loved you and he wanted better for you. Me. Can you imagine? He must have known he would leave you too soon."

"I can't believe you did that," Mary said, wiping away tears.

"Yeah, I can't either. I don't believe I would do the same thing today. I'm a lot more selfish, I guess, especially after living without you for a few weeks."

"That's very nice to hear," Mary said smiling.

"You see, Alex was right," Ted continued. "The last thing he told me was everything would work out."

"That's what he believed," Mary said.

"Let me think," Ted said. "That's right, he said, 'Every romantic knows it will all work out.' I suppose he was referring to me. Although I don't really think of myself that way."

"But you are, Ted! Here you are in a graveyard, playing hooky from work, running around with an orphan college girl, trying to give your son a good birthday."

"No, Mary. I only wanted to know if you needed me, if you were okay."

"Oh God, Ted. I need you. I want you. I want us, all of us, for as long as I can have it. In fact, I want as many people as I can fit in my life, for as long as I can have them. Maybe then I can figure out why some people are gone and I'm still here."

"Mary, you still don't understand your own significance. Alex was bright, yes, but that doesn't make his life any more important than yours. You touch people too. Everyone does. Look at Cathy. She gets it. She allows time to mourn and time for fun. Her mother's death is sad, but also liberating. You have children, you made a home, and maybe it's time to do something different, but not because the world thinks so, because you think so. You'll figure it out."

"I'll figure it out from home," Mary told him.

"Really? That's good. That's great." He nervously laughed, and then to hide his delight, joked, "The place is practically recognizable."

They stared at each other for a long moment and hugged, neither in a hurry to let go. Mary's mind raced back home, to all that would be waiting for her.

"I think it would be best if you got the cake, and if I got the gift. I know you usually pick out the boys' presents, but I've got a really good idea," Mary said, planting a quick kiss on Ted's mouth, and bounding away as though she had a million things to do. She was half jogging when she yelled back to him, "And we'll just order pizza when I get there."

"So you mean, you'll actually be there for dinner?"

"God, yes," she answered. "I can't imagine being any- where else. But don't tell Matthew, he needs a surprise."

"Sure," Ted answered. "Take all the time you need."

"Take Cathy back home with you. She's great at decorat- ing."

"Okay. I'll see you back home then."

At the town deli, Mary got a turkey sandwich and a coffee to go. She couldn't remember being so hungry. There was a feel- ing of urgency. It was Matthew's last year at home. And she had only really been half there since her mother's death five years ago. He had been in seventh grade when the veil had fallen over her eyes.

The year her mother passed away, Matthew had been twelve. She could remember him watching her as she cried into her cake batter, his feet still too big for his growing body, his hair combed without any reminders, his voice so low, peo- ple thought he was Ted on the telephone. Brian had already demonstrated potential for comedy. But Matthew grew even more serious, held in his laughter as though it were a sign of weakness, and began avoiding eye contact with her. He went out for more and more sports, determined to imitate his dad. He hid his literary books and would only carry sports maga- zines with him into the den.

Mary's memories were rich with spills and scrapes and smiles from swings and car seats and bikes. In an instant, she could recall the surprise she felt the first time she beheld his newborn face, how she and Ted kept looking at each other for reassurance, how the moment she held him, and looked into his tiny eyes, she knew there was nothing else in the world she would rather do than be with him. When she was pregnant with Brian, she worried whether she could ever love like that again, worried that Matthew would have less of everything, couldn't possibly imagine loving her second son the way she had loved her first. But that was before she had ever held Brian, before she had learned that the heart had an infinite capacity to love, before she realized how absolutely precious each human connection could be.

The porch was draped in orange and brown leaf garland for Mary's arrival, a painted pumpkin sat on each step, and tall, golden cornstalks had been wired to the posts. On the door hung a happy birthday wreath of dried red and yellow flowers, little five-and-dime-store boats, trucks, cars, candles, and penny candies. There were a few crows perched in the neighbors' trees, a hum or two of a distant motor. The living room lamps were lit, the pinch-pleat ivory drapes had been drawn open, as Mary always positioned them when a visitor was expected. As she stepped out of her car, she smelled the wood smoke from her fireplace.

Brian, in jeans and a sweatshirt, had run out to greet his mother, hugging her right there on the street. Arm in arm they walked into the house.

"Thank God you're here. You have no idea what I've been eating. Until Beatrice and her casseroles, we were living on fast food and toast. They have no idea how to feed an adolescent here."

"I missed you too, honey."

"Hey, wait until you see how Dad wants to fix up the basement for Cathy. Did you know she knows her way around tools? Impressed the heck out of us, although Dad and Matt would never admit it. They just act like they know as much as she does. She's the first girl I ever met who took shop in high school."

"She's amazing, isn't she?"

Mary went through the doorway. She smelled coffee, pizza, popcorn. She greeted Cathy, Ted, and finally Matthew.

"Happy Birthday, Matthew," she told him, reading in his eyes that he was really happy she was home.

"Thanks, Mom. I know it's a long drive," her older son said, embracing her.

"Very long. Too long," she said, moving toward the door. "Could you help with my stuff?"

"I'll help!" Brian said, leaping into action.

"I think Matt can handle it," Mary told him, gesturing that there was something for Matthew in the car.

"So, how does it feel to be eighteen?" she asked him as they walked to the car.

"Not so bad," he said. He opened the car and immediately noticed her overnight bag.

"Wow. You're not going back tonight?" he asked, momentarily optimistic and unguarded.

"I thought I'd move back in."

"That's great, Mom," he said, blinking slowly, now hugging her more intensely.

"I'm sorry, Matthew. I'm so sorry I made you worry so much. I just wasn't myself when Grandma died. And now here you are, all grown up and ready to go to college. Soon you'll be married and have a family—"

"Mom, slow down. I haven't had a date in months," he sighed, in embarrassed frustration, raising that one eyebrow.

"Yes, but you will now. I bought you something to help."

"Oh, God, not a how-to book. Brian will really give me a hard time."

"No. It's in the car," she said, taking the little cage from the backseat.

"A puppy. All right! A beagle? Wow. Look at him, he's so cute. He's sleeping. Should I wake him up?"

"She," Mary corrected. "I'm trying to balance the house with male and female energy. Of course wake her up. She should be at your party."

He hugged the black and white puppy to him, and within seconds, was having his face licked.

"Thanks, Mom," he said. And then, to the dog, "We need to get a name for you. Come on, Mom, I need a girl's name."

"Oh, let's see. How about Sis?"

"No way. It will start out Sis, then before you know it, someone will call her Sissy. It sounds too wimpy. I need a name that girls will respond to."

"Venus, Chloe, Abby, Charity, Mercedes."

"I like Mercedes. It sounds rich. What do you think, Mercedes?"

Mary watched as he rubbed the puppy against his face, and seeing that he was being watched from the window, Matthew showed his puppy to his admiring family.

Mary couldn't help but smile.

Cathy and Ted were in the den planning how to maximize the space in the basement, studying kitchen counters in building magazines for ideas about work and storage areas. Mary ate a second piece of cake while the boys took Mercedes outside to roll in the leaves. She looked around, enjoying the warmth of her kitchen, her family, her home. Yes, this was far better than that campus apartment, she thought, wiping the crumbs from her tablecloth, positioning the sugar bowl at the table's center.

"I'm so happy to be home," Mary announced from the doorway, her mind still rebounding from her long day's adventure.

"You should turn in," Ted told her. "You look beat."

"You do," Cathy agreed. "And it's not even midnight," she commented, sitting cross-legged on the rug, smiling up at her.

Mary nodded and went up the steps. She could hear Ted and Cathy disagree about the height of some structure, David Letterman's studio audience laughing, the vigorous crunching of leaves as her sons played with Mercedes.

She showered, brushed her teeth, slipped into bed, and drew up her quilt, the one her mother had made for her so long ago. The window was opened slightly, and she could feel a cool breeze blowing on her face. Home had never felt so wonderful.

Tears for Alex began slowly rolling out of her eyes, down into her ears. She told herself time would help. But the sound of her sons playing upon the leaf-covered lawn just made his death that much harder to overcome.

There was a question she had yet to ask, that could perhaps shed some light on things. She tried meditating, hoping to get back to that perfect beach where she last saw him. She spoke in phrases to her own mother.

"No use laying down if you're not going to sleep," her mother's voice told her.

Mary sat up abruptly, deciding her mother was right. She grabbed her robe and went back downstairs.

ed and Cathy had moved to the kitchen table and were still energetically drawing, erasing, measuring.

"Mary," Ted said, looking up from his drawing tablet, surprised.

"I just had a thought," she began. "Cathy, I wanted to ask you if maybe you could contact your grief group and ask if they know who put that picture of my friend on the wall?"

"Sure. What was his name?" Cathy asked, dragging the pencil from behind her ear, and taking one of the cowboy napkins she had bought for Matthew's birthday to write on.

"Wyatt," Mary said softly, opening the refrigerator door for some milk, to hide her pain from her husband. "Alex Wyatt."

Ted was the first to notice that Cathy wasn't writing, that she seemed frozen in space and time, absent from all that was real. For a moment, it seemed the young girl couldn't breathe.

Ted put his hand on her back, while Mary, still in search

of the milk carton, chatted that she was pleased to see so many fruits and vegetables, even broccoli, there in her absence, and that perhaps whoever was doing the food shopping could continue in that role.

Ted lifted Cathy's chin and looked into her blue eyes that yesterday had seemed so intensely green, looked deeply into her very soul, studied her blond hair, the shape and angles of her jawbone, her nose.

"It's okay," he told Cathy, taking her hand, feeling heat in his own throat, behind his eyes. He called for Mary, still keeping his eyes steadily upon Cathy, feeling that she might melt away, right there before him, if he didn't continue to hold her.

Mary was staring now, knowing, not quite comprehending, rationalizing what she couldn't possibly deny.

Ted put his hand out for her. He called to her more loudly, "Mary come here."

Mary didn't feel her feet moving, couldn't feel anything but the thumping heat of her heart, but somehow she made it across to the round table without ever taking her eyes off Cathy. She looked to Ted who seemed almost as stunned, his kind eyes filling up as he held tightly onto both their hands.

Mary moved closer. She knelt down between Ted and Cathy. She took the young woman's face into both her hands, having the same need as Ted to touch her, to stroke her hair, to examine the evidence, and she smiled.

"Mary, Mary, quite contrary . . ." For a split second, he was there, green eyes glowing, blond hair shining, the curve of his lips, but then Cathy reappeared.

Mary could feel Ted's hand on her back now, steadying her. She studied Cathy, transfixed by her, the blue eyes looking green in the dim light from the stove, her lemon silk hair, the nose, the generous curves of her mouth. Alex's daughter. In undeniable flesh and blood. In absolute truth. In brilliant beauty. In loving spirit. Part of him was sitting there in her kitchen chair. He was looking at her. He was touching her. Part of him was joyously alive.

Mary lifted a long strand of Cathy's golden hair and watched it drop. She rolled her hands down the girl's neck, each hand tracing a shoulder, until she had reached the tips of her pink-and-white-dotted fingernails, the tightly clasped hands of Ted and Cathy. Mary sat back into her husband's lap.

"He was in California with my mother," Cathy began, regaining her composure. "She was never the same after he died. She carried his picture in her wallet. A few days after I put my mother there, I put his picture there too. It just occurred to me one day. I don't know much about him," Cathy finished, wiping at her eyes. "I don't even know how he died."

Ted tightened his grip on Mary and leaned forward to Cathy. "He had to have been your father," Ted told her, holding on to both women. "I see it in your smile, in your eyes. He—they, he and your mother, must have wanted you to be with Mary."

"With both of us, Ted," Mary said, holding up the chain of their held hands, remembering how Alex had placed her hand into Ted's so long ago, for safe keeping, for security, for unconditional love.

Ted looked down at his right hand, still holding on to Cathy, trying to recall bits and pieces of his last conversation with Alex.

"But she's in love with you," he had announced to Alex, on Mary's behalf, even though it hurt him to admit it.

"It will pass," Alex told him. "You're so much better for her. I'd only destroy her."

"Why am I better? Because I'm so ordinary?" Ted had demanded, insulted by his implication.

"No. You're extraordinary. You're able to love her in that same way she loved me, that nurturing, peaceful way. I torture her. I don't mean to. But I torture myself, and that hurts her. It's a dirty job, but someone has to do it," he had joked, offering Ted a second beer.

"What is wrong with you?" Ted had asked, shaking his head.

"I really don't know. We are what we are. You have to do what you do. Make Mary happy. We need more couples like you in the world. Be fruitful and multiply. Someone has to perpetuate this madness. You and Mary would be excellent parents, don't you know that already?"

"What is this martyr act? You're anything but celibate."

"Marry her, Ted. Take care of her. She needs you. She needs a family. She needs a home. I prefer living a more haphazard life." He had shrugged, unapologetic.

Ted had become angry. "You know, if you could get past the brooding poetic crap, you'd have a chance to be happy. I mean, if you tried, you could get it together—"

"You don't get it. I don't want it together. And that makes all the difference in the world. You can't will something into being."

"So Mary's just supposed to accept this?"

"Yeah, I really think so. Look, Ted, you guys belong together. I saw it the first time I met you. Did you ever have that feeling about people? It hits in an instant, boom, thunderbolt. Not love at first sight. Something deeper. Something spiritual. Something that rings true. The sound of two hearts connecting. Something that says, Ted and Mary, sitting in a tree, k-i-s-s-i-n-g . . ."

"Impossible to talk to you," Ted huffed, nearly laughing.

"Hey, you're a fine man. Accept it. Accept Mary. I trust you with her. This was a very noble gesture on your part. One day, maybe you'll see that I was making one too," he had grinned. "Despite the brooding, poetic crap," he added.

"Well, I tried," Ted had sighed, standing to leave.

"Hey, cheer up. It will all work out. You'll see. Every romantic knows it will all work out."

Mary remained transfixed, staring at Cathy, that familiar face looking curious, a treasure contained within her.

"Mary can tell you all about him," Ted offered.

Mary moved to Cathy and embraced her, crying openly. She could feel him in the texture of her hair, in the coolness of her face, in the warm breath as she sighed against her. It was what she had always hoped for, a daughter, but to have something of Alex to hold on to seemed no less than miracu-

lous. Mary kissed Cathy's cheek, again and again, a lost treasure, a most precious gift.

"I look like him?" Cathy asked.

"Yes, yes. Oh, God, I don't know why I didn't see it in
you before. I can't tell you how it feels to find someone you
can wrap your arms around and love, from someone you already loved. I always knew how much I wanted you, Cathy. I
wanted you for so many reasons. I did covet other women's
daughters in the mall. But if we'd never found out who you
were, I wouldn't have loved you any less."

"I know that."

"But now that I know, I'm so grateful for the chance to
be part of your life. Your father is the reason Ted and I came
together. Look at you. You are the best parts of him. His
eyes didn't change color. They were always green. But his hair
was just as gold. Didn't you think that when you found his
picture?"

"No. I only kept asking Luke if he could talk my mother
into helping me find my father. Of course I was thinking he'd
be alive. But I really wanted a family."

"Well that much we've already managed," Ted told her.

"That's what Luke said. That we were all meant to be together. You're really very generous, Ted," she said, hugging
him.

"Thank you, but considering how beautiful, loving women
seem to just fall into my hands, and forgiving Alex his dramat-
ics, I'm now inclined to think he was the generous one."

～ 40 ～

𝒯he light shone through the large beveled glass windows of the luncheonette as Mary refilled her Coke glass, continuing to nibble at the chocolate chip cookie she had, in her opinion, baked to perfection. It was the Wednesday before Thanksgiving, the schools had half days, and the high school crowd had promised to be in for burger lunches. Ted and Brian had rearranged the layout to include a jukebox, and an additional cold case for milk and dairy products to accommodate the older customers who came in to play the lottery, and didn't want to make another trip out in bad weather.

The countertop was stocked with pumpkin pies. Cathy's fall work, wreaths, fruit centerpieces, candleholders in autumn colors that had been displayed or hung in the back, was now changing over to Christmas crafts, and Mary was sure, before long, they would be able to reconfigure space in the back room for classes. They had barely an hour before their rush, and Cathy was insistent that the twinkle lights be up and ready for customers, so she was busily attaching holly berries and long swags of green garland, while Mary tried yet another recipe for baking strips of potatoes into fries, since the place was equipped with only a side by side oven and a grill.

"How does that look?" Cathy asked, pointing to a perfectly shaped gold bow. "Do you think red will be better?"

"I think it's all beautiful," Mary said, admiringly.

"I'm testing the gold for Fallon's Jewelry Store. They've asked me to do their display."

"Word is getting around about you," Mary smiled.

"And you too. Didn't I hear you take orders for six more pies yesterday?"

"People come in, they smell the pie, and they just can't help themselves."

"How are the fries coming?"

"Here, have a taste," Mary offered, salting a small plateful.

"Not quite there yet," Cathy admitted. "But with some ketchup."

The cowbell on the door rang and Brian stepped in, yelling hello, grabbing for an apron. Mary held out the plate for further testing.

Brian sampled one and scrunched his face.

"Mom, give up on the fries already. Nobody knows the difference. Use the precooked ones."

"Never," Mary insisted.

"Where's Dad?" Brian asked, looking toward the stockroom.

"With you, I thought," Mary responded.

"I haven't seen him since breakfast."

"He was supposed to do burgers today. I'll just bet he's dragging out that train platform already."

"Cut him a break, Mom. He needs something to do when the grass stops growing."

"How's that?" Cathy asked of her decorating, having changed one of the gold ribbons over to red. "My mom always liked to use some gold."

"Gold's good too," Brian offered, sympathetically.

"Red's better," Matthew said, coming through the door, having tied Mercedes outside. "Red's always better. It's traditional. Hey, Mom."

"Matthew, I didn't think you'd make it back from school this early," Mary commented.

"I missed my dog."

"Thanks a lot. I've been with you longer," Brian groaned, tying his apron.

"I was talking about you. Mercedes is my girl."

"Really, still? I'd have thought you would have moved on to the two-legged variety by now," Cathy teased. "The prom is only five months away."

Matthew gave Cathy a thumbs-up and pointed to Mercedes, who was wearing a pink bow, compliments of Laura. "I wanted to get here in time to help put up the lights," he said, changing the subject.

"Cathy's doing great," Brian told him.

"Yeah, but now that we have my expertise we can get

everything done faster. We need time off to get the tree on Friday afternoon, right?"

"How do you feel about closing early, Cathy?" Mary asked.

"How do I feel? I'll make a sign: GONE TO GET TREE."

"Thank goodness we have your opinion," Brian whined. "Matt and Dad don't care about needles or how good a tree smells. They always outvote Mom and me."

"We're still getting the biggest one," Matthew insisted.

"I guess we need to get one for here, Mary," Cathy suggested.

"Or not," Mary said, watching out the window as Ted pulled a full-sized tree out of his Cherokee. "Will you look at the size of that thing! That must be why Dad never objected to our taking over this place—the high ceilings. You know he was just picturing a big tree."

"All right, Dad!" Matthew yelled. "Come on, Brian."

"Now I'm going to have sap up to my knees," Brian groaned.

"Yeah, but at least you've got the apron for it," Matthew teased.

The boys ran out to help with the tree. Cathy and Mary stood together at the window, watching, arm in arm.

"I love this place, Mary. I'm so glad we're back here."

"It's perfect for me too," Mary answered. "It sure beats trying to waste time at home, or trying to concentrate on homework. Now I get to see those babies in strollers, and the teenagers with the four earrings, and I can still have tea with the seniors."

A timer sounded.

"There's my next set of pumpkin pies."

"They're putting us in the black," Cathy told her.

"My mother's recipe."

"I wish I could cook like you."

"Maybe someday. But for now, it's enough that I see you using my mother's knitting needles. I could never get the hang of them."

"That's because you didn't see them as an extension of you. It makes all the difference in the world. Hey, that reminds me, this should make you proud. My grief group's planned a field trip to visit us here. Sometime after exams, but before Christmas."

"That's so great."

"We've become a happy stop. And we didn't even need accordion lessons," Cathy joked.

"You know what I forgot to tell you? I had the jukebox man install some Christmas polkas," Mary bragged.

"I never knew there were such things," Cathy admitted.

"It's all out there, Cathy. You just have to look for it," Mary mused. "A very wise young lady once told me that."

"We should make a videotape of your family trying to get that big tree out of the car."

"Our family, unless of course you find them too ridiculous to admit to at the moment."

"They are extremely ridiculous. But exactly what I've always wanted."

"You know, me too," Mary agreed. "I see a whole different side of Ted and the boys now that you've joined the family. Not only do I feel like I've inherited a daughter, it's like everything has suddenly swung toward Brian's agenda."

"Total absurdity," Cathy agreed.

"Thank God," Mary replied, laughing. She watched as the rope snapped from the tree, and its branches swung out in all directions, slapping Matthew and Brian backward. It was huge. Ted looked at the store window and waved. Cathy gave him a thumbs-up and Mary blew him a kiss, noticing how many people had remained in place, smiling at the spectacle of her family.